AFTER THE
Fall
Jason's Tale

A Novel

David Nees

Copyright © 2013 David E. Nees

Revised June, 2019

All rights reserved.

To keep up with my new releases, please visit my website at www.davidnees.com. Scroll down to the bottom of the landing page to the section titled, "Follow the Adventure" to join my reader list.

You can also click "Follow" under my picture on the Amazon book page and Amazon will let you know when I release a new work.

ISBN 9781530563203

Manufactured in the United States

For Carla

*Without your support and encouragement, this
book would never have happened.*

Special thanks go to Diana, who told me that the story
was worth writing and Lynette for her detailed critique
and beautiful cover art. I am indebted to the rest of my
family, David, Andrew and Lilith for their encouragement
and faith in me. Thanks also go to my two good friends, Ed
and Jim, who believed in me and encouraged me when my
work was not very good. My buddies from school also were
a great encouragement: Greg, Richard and Ron; thank you
guys. It means a lot to me.

After the Fall

Jason's Tale

"Every new beginning comes from some other beginning's end." –Seneca

"What we call the beginning is often the end. And to make an end is to make a beginning. The end is where we start from." –T.S. Eliot

Prologue

The tramp steamer plodded across the Atlantic, a beast of burden laboring without complaint through the ocean's waves, the bow rising and falling in response to the heavy swells. The diesel engine rumbled in its efforts, the vibrations continually coursing through the ship. The superstructure was unkempt. Rust attacked it everywhere; its owners long since having given up the fight. It was a tired, old ship that should have been taken out of service years before, yet still continued to subsist on the fringes of world trade, scrabbling for any dollars it could make. This voyage, however, would be its last.

Mahmood stood in the wheel house looking out over the ocean. The gray water and leaden sky merged without a horizon, holding a hint of danger to come, as if the ocean were saying, "I can turn deadly. I can hurt you."

He did not like the sea; he preferred the mountains. Man was a land animal and being on the water was foreign to him. One could not live out here. One could only pass through. Yet being in the wheel house was better than being below, closed up in the steel of the ship. The comforting smells of familiar cooking, the lamb, the onions and peppers, the garlic, the odors that brought up sharp, welcoming images of his village home in Pakistan, now did not comfort him. Inside the ship they mixed with the ever present diesel and sweat to produce a nauseating haze of scent that violated all his cherished memories, making the comforting now sickening. He had passed through the initial round of sea sickness, but the uneasy possibility of throwing up always came back when he stayed too long in the bowels of the ship.

He turned needlessly to the charts where the ship's dead reckoning plot was updated every four hours. He forced his impatience down. The pace was slow but that didn't matter. All that mattered was that they arrive at the coordinates at the right time. He knew they were still days from their position. The GPS and AIS identification system were turned off, the ship was out of communication with the world, and, Mahmood hoped, the world was ignoring its presence as well.

Half way around the world, in the Pacific, another indistinct, small freighter also slowly made its way to pre-arranged coordinates off the shore of the U.S. The two freighters had a common purpose, more than two years in the making. In the hold of each of them, hidden in containers, was a missile that they would fire at a set time. Each Sajjil-2 missile was topped with a nuclear warhead. It was a solid fuel rocket with a range of 1,300 miles; more than enough to reach their targets. The targets were not on land, but were points in the upper atmosphere over the U.S. They would be launched simultaneously and aimed so each would explode over part of the U.S., effectively blanketing the country with an electromagnetic pulse or EMP.

Mahmood recalled the efforts of his mentor, Nusair, in convincing the al Qaeda leadership, most of whom did not understand his plan. They wanted the rockets to drop on major cities. They wanted to see death and destruction come with fire and explosions. At first they seemed unsatisfied with what his mentor proposed which would cause the U.S. to die from within. It might not be as immediately satisfying as raining fire and destruction from the sky, but his way would be more complete. Nusair had to educate them on how dependent the people in the United States were on having all goods and services delivered to them.

As the picture emerged the leadership grew more enthusiastic with the plan. If the blast could knock out microprocessors throughout the country, all would come down. Cars, trucks, planes and trains run on microprocessors. The EMP burst would destroy them which would stop the vehicles from running. If they stopped transportation, they would stop the distribution of food, fuel, medicine, clothing; just about every good and service required for maintaining modern civilization. Additionally, communications would shut down, ending any attempt to coordinate relief efforts.

Next, the burst would knock out the energy grid and the power throughout the country would go down. The country would be blacked out, factories would shut down, buildings couldn't be heated and the pipelines that control distribution of natural gas would stop flowing.

No food, no fuel, no energy, no support systems needed to maintain the massive population. Nusair won them over. The leadership relished his vision of massive starvation and the collapse of civil society. The terrifyingly powerful U.S. army would have to turn homeward to handle the chaos that would ensue.

Mahmood did not know the effect of launching the missiles from the ship's hold. The blast of the rocket could very well sink the ship even though they had added reinforcing plates to the bottom of the hold. So be it; Allah will be pleased and Mahmood will be honored by his companions in arms. He could imagine the tales told around the villages of the man who brought down the great Satan.

If the hull held together and he lived, so much the better; the ship would turn towards North Africa and they would flog the engine for as much speed as they could generate. If they reached the coast they would run the ship up on a beach and disappear into the interior. He would be assured of his place of honor and power in the new caliphate that would emerge. There might be retaliations but Mahmood knew his people would survive them; they were used to the wilderness—the caves in the deserts and mountains. They would wait until the fury of the response faded. When the U.S. forces had to turn to the collapse of civil order at home, they would go away and his people would come out to reclaim their lands and then take the soft, fat European countries that would not have any protection from their benefactor across the ocean. He smiled at the thought of the new order he was soon to initiate. *Tomorrow, I will trigger an end...and a new beginning.*

The launch day dawned clear. As the sun climbed higher, the ocean turned a sharp blue in reflection of the sky. The tired ship was throttled down and turned into the gentle breeze. The swells were long and regular and the old freighter slowly rode up to meet each one; its motion now more gentle. The captain had taken full control over the ship's steering and engine as he expertly kept the vessel holding its place in the water. The technicians had all retreated to the farthest corners of the freighter taking the crew with them. Only Mahmood remained in the wheelhouse with the launch technician and the captain. Everyone was wearing smoked goggles and ear protectors.

At the appointed time Mahmood pressed the launch button with his breath held. Suddenly it was as if the fury of hell erupted in the ship's hold. The violence of the ignition threw them onto the floor where they lay, curled up as the roar of the rocket, heightened by its close containment reached two hundred decibels, piercing the ear protectors and smashing into their ears. The blast thrust shattered the windows of the wheelhouse as the missile cleared the hold.

The old freighter shook, its metal plates screamed as they were suddenly heated to over 5,000 degrees, stretched, melted and warped. Sections of the ship buckled, the rivets holding the steel plates bursting free and shooting through the hold and across the deck in a massively lethal crossfire over the ship. The hull plates in the now-empty hold pried loose, and leaks sprang open. The hatches were partly melted and distorted from the rocket's flaming exhaust; no covers would go back on them again.

And then it was over, the rocket now a point of fire receding in the sky and already beginning to angle westward towards its assigned detonation point. The ship was left open and vulnerable to any assault from the ocean's waves.

On board no one could hear. They turned to one another, deafened and dumbstruck from the ferocity of the launch. The ship was still protesting the assault on it, though no one could hear it. The engine was struck dead from the rocket's heat and fire and could not respond as the captain recovered his wits and attempted to get the freighter under control. The ship slowly turned side-ways in the swells and began to list to one side as she took on water. The captain shouted for his crew to man the pumps, but no one could hear him. After some time, he was able to gather and direct them, but the pumps did not work well; it was too little too late. The ship slowly listed further and the stern began to sink. In an hour, the old freighter ended her life at the bottom of the sea, taking Mahmood and the rest with her.

.

Book I: Into the Mountains
Chapter 1

H e lay on the ground behind the rhododendron bushes. Their leaves remained through the winter, giving him cover. The earth was beginning to thaw on this February day. The south facing ground on which he lay hungrily drank in the sun's rays. The long, unkempt grass though was still dry and dormant under him. Only the faint, musky scent of dry vegetation registered as he pressed his body close to the ground. The cold grip of winter had not yet fully given way to the freshness of spring.

Jason carefully pulled aside a branch to study the road ahead through his binoculars. He was hidden at the top of a gentle rise a quarter mile from the interstate. The road he was following went north under the highway. The houses had thinned out here, like a forest giving way to grassland. They stood with doors opened and broken windows, like sightless eyes looking out at the world, giving mute testimony of their violation. Grass had grown long, only challenged by the weeds which grew in riotous abundance after being left alone. Bushes once well trimmed were now beginning to assume their wilder shapes. He could see no movement, but still he waited. Going down the hill he would be exposed.

The underpass carried the interstate highway on its back. It was low and narrow, only having room for the two lane road which he followed. Above, the four lanes were split into two sections as they went over the local road. Abandoned cars were scattered along the interstate as far as he could see. The electromagnetic pulse burst had killed them all in an instant. Jason could see some crashes had occurred when drivers had lost control. Many cars sat with their trunks and doors open. Where had all the people gone, he wondered? It didn't really matter now. What concerned him was the underpass made a good spot for an ambush. His route so far had skirted downtown Hillsboro. He had no desire for another encounter with the militia or gangs, which seemed to be one and the same. To the north of the interstate lay the national forest and the wilds of the Appalachian Mountains, his goal. This was the last obstacle. But there was not enough cover to allow a furtive approach. He would be exposed as he hiked down the hill.

The empty houses in the suburbs spoke of a retreat. Death first reigned among the elderly and sick, but without the delivery of food, life quickly became untenable for even the average citizen. And the ones who remained alive looked to the town authorities to provide for them. They migrated into the city when they ran out of food, needed medical help or were threatened by scavengers. They were looking for food, shelter and safety. In Hillsboro they found a limited amount of all three, but they came with a price.

Personal freedoms disappeared as strict rules were set up to stave off chaos. People were catalogued, assigned where to live, where to eat and to what tasks they would have to perform as the price for the succor they sought. Hillsboro was turning itself into a medieval city. As martial law was established, Jason had watched personal freedoms disappear, and decided to strike out on his own in the forest. Crossing the interstate was his last challenge.

From there he would be putting the city and its control behind him.

Over the winter he had made himself a copy of an Indian travois using aluminum poles and putting wheels at the end. On the webbing between the frames were two backpacks loaded with food, tools, weapons and camping gear; all the supplies he needed to survive in the mountains. He was ready to depart.

He would wait until night. It would be harder to see, but also harder to be seen. There was still no sign of movement around the underpass. Jason crawled back twenty yards through the tall, dry grass. When he was far enough below the rise, he got up and walked to an old oak tree and relaxed against it. *Get some rest. Don't be careless now.* He resisted his desire to hurry to the forest. It felt like freedom lay just on the other side of the interstate.

Late that night, with a quarter moon barely softening the pitch darkness, Jason lay in the same spot, studying the road. His binoculars pulled in more light than his naked eye, but it was still shocking how dark the nights were with no lights. There was no movement.

It was time to go. Again, he backed down from the rise, then shouldered his backpack. Jason carried a Ruger .223 Mini 14 Tactical carbine and a 9mm semi-automatic pistol. The Ruger held twenty rounds in its magazine and the 9mm held thirteen rounds. He pulled the charging lever back and with a click chambered a round in the rifle. He then pulled back the slide on the 9mm chambering a round. Each weapon was now ready to fire. He flipped their safety levers on and, with a deep breath, set out. He held the carbine in his right hand and pulled the travois in his left. He had encountered scavengers and militia on his journey out of town. Both were dangerous. Jason hoped there would be no encounter this night.

Quietly he walked down the road towards the underpass. He stepped carefully in the dark trying to not make a sound. He did not want his boots thumping on the pavement. Nearing the underpass, he stopped and crouched in the ditch along side of the road and listened. The night was still. That would change. With spring approaching there would again be refugees on the move from Charlotte and cities to the east. *Hillsboro is getting its defenses ready for them.*

He stood up and stepped into the opaque underpass. Carefully he walked forward, blinking, not yet seeing properly, the darkness closed over him. His left foot stepped on a branch that snapped with a loud crack. His right foot was tripped by the rest of the branch as it sprang up. Cursing under his breath, Jason stumbled forward.

A car door opened on the road above; then another; then some muffled conversation.

"Wake up. I heard something below us." A man whispered.

"What's up?" another voice asked loudly, in reply.

"Shhh. I think I heard someone underneath the highway."

"So what? Probably a deer." came the now whispered reply.

"There ain't any deer in that underpass. Must be someone down there."

"What would anyone be doing out this time of night?"

"Hell if I know."

The voices were hard edged, rough. They spoke quietly but the sound carried easily in the still night air.

"My guess is they got something to hide, stuff we can use."

"You think?"

"Yeah. We ain't found much along the interstate, so I say we take a look. If there's someone down there sneaking stuff out of town, we can take it. Get Jake."

Another door opened. "Damn, I was sound asleep 'til you woke me. What's up?" A new voice entered the conversation. It continued over the possibility of someone beneath them; someone with supplies they could take.

"Bring your guns; we don't know what we're gonna find."

"Shoot first, look second?" one of the men asked.

"Maybe, if they give it up, we may let them off easy. Be ready for anything."

The men had been working their way west on the interstate, scavenging from the abandoned cars and using them for shelter at night. Sometimes they could siphon some gas and barter that for food. They were looking for a gang to join in Hillsboro.

Jason kept still, not wanting to confirm his presence by moving forward. He couldn't make it to the end of the underpass before they would intercept him and to retreat would only expose him to the highway above. The conversation became muffled, but he understood enough to know they were coming down and they were a threat. There were sounds of movement now from above.

The sounds were coming from the direction he was headed. Were any of them coming from behind him? Jason quietly laid his trace down and unshouldered his backpack. His Ruger was at the ready position. He ruled out running. They were too close and he didn't have a head start. He couldn't move fast with all his gear, the travois and backpack, and would be an easy target. His only advantage was the men above didn't know exactly where he was. Be still and wait. Let them come to him.

He was in the dark of the underpass, just before the pale light that spilled down from the gap in the lanes, splitting the dark tunnel into two segments. They could come from the end or the middle. His eyes were now adjusted to the dark of the underpass; he would have a moment's advantage and he knew he had to use it. Adrenalin rushed through him. He began to shake.

They sound so casual about taking everything from me. They'll kill me just as casually. He knew there would be no negotiating his way through this encounter. Images of the wild chase two days ago flooded his mind. This time there was no outrunning them and no hiding from them.

Three men came down to the road level at the far side of the underpass. He could hear them talking. They were still sheltered by the abutment.

"Do we go under?" one asked.

"He may be armed," the leader replied.

The men waited, not sure what to do next.

"I don't hear anything. Think he's heard us?"

"Maybe, one of you go back up and be ready to come down in between the lanes in case this guy's armed," the leader directed.

Jason heard movement but no one came into view. He waited forcing his breathing to slow and listened carefully. *They have to give themselves away when they move. Don't move, wait.*

Then two men stepped into view at the far end of the underpass. Jason took aim. He knew they could not see him in the greater darkness. Before they stepped out of the moon light, he opened fire. One man went down immediately; the other fired wildly into the dark and then fell from Jason's return fire.

Where was the third? He listened. There were footsteps above. Jason backed out of the underpass and crawled up the embankment on the south side of the highway. He saw the man's shadowy image coming across the far set of lanes. Jason fired at the shadow. The man fired wildly back. A few more shots from Jason sent the man running west on the lanes towards Hillsboro. Jason climbed up on the road and shouted as if calling to another shooter, "He's running west, see him?" He then fired one more round in the direction the man fled.

It was over in a moment. Jason stood shaking and panting.

Are they dead? Then a panic began to rise in him. *Get moving!* He didn't know who might have heard the gunfire and how quickly anyone might come. He didn't want to be there to find out. *Got to get to the woods.* He ran back down to the local road, shouldered his pack, grabbed the travois and started running through the underpass, past the men he had shot. One lay still. The other made sucking sounds as he struggled to breathe. Jason shuddered but kept going.

On the other side of the underpass, he turned right and climbed up the embankment to the still-raw slope where the interstate sliced through the side of the hill. Jason ran along its base away from the underpass until the slope became less steep. He strapped the travois to his waist and shouldered his backpack, then moved diagonally up the slope, crawling, scrambling and fighting the drag of the pack and travois. He needed to reach the cover of the trees at the top. From there he could defend against anyone following. His hands clawed at the rocks and dirt, trying desperately to gain the top of the slope and the cover above. The stones scratched and cut his exposed skin. He struggled with the loose slope, pressing his body against it when he started to slide backward, then crawling upward again.

Finally Jason got though the bushes at the top and into the cover of the trees. He lay down, drenched in sweat and blood, completely out of breath. After a few moments he crept back to the edge and looked out to see if anyone was coming after him. The road below was silent. Through his binoculars, he thought he saw a shadowy figure moving south on the local road he had used. Otherwise, all below him was still.

Jason returned to his gear and with great effort dragged it a few more yards into the underbrush and lay down in a laurel thicket. The fear, the panic and now the realization that he had killed without warning and maybe without need overwhelmed him. He started to shake.

He sensed a line had been crossed; what effects it would have on him, he could not say. *Are we going to become barbarians? Is this what it will take to survive?* Finally, the adrenaline drained from his system. His shaking subsided as he sank back in exhaustion. Slowly his body relaxed and sleep began to envelope him.

Jason awoke some hours later as the eastern sky began to promise the sun's arrival. He had a raging thirst. He was covered with dirt and blood. His hands were cut and sore from clawing his way up the hillside. He fumbled around in the pre-dawn light to retrieve his canteen. After several huge gulps, he splashed a little on his hands and face. He avoided thinking of the night's events. Sitting against a tree, he stared at the bluing sky, then searched his surroundings with his ears, listening for anything out of the ordinary. Nothing. His mind drifted back to the day of EMP burst that previous summer.

Chapter 2

J ason was at his computer in the fitness gym he owned when the power went out. It was four in the afternoon in Hillsboro on a Thursday, a bright, late summer day. Stepping out of his office, he realized the whole gym was without power so he went to the circuit breaker box in the rear of the building. All the breakers were in their normal position. Puzzled, he went back out to the front of the gym and stepped out onto the street. He was not alone. The gym was located in downtown Hillsboro, in a mixed-use block with offices, shops and restaurants. Horns were blaring, cars were stopped dead in the streets; some had hit other cars. Drivers were shouting; people were standing around outside the buildings. Many were looking up in the sky, as if expecting to see something.

"The power station must have had a problem," one man standing next to him opined to no one in particular.

"Was there a lightning strike? I don't see any storm clouds," another person spoke.

"What happened to all the cars?" another asked.

Jason wondered himself. There was something more serious going on than the local power station shorting out. He tried his cell phone...nothing. Going back inside, he had the receptionist try the land line with the same result. No electricity, no vehicles running, no computers, no cell phones; this was not a simple power outage. A further check revealed there was no radio or TV either.

Jason had read about EMP bursts and the threat they posed to the U.S. He began to think the unthinkable. He hurried to the back room and made sure the service door was locked. Then he stood on a bench in the gym area and announced that due to the power outage, the gym was going to have to close and no showers could be taken. People began mumbling and grumbling, many coming up to ask questions that Jason could not answer. All he could tell them was that he couldn't keep the gym open without any power and he needed to let his employees go home. The power seemed to be out over a wide area.

After the members had departed, Jason gathered his staff together.

"The power seems to be out all over town. You'll probably have to walk home. Cars don't seem to be running. Get some bottles of water and grab some snacks from the vending machine. I'll open it for you. If you're going in the same direction, walk together as far as possible just to be safe. Some of you have a long way to go so don't delay."

"Is it dangerous?" one young instructor asked.

"I don't think so, at least not right now. But it's best for everyone to get home as soon as possible. I'd stock up on essentials right away, just like if you were facing a big snow storm. There's no telling how long the power will be out."

"Should we plan on coming in tomorrow?" another asked.

"No. Don't come to the gym until the power returns." What he left unsaid was that the power could be out for a very long time, if this event was what he thought it was.

"What about our cars?" another asked.

"What can you do? If they don't run, you got to leave them."

"And our phones don't work." There were murmurs of agreement; everyone had tried unsuccessfully to phone or text someone.

"Yeah, I don't know what's up with that either." Jason responded. "The only thing I can think is that everyone is better off at home. Downtown may get a little crazy if everyone is stuck here."

With that Jason opened the vending machine and handed out the power bar snacks to everyone. Soon the gym was empty. Jason collected the remaining food from the machine and the back room, put it in his backpack, grabbed half a dozen water bottles and put them in the pack. Then he emptied the register and safe of all the cash. As he was leaving, he suddenly froze in the doorway: Maggie was flying home today. She had called Jason earlier, from the plane, to let him know when she would get into Charlotte.

Jason and Maggie lived in the hilly suburbs just outside of Hillsboro which was located in the northwest corner of North Carolina. It was a medium sized town of approximately 200,000 people, nestled in a small valley of the Appalachian Mountains. The economy was supported by some small, local manufacturing, and an old nineteenth century inn which enjoyed a modest tourist trade. It had the problems of urban blight and unemployment found in many mid-sized cities along the east coast. With those problems came its share of the usual accompanying vices: addictions, theft and prostitution.

He quickly locked the door to the gym, grabbed his mountain bike and rode over to the local airline ticket office. His mind raced. *What time did she call? Did her plane take off before the power went out?* As best he could remember, she called him from the plane at three pm, about an hour before the power went out.

The manager was alone in the ticket office when he arrived. She was confused and flustered about what had happened but Jason could offer no explanation. After he got her settled down, she checked her printouts for departure times. They confirmed Maggie's call; the plane had taken off before the power went out. It had probably been over Maryland or Virginia at the time of the event.

Jason wondered how extensive the power outage was. Could a plane survive it? He was afraid of the answers. Another man came into the office to check on a flight. He spoke of seeing a plane literally fall out of the sky when the power went out. It must have crashed more than fifty miles to the west. This was not a local phenomenon.

Jason slipped out of the office as more people were coming in, anxious to find out about loved ones flying. Downtown there was a growing panic as people tried to comprehend the situation. Some people were shouting that everyone should go to City Hall. Some were shouting everyone should go to the police station, they would know what was going on. Most people were just standing around, still confused and not knowing what to do. Leave my car, here in the street? Walk home? How do I contact my wife or husband? What about my kids at school? Some people were asking everyone around them these questions. When asked, Jason's advice consisted of, "Leave your car. You can't do anything about it. Go home or go to school and get your kids and then go home. Stock up on food and water, just like for a big snow storm."

As he pedaled home his thoughts kept returning to Maggie. The sky was ominously quiet, which only lent credence to what that man in the ticket office said he saw. Could she really have crashed? A knot grew in his chest. She had picked this day and flight to avoid the crush of business travelers heading home at the end of the week. Now had that choice proved deadly? Who could have known? The 'what ifs' plagued his mind. He began pedaling faster and faster, covering the ten miles to his home in record time. The conviction that Maggie was gone kept growing inside of him.

At home, he went from room to room, not knowing what to do, his mind paralyzed by the awful realization. The silence was unnerving. Out of habit, he kept trying his phone and the television. Then he went into his bedroom. He found himself pulled towards the closet. It was a large, walk-in space that he shared with Maggie. Reluctantly he opened the door and stepped inside. It smelled like her. Jason reached out and pulled one of her dresses close to him. It was her favorite party dress. She'd last worn it on their anniversary when they went out to dinner and dancing, something Jason didn't really enjoy but Maggie loved. He pressed it to his face and breathed deep. Her scent filled his nostrils. He began to sob into the cloth.

Wrenching himself away, he stepped back out into the bedroom. He approached her dresser and began to touch the items she had placed on it; her hand mirror, perfume, powder, the picture of the two of them at the beach. He gently opened the dresser drawers taking her clothing out, touching the items and pressing them to his face. He tried to pull her back to him with touch and smell. Ever more frantically he began to open each drawer, grabbing the clothing, pressing it to his face; faster and faster until the drawers were all opened and clothing strewn around the floor. Choking on his sobs, he collapsed and pulled all her garments up close to him and just cried. He spent that night working his way through a bottle of whisky, alternately pacing the rooms of his house or slumped on his couch.

The next day dawned bright and clear. Jason awoke with a throbbing headache and a twist in his gut. He checked his phone, TV and computer...nothing. The situation was serious. Even in the worst disaster, one had some communication. Now there was silence. What to do? He paced around his living room for some time, disoriented by the information blackout. His thoughts turned to his family. His mother lived alone in Florida, in a retirement community and his only brother was in California. His father had left the family when Jason was eight. He had lost his job and fell into a depression. Finally he just cut and ran, leaving the family to fend for themselves. He disappeared rather than face the daily needs of his family when he couldn't provide for them. Before the power went out it had been easy to transcend distance and keep in touch. Now they were so remote, with a possibility of never seeing or hearing from them. The thought was so odd, so final that he dismissed it from his mind.

Energy. Was the gas still working? He checked and it was, but he needed the barbecue lighter to light the stove. *How long will that hold out?* He knew he could not count on the gas for long. He began to take stock of his situation. He checked his propane tanks, camping stove gas and gas left in his vehicles. Food needed to be inventoried as well. Jason was a bit of a survivalist and kept a six month supply of emergency food in the basement. Maggie accused him of being a closet Mormon, to which Jason would reply, "Yep, and I'm thinking about a second wife." Maggie would then respond with something on the order of, "Over my dead body...or hers." And they would chuckle over this running joke. He loved Maggie's possessiveness. The memories kept coming. His sadness grew with each one.

Maggie was quite glamorous. Jason always said she could have been a model and joked that he had married above his station. That comment had seemed to become more painfully true over the last two years. Maggie had always said that Jason seemed to have the spirit of a golden retriever, loyal, protective and always trying to be helpful. He realized there was some truth to her characterization. She was so successful that he sometimes didn't see how he fit in to her life. He was not sure how he helped fulfill her in their relationship.

Maggie was a rising fashion executive and spent much of her time in New York. Their being apart so much of the time did nothing to help cement the marriage and Jason feared it was only a matter of time before he got the notice from her that she had decided to relocate to New York, something Jason would never do. He loved the mountains and woods, and the thought of living in New York City made him shudder. He loved Maggie, but deep inside he knew something would always be missing in their marriage. Bittersweet tears came again and again as he thought of her.

After writing out a list of things to do, he made some coffee and had a small breakfast. Then he just stared at the list. Taking action seemed to elevate the improbable into reality. He kept waiting for the TV to come on and explain everything. Outside, it was unnervingly quiet. The quiet you hear when a snowstorm blankets the town. But now there was nothing moving, no cars on the roads, no planes in the sky. He stepped outside and listened carefully. The background hum from the interstate that ran past the town to the north was absent. No contrails or noise from jets flying overhead. Jason stepped back in the house and sat down. This was real. This was the big event. The unthinkable had happened. With a snort, he stood up.

If the worst has happened, what do I do? What do I want to do?

Chapter 3

I n the first few days after the EMP burst, Jason took inventory of his supplies, and then set out to fill the gaps. His supply of food would last for many months if supplemented with what he could forage and hunt from the woods and fields surrounding his home. He also set out to supplement his supply of ammunition. Along with his 9mm semi-automatic pistol, a .223 Ruger carbine, Jason owned two shotguns, a 20 gauge, which Maggie shot occasionally, and a 12 gauge.

The Ruger was his pride and joy. It was modified with a longer, heavier, match barrel, which was bedded in and a re-worked trigger. The result was a very accurate rifle that was light, compact, and rugged. It was equipped with a low power, bush scope which worked well in the woods.

In addition to the guns, Jason also owned and was proficient with a hunting bow. He had enjoyed mastering the weapon and hunting with it. Now that skill might make the difference between life and death. If the power didn't come back, the bow might be the only weapon of value when the ammunition ran out. In those first days, Jason suppressed most of those thoughts, remaining hopeful that his worst fears would turn out to be unfounded, that the power would be restored, that Maggie had somehow escaped the plane crash and all would return to normal.

He lived on a back road that went up into the foothills. The houses on the road were well spaced apart. On the second day after the EMP, Jason decided to check on his nearest neighbors.

Tom and Mary Phillips lived closest to him, a quarter mile down the road. They were an older couple, retired and living alone. Tom came to the door to greet Jason.

"Hi, Jason, it's good to see you. Come in."

"Good to see you as well Tom. How are you and Mary doing?" Jason asked as he followed Tom into the living room.

Mary sat on the sofa with a worried look on her face. "Come, sit down," she said.

"Do you know what happened? Nothing works, not even the car," Tom said.

Jason explained his theory of the EMP burst and its effects. They followed his explanation with increasing concern.

"If what you're saying is correct, then we may be out of power...with nothing working," Tom gestured around with a wide sweep of his hand, "For some time."

"Yeah, that may be what we're in for."

"What about Maggie? Where is she?" Mary asked.

Jason paused, "Her plane took off an hour before the power went out." There was silence in the room. Tom and Mary didn't want to press Jason about what that most likely meant.

"So what do we do?" Mary finally asked. "How do we get medicine and food? Tom has high blood pressure that's controlled by medicine and I have diabetes."

Jason looked down at the floor; there were no good answers to her question. "I'm going to go into town to try to buy some things before they run out, if you have a prescription, even an old one, I'll take it and try to get it filled."

"Jason, thank you," Tom said. "But that may only be a stop-gap solution."

"Maybe so, but it's the best you can do for now. I'm thinking I should go pretty soon, there's no telling how long the supplies will last." Jason stood up. "I'll go back to my house and get my backpack. Find some prescriptions and write a note giving me permission to get them. I'll stop by on my way to town."

Tom saw him to the door. "Do you think this will last a long time? I don't want to panic Mary by digging into how bad this could be in front of her. I can get along without my blood pressure medicine, but Mary has to have a supply of insulin."

"Tom, I just don't know. If it's regional, help will come shortly and we'll be okay. If it's national in scope, then I'm afraid we're in for a terrible time. I don't want to sugar coat it for you."

"Could this problem really be national in size?"

"Under the right conditions, yeah...it could." After a pause, "You should clean your bath tubs and fill them with water. Be prepared to use the water in your pool as well."

"The water's going to run out?"

"It runs on gravity. Yours is the last house on this road with city water, and when the storage tanks run down, the water won't push up this far."

Jason rode back into town with his backpack, his 9mm pistol under his shirt, money and the prescriptions for the Phillips. He entered the first drug store; the pharmacy counter was at the back. There was a long waiting line. Other people were scrambling around the isles, grabbing soda bottles, bottled water and over the counter drugs and taking them by the armful up to the counters near the front door.

Jason's turn finally came. He showed the pharmacist the prescriptions and notes from Tom and Mary. "I'm picking these up for my neighbors," he said.

The pharmacist scowled. "We're in an unusual situation here. I can't even confirm insurance coverage for people who are presenting proper prescriptions, now you want me to let you pick up other people's prescriptions?"

"You must know these people. They get their prescriptions filled here. They're my neighbors. Look at the address, they live outside of town. You know cars don't run. They have no way to get here. I'm trying to do them a favor, helping them to get some needed medicine."

"I don't know..."

"Here are their prescription cards. I'll pay the amounts needed—in cash—so you don't have to worry about insurance reimbursement. Things are going to return to normal, but we all have to help one another while this disruption lasts." Jason felt that he might be lying about things returning to normal soon.

"Well, we're out of the insulin, but I have the blood pressure medicine in stock."

"I'll take it," Jason said quickly. The line behind him was becoming restless. He didn't relish the pharmacist's situation as his supplies ran down. The tension was growing. The girl at the checkout counter up front could not process any credit cards which upset some of the customers who refused to give up their supplies but didn't have enough cash to cover them. With the blood pressure medicine in hand, Jason pedaled away in search of insulin. It took three more visits to drug stores and their pharmacies to find one with insulin, but he was finally successful.

After the medicine, Jason went to a gun shop for additional 9mm and .223 caliber ammunition. The lines there were beginning to grow and the shop was posting its own armed guard. He was limited to purchasing one box of each type of ammunition, cash only. Jason pedaled off to two more gun shops and was able to purchase more rounds for each of the guns. Later in the afternoon, he headed back home. In the distance, back in town, he heard gunfire. *It's started already.*

The next morning, he was in the garage working on an old generator, trying to get it to run. Jason figured this older engine, with no electronics, might be made to work.

With it, he could not only run some lights, but also an electric motor that could be made to pump water from his well. A steady supply of clean well water would be invaluable over time. He paused as he heard someone walking up the driveway. It was Jim Miller, the only other neighbor Jason knew on the road. Jim and his wife, Cathy, lived a mile down the hill with their two kids, Tim and Carrie.

"Jason, are you around?" he called out.

"In the garage," he responded. "Come on in."

"What can I do for you?" Jason asked as Jim entered the garage.

Jim was in his thirties. He and his wife both worked. Their kids, Carrie, twelve and Tim, nine, were both bright and enthusiastic. Carrie idolized Maggie and had made her promise to help her get a job as a fashion model when she graduated from school.

"Just wanted to get your thoughts about what has happened. I can't figure it out for the life of me."

"Did you get the kids back to the house?"

"Yeah, Cathy and I wound up meeting at the school; I came from work. It was her day off, so she rode her bicycle from the house. The school was holding the kids until parents could come for them."

"I hope all the parents were able to pick up their kids."

"I think some of the staff were planning to stay overnight with the kids if their parents didn't come. Hopefully everyone got picked up by yesterday. So, you have any clue as to what's up?"

"I do. I think it was an EMP burst, possibly over the eastern half of the US." Jason went on to explain the effects of such an event.

"If it shut power down all over the east, we'll be quite a while recovering." Jim was going where Jason had already been.

"I think this was an attack; it didn't happen by accident, and if it was, there might have been multiple bursts to cover the whole country."

"Holy shit," Jim murmured, "That would be a first class disaster."

"More than you can imagine. I went to town yesterday to get some prescriptions for the Phillips. There are already lines at the pharmacy counters for medicine and that will only get worse. It's good your family is together; I think I heard gunfire late yesterday when I was coming home."

"Rioting?"

"Maybe, or looting."

"What do you think we should do?"

"Fill your tubs and any containers with water while there's pressure. That's the first thing. Next you should inventory your food supplies and, this could be dangerous, you should go out right away to buy what you can. Food and water are going to become scarce soon, get what you can now."

"You're freaking me out, you know that."

"I'm telling you how to deal with what we're facing. Who knows what's going to happen, but I can't imagine many rosy scenarios. Jim, do you have any weapons in the house?"

"Christ, no."

"Well, it's too late to buy any. I'll loan you my 20 gauge shotgun. Do you know how to use it?"

Jim took a deep breath, "I can learn quickly."

"Fine, let's go inside." He put down his wrench and headed into the house. After getting the shotgun out, Jason showed Jim how to load and unload it. It held four shells in the tube magazine and one in the chamber. In defending his house, he instructed Jim to chamber a shell, then put another in the magazine and, if possible, never shoot the magazine dry so he wouldn't have to spend too much time loading shells. Jim followed along as Jason went slowly over the operation of the weapon. He looked close to panicking as the lesson and the implications of what it meant sank in.

"I'll go back down to the sporting goods store on the Ridge Highway, the one on the way to town. I'll see if I can get you a couple of bow and arrow sets. People may not have thought of buying them yet. They're quiet and the ammunition is reusable."

"I'll go with you," Jim offered.

"No, I've got no one here at home. Stay with your family. Show them how to use the shotgun. Make sure they can load and unload it and aim it. For God's sake, though, don't fire it. Shells are precious and you'll scare the Phillips to death."

Jim smiled thinly at Jason's humor attempt. "What about Maggie? She's away?"

"Yeah, she was on a plane when the power went out."

There was a pause. "Does that mean what I think it means?"

"I think it does." Jason could say no more. His eyes teared up as he thought about Maggie.

"I'm sorry," was all Jim could say.

Chapter 4

The first casualties were the very sick and very old. Next to die were those who were kept alive by drugs that were no longer available. It was heart wrenching for everyone who knew people in these situations. Mary Phillips passed away after six weeks. Jason helped Tom bury her in the back yard. Tom then set out to walk to town to seek help from the authorities in charge. Two weeks later, Jim and Cathy decided to go to town with their kids.

"Are you sure you want to put yourselves in the hands of the town authorities?" Jason asked.

"We're running out of food and water and we can't ask you to support us. You've been generous, but it isn't right to eat up all your supplies. I hear there's a regular supply in town. It's better than starving. You sure you don't want to come?" Tom asked.

"No. I can make it through the winter. I'll see how things are in the spring. Don't let them split up your family," he warned. "And don't tell them about me."

In different trips into town Jason saw order restored under martial law. There were cops or a militia on every block. People were being organized by blocks, told where to live, and what work to do. Work was begun on repairing old vehicles, gardening, digging wells or digging latrines around town as the toilets couldn't be flushed. On his trips to town, he was shaken down for money, then, as that became useless, the stops were to search for food, weapons, ammunition or medicine. Jason had learned to go to town unarmed except for a knife. The police and militia would confiscate anything else of value. As the environment in town became more controlling, he ventured there less often.

After saying goodbye to the Millers, Jason retreated more and more into himself, staying alone in his house as the city became more controlling. As food and water became more difficult to find, hunger became the driver of people's behavior. Autocratic control was the response by those in power.

Often Jason spent hours at night thinking about Maggie. When he couldn't sleep he would take some of her clothing into bed with him and hold it tight to his body until exhaustion had its way. Waves of sadness would envelope him without warning. He gradually came to accept that he would never see her again. This acceptance did not end his grieving but allowed him to move forward.

One late fall day, Jason heard some commotion on his driveway. Going to the window, he saw a group of five men and one woman approaching the house. They were armed with bats, an ax and a couple of pistols. Quickly grabbing his Ruger .223, he yelled out of his window.

"Stop or I'll fire! I've got an automatic rifle and I can take all of you down before you get to the door!"

The group hesitated. They looked at one another. Clearly they had been going from house to house, scavenging what they could, and had found either little resistance or no one home. They had not expected a confrontation.

"We're hungry," one of the group members called out. Jason noted the speaker, figuring him for the leader.

"Everyone's hungry," Jason replied. "Go to town and get in line to be fed."

"They take everything from you when you sign up for a ration card," the leader complained.

"Still better than starving...or stealing from others. Trying to steal from me is going to get you killed." Jason hoped they understood how serious he was. He didn't want to shoot them, but he was not going to let them steal his resources.

"Can you give us some food?" the leader called out after considering Jason's threat.

"Sorry, I don't have any extra to give you."

There was a conference among the group. Jason waited for them to accept that he should not be challenged. "I guess we'll just be on our way," the leader finally called out to the house.

"I'm going to be real clear with you," Jason answered. "I'm the last house on this road for five miles and you can bet any people further out are also armed and willing to shoot trespassers without warning. You need to turn around and go back. This road holds nothing of value for you anymore. And if you try to sneak up on me at night, I have power and trip lights rigged. I'll shoot you on sight now that I've warned you." Jason was bluffing about warning lights. He didn't want them trying the house at night even though he had secured it against easy entry.

The resolve of the leader visibly sagged. "You won't have trouble from us."

"Good luck, then," Jason replied as he watched them slowly trudge down his driveway and off in the direction of town.

It'll be a light night of sleeping. He sighed.

As winter approached, wild game got more and more scarce. The deer population had either been killed or had moved further into the mountains. Jason began to wonder if he should stay. His food supplies would not last forever and local game was scarce. He could still survive but only by going further and further afield to hunt and gather.

He spent many nights sorting out his thoughts, pondering what to do. Hillsboro was only partly under control. Food was still scarce and what was available was controlled by the town's safety committee. There was no input from the general citizens. The emergency laws were put in place by the committee which consisted of Frank Mason, previously Chairman of the Town Council, two other Councilmen and Charlie Cook, the Chief of Police. Jason suspected that Joe Stansky had a hand in much of what was going on as well. He had heard his name invoked by the militia on some of his trips to town. Joe ran a local strip club and was suspected of controlling much of the drugs and crime in the city. There were still gun fights between either the police or militia and scattered groups trying to steal supplies. However, most of the public had been disarmed, if they ever had been.

The ones who wanted to be fed, who signed up for ration cards, were stripped of all weapons and forced to abide by a set of emergency regulations set up to control them. The regulations directed where they could live, where they could eat and the work they had to do on the town projects. Top down control was established in the name of civic order. Most people went along with it since it meant regular, if limited, food to eat. In addition the town was building up its defenses—walling itself in—to keep out wandering refugees and roving gangs.

On his last trip to town, Jason was stopped by some of the militia. They wanted to know where he lived and why he didn't have a ration card. When Jason protested that he didn't have to answer such questions they grabbed him and handcuffed him. During the struggle a crowd began to form. Finally a man came up who seemed to be in charge.

"What's going on?" he demanded.

"This guy doesn't have a ration card and won't tell us where he lives," one of the militia replied.

The man walked up to Jason who was glaring at everyone. "Why the reluctance to tell us about yourself?" he asked.

"It's none of your business," Jason replied.

"Well it is. I'm in charge of the town, my name's Frank Mason. We have to restore order, so questions like these are necessary. We'd like you to cooperate."

"I don't live in town. I live outside, in the western suburbs," Jason lied. I don't have a ration card because I don't need one. I can feed myself." He glared back at Frank. "So is that enough information for you?"

Frank looked thoughtful. "That explains a lot. But you should know that you may not be able to enter town soon. If you're going to be on your own, you're not going to have the town to lean on. We can't have people using our resources and not joining our team and becoming part of our rebuilding work." He turned to the militia man in charge. "Let him go and see that he leaves town. If he comes in again, arrest him."

They released Jason and escorted him west out of town. When the militia departed, he circled back to the south and arrived at home much later that night.

Jason knew it was only a matter of time before the militia showed up at his house. He guessed he would he be forced to give up his food and his weapons; forced to move into town, to 'donate' his resources and be stripped of everything for self-sufficiency. He would become a ward of the government with this new system, under the control of those few in power. He wanted no part of it.

What to do? The choice was to either submit to the dictatorship of martial law in town and be stripped of his independence, or...head out into the deep forest, on his own, alone. Jason was comfortable in the woods, but living alone? And how would he get through the winters? Would there be anyone out there who would accept him into their household? He thought about his own situation and decided it would not be likely. Most people were probably just hanging on, even in the countryside, and they would be suspicious of strangers, having had to rely on themselves to defend against any gangs.

After a few more run-ins with wandering scavengers, Jason knew he had to leave. Word was going to spread that he had supplies. The stories would get passed around, growing as they circulated and soon the authorities would focus on him. He would put his trust in his own survival skills. He would head north, into the Appalachian Mountains, away from cities and the corruption that came with them. With his food supplies, his camping gear and weapons, Jason figured he could find a remote place to hole up until this catastrophe passed. And if it didn't, he would at least be safe, if alone, in the mountain woods. While confident of his skills in the woods, a kernel of doubt still remained in the back of his mind about being so alone.

With his decision made, he set about building a travois. He made a modern version of the old Indian device, working day and night, racing against the day when the militia would show up. The travois would allow him to carry a large store of supplies until he could set up a new living situation.

Chapter 5

One morning in late February, Jason stepped out of his front door. He breathed in the crisp air; clear, still without the rich smell of spring to come. He walked over to the garage and opened the door. Then he brought out his travois loaded with two large packs. He had a third backpack that he shouldered himself. Setting everything down in the driveway, he paused and stood looking at his house; his and Maggie's. His mind raced over the memories of their time together. There was so much joy and laughter. The house had been filled with it. Now it was only memories and emptiness.

He stopped himself from locking the door. *I'm not coming back. There's no need to keep anyone out.* He was leaving behind his possessions, things from a world now passed. A wave of sadness swept over him flowing deep into his bones. He shuddered, trying to shake it off. *Maggie's gone. Life as I have known it is gone. I love this house but there's only memories here now. It's time to leave.* He turned away with a sigh. *Got to look forward.* Then he shouldered his backpack, hitched up his travois and headed down the driveway.

He had packed his camping gear and all the food rations he could fit on the travois. For weapons he chose the Ruger .223 rifle, his 9mm pistol and his hunting bow and arrows. He included the bow because it was stealthy and the ammunition was reusable. A survival knife, a multi-purpose tool and small camp ax rounded out the hardware. He packed as much ammunition as he could carry, which increased the weight of his rig dramatically. Weighed down with 50 pounds of backpack and 120 pounds on the travois, he was not going to move fast, but as he got the hang of controlling the load, he managed slow but steady progress.

His plan for getting to the forests was to go around the center of town on his way north. He knew he couldn't go straight through town. He would be stopped, disarmed and stripped of supplies. Three miles down the hill, his street connected to a county road running east and west. He planned to hike east for ten miles, avoiding local neighborhoods. He was familiar with the county roads and planned to go east far enough to avoid the denser parts of town before turning north. Within two hours he crested a rise in the road and saw a small, ragged group on the road heading towards him.

Uh oh! Too late to hide. Keeping his eyes on the approaching group, he stepped to the side of the road, unhooked his travois, slid off his back pack and slid everything into the ditch on the side of the road. Then with the Ruger held at ready, but not pointed at anyone, he watched as the group approached. They were looking intently at him as they came closer. When they were thirty yards away, one of them motioned to the others and they began to fan out.

Jason called out, "Stop! I'll let you pass, but I'm going to shoot if you spread out. I won't let you circle me." He pulled back the charging lever on the Ruger. He couldn't tell who was armed and what weapons they had, but he hoped his rifle presented a significant threat. The group paused and Jason took advantage of the indecision.

"If you try to spread out, I'm going to shoot, starting with you in the blue jacket." He addressed the one who gave the gesture to fan out, thinking he might be the leader. "You'll be the first to die."

"We're not looking for trouble," the blue jacket called back.

"If that's true, get back together. I'll step to the side, then you can walk past on the other side of the road."

"How do we know you won't attack us?"

"You don't have anything I want. I'm on my own journey and I don't have any interest in you."

"Where are you going?"

"Out of town. On my own."

"You been in town?"

"Enough."

"Things ain't good there. They work you hard and don't feed you much."

"At least you get fed."

"We've managed so far," blue jacket responded.

"Long as you keep ahead of the police and militia." Jason suddenly had a thought. "When you're safely past me, I'll tell you where you can find more food and clothing."

"Where?"

"When you move past me in a tight group."

The leader turned to the others and they held a whispered conversation. Blue jacket then turned back to Jason.

"You're not just puttin' us on, are you? You're serious?" Hope resonated in his voice.

"You won't know until you go to the place I'll tell you about...it's my home. It's got supplies. I couldn't take them all. There's clothes and a working well, if you know how to use it. I figure it's a good trade. You don't try to overpower me, I don't kill any of you and you get to use what I left behind."

The group huddled for a whispered conversation.

"All right, we'll go on by, but if you're lying, we'll hunt you down."

"I'm not...and don't try to come after me or follow, I'll shoot without further warning." Jason shouldered his rifle as the group filed past him. Some stared at him with a dull look in their eyes, others glared in resentment at him and his possessions.

When they were past, Jason gave them directions and watched them trudge off, the way he had come. When they were out of sight, he shouldered his pack, hitched himself to the travois and set off down the road. He walked late into the night pausing at times to watch the road behind him for any sign the group was following. The road remained empty. The group probably was feasting on what they had found. They could stay there for some time, but the militia would come eventually. He couldn't help that. The group had to deal with them on their own. Later that night he worked his way far off the road and set up a cold camp in a dense cover of trees.

Could he have shot them? Jason didn't know the answer. He was glad his show of force had deterred the group. They had reacted the same way as other scavengers he confronted. Would his luck hold? Jason's gut feeling was that if he encountered any of the local militia, his bluff would not work. He shivered at the thought as he lay wrapped in his sleeping bag and ground cloth.

After a fitful night's sleep, waking at every sound, he started out again early in the morning. An hour down the road, he turned north. The road cut through the eastern suburbs of Hillsboro, but it led to the closest point where he could enter the National Forest. That would be his route north, further into the Appalachian Mountains. He walked more carefully now, stopping at every rise in the road to scan ahead with his binoculars. Twice he saw militia patrols ahead. He turned off the road to give them a wide berth, preferring a slower, more circuitous route to any encounters.

Around noon, he stopped and refilled his water bottle from a small creek, dropping in the purification tablets. Later in the afternoon, as he approached a rise in the road, he unhitched his travois, hid it with his pack in the bushes in front of a house and crawled to the top of the rise to check the road. He lay in the un-mowed grass with his body pressed down against the still-hard ground. Ahead the houses gave way to a small strip of stores. There they were, five armed men purposely checking all the stores in the center. These were not scavengers; they were armed and moved purposefully as if they had a job to complete. The stores had most of their windows broken out. Some had no doors. The men were focused on two of the stores that still seemed closed up, perhaps protecting something valuable. The doors were apparently strong having weathered the initial round of looting.

While Jason was studying them with his binoculars, trying to decide what to do, he suddenly noticed a sixth man scanning the area, also with binoculars. His slow swing stopped when he was pointed at Jason. Had he seen the glint of Jason's binoculars? Suddenly the man jumped up, called to his companions and pointed towards Jason.

Jason quickly slithered back down the slope. He could hear them running towards him. Where to go? He couldn't get away burdened with his pack and travois, so he left them hidden.

He had to lead them away from his gear, so he quickly ran east, through some of the yards, away from the road. He heard a shout as he bolted between houses. He was seen. Now he needed speed. He ran across the next street. On the other side there was an older house, the original property from which the small subdivision had been created. He sprinted for it. As he rounded the corner of the house he saw an old wooden shed in the back yard. The urge to hide was overwhelming. The shed door was ajar. There was a hasp with a lock left on the loop. Jason ran to the shed and, after closing the door, reached through a hole in the siding to slip the lock on the hasp.

He had just locked himself in. Panic rose. What had he done? He had hidden himself, but he had also trapped himself. *They won't think I'm in here if the door's locked.*

If I'm quiet they'll stop searching. Jason put his eye close to a small hole in the siding and looked out.

The men came around the side of the house and stopped running.

"I saw him cross the street, somewhere around here." One of them said. "He can't be far." There was a wild energy in his voice.

"See any prints?"

"No, the ground's too hard."

"Why are we bothering?" another asked, puffing from the effort of their run.

"He was checking us out with binoculars. He wasn't just another scavenger."

"You think he's got some supplies?"

"I don't know what he's got, or who he's with. He may be part of a gang. He could be trouble. We need to find him." This was the leader talking.

"I'll check the house. See if he broke in." Another said.

Jason watched through his peep hole. The men had a wild look in their eyes, inflamed by the excitement of the chase. They were fierce looking. There would be no negotiating if they found him. He shrank back to the darkest corner of the shed, listening to the discussion going on outside. He heard someone approach the shed.

"I wonder if he's in here." The speaker tried the lock on the door.

"It's locked, ain't it?" the leader called out.

"Yeah, but something's not right. He just didn't disappear. We saw him come this way and now...no sign of him." He began a careful walk around the shed, like a dog hunting for a scent. Jason was sweating in spite of the cold day. He muffled his breathing in his arm, forcing himself to breathe slowly though his body was screaming for more oxygen. As the man came by the wall near Jason, he held his breath. Once past, Jason opened his mouth and slowly breathed into his sleeve again.

"Gone to ground," another chimed in.

"The house is closed; he didn't go in."

"He's either in one of these houses, or he got to that patch of woods." The leader pointed to a small patch of woods at the back of the large lot the old house sat on. "From there he could sneak off in any direction."

"I didn't hear him going through the woods." The man near the shed declared.

"How the hell would you with all the talking we've been doing?"

"And who's to blame for that?"

"Stuff it. If push comes to shove, I'll make you take the blame for it."

"So what do we do now?" asked the man who was short on breath and not looking for more running.

"Check the two houses next to this one; if he's not in them, we go back, finish what we were doing and head back downtown."

The group dispersed to search the nearby houses. Jason lay back and took large gulps of air, like a man coming up from near drowning. His heart raced, his head pounded. He just lay there, exhausted from the chase and the fear that flooded him. Long after the men left, long after the sun went down, Jason finally stirred.

He wondered about his resolve. He had killed in the army over in Iraq. But civilians...he wasn't sure. *These people would kill me in a moment for my supplies*. He thought about the wild look in their eyes as they came around the corner of the house, a blood lust that spoke of no mercy. *Remember that look* he admonished himself as he set about prying open some boards to free himself from the shed. The next night, he had his answer as he went through the underpass.

The morning light had grown stronger while Jason was lost in reverie. A stray breeze stirred the woods and startled him out of his thoughts. He sighed deeply from the roots of his body as the memory of the previous night's confrontation in the underpass came rushing back to him. Slowly he stood up and moved to the edge of the woods to peer back down at the highway with its litter of abandoned cars and trucks. There were no people. The emptiness, the deadness of it saddened him. Were the men he shot last night in the underpass dead or alive? He would never know. He knew he should go. It might not be safe to be here, even up on the ridge, if the militia found the men he had shot.

Heading into the mountains was going to be a lonely adventure, but he had no partner. He had to go it alone. Who knew how many people he would see after this? He turned his gaze from the roadway and went back to his gear. He drank some more water and ate a cold MRE. Then he slowly strapped on his gear and without looking back started his lumbering climb into the mountains.

Chapter 6

Jason hiked north. The remote country lay in that direction. He headed for the areas of the forest that had not been logged in a hundred years and were dominated by large climax trees, leaving the undergrowth open and easy to navigate. He tried to stick to established trails which provided easier travel, however to the north, the terrain got steeper, tougher. There were fewer farms; the forest taking over more of the land. He was looking for that country.

The second day, following a well worn trail, he came around a bend and there sat half a dozen people. He stopped, cursing himself under his breath for being careless. No one moved. The group stared at Jason as if he were an alien from space. He stood and stared back. *Don't threaten them.* They were young. Some of them were armed. They were a mix of men and women. They didn't have much gear with them, only an assortment of book bags and backpacks. Some of them had on hiking boots and some had running shoes. They didn't look ready for the wilderness.

"I didn't mean to startle you," Jason finally said. They just looked at him. He unhooked his travois without taking his eyes off the group. Next he slid his backpack off. His 9mm was in a holster at his side.

One of the men responded, "You did." He stared at Jason. They outnumbered him. No one moved.

"Where're you headed?" one in the group finally asked.

"Where are *you* headed?" Jason countered.

"We're just trying to find a place where we won't be bothered by the militia telling us what we can and can't do."

"Where do you think that will be?"

"Somewhere away from Hillsboro we figure."

"Was it hard to get out of town?"

"We all got out okay. We met up after leaving town."

"Better watch out for gangs. They'll take all your supplies."

"That's why we're in the woods."

"Are you going to try to rob us?" another asked.

"No. I'm not interested in robbing anyone."

"Looks like you're pretty well equipped," someone else said.

"I planned it that way. I'm also ready to defend what I have."

One of young men edged closer to his backpack propped against a rock.

"I wouldn't reach into your pack. It's liable to get you shot," Jason stated. His hand edged closer to the pistol on his belt.

"You going to try to shoot all of us?" the young man replied.

"If I have to."

"You can't get us all," he challenged.

"Yes, but who will I shoot first? If this turns into a shootout, none of you know who'll get shot. I'm a good shot, I don't miss." Jason continued as the tension grew, "I've done this before and survived, so I don't recommend you do anything foolish. I'm no threat unless you threaten me."

"How about coming with us?" one of the girls spoke up. She eyed him intently. "We could use an extra man like you." Her look was both challenging and inviting.

Jason stared back at her. She was pretty. She stared at him, provocatively measuring him. But behind the invitation there was a hint of desperation in her eyes. He ignored the implied offer. "No, I'm going alone. You better get some supplies. You have any weapons?"

"We've got enough," one of the men said.

Another said, "I've got a 9mm in my pack."

Jason could see a rifle laid against another backpack, "What caliber is that?

"It's a .22," said the man nearest the rifle.

"Good caliber for hunting small game. It's quiet and the bullets don't weigh much. I hope you brought a lot of ammunition."

"Do you think we'll run into gangs here in the woods?" another asked.

"You ran into me. You could run into anyone."

"We thought being off the roads would keep us safer."

"Probably, but there's no guarantee. My advice is to find a place soon and gather supplies. It's that or go back to Hillsboro."

"And get raped?" the girl spoke up again.

Jason turned back to her. There was an angry look in her eyes. "Did that happen?"

"It almost did. Lots of other girls experienced it. It was that, or become someone's mistress, same thing if you ask me. Why don't you help us out?"

Jason stared at her. He didn't know what to say. The urge to protect rose up inside of him but this group didn't look prepared to survive. They had no structure, no organization. There would be the inevitable jockeying for dominant status with the males. Then there would be paring up issues with the two females that would fuel more discord. Their situation didn't look promising. Yet Jason's sense of duty nagged him. The practical solution was to leave them to their own fate. The problem was he knew what that would be.

Finally he answered, "I can't help you. We're all going to struggle to survive. I'm going to do it on my own. That's my plan."

"We're going the same direction, shouldn't we hike together?" the girl asked.

Again, Jason paused, wrestling with his conscience. "No. You go on. I'm going to take a different route." The group gathered their gear and began to walk away. Jason stayed where he was, watching them go up the trail. His mind churned with conflicting thoughts. Was he someone who cut and ran...like his father did? He couldn't save everyone. He had just reinforced his decision to strike out on his own—to save himself. After they were gone, he set out for higher ground.

It was the fifth day and the way was harder now. The steeper terrain was rougher than the ground on which he had practiced. The hiking was a constant wrestling match with the travois—his 'anchor' as he came to think of it. He made only a few miles progress each day and his hips and shoulders were rubbed raw as he struggled to adjust the harness and backpack. Comfort remained an elusive goal. Some routes became impassable with the travois and he had to retrace his steps to find another way north. It was always north, or as close to it as he could maintain. At night he often sank, exhausted into his sleeping bag without making any shelter, just pulling a tarp over him. Each morning he awoke in pain from his hips and shoulders. When he found a game or old hiking trail heading in a generally north direction it was a huge relief, as he could make a couple of extra miles that day. He drove himself to keep pushing, keep moving. Each day he fought with the terrain, not willing to give an inch to it, driving himself onward.

The trail was so faint he almost missed it. It was narrow but promised more miles north. An hour along, the trail wound around the shoulder of the mountain following the twisting spine of the ridge above which crooked and curved like an arthritic finger. The trail bed was a narrow bench cut into the side of the mountain. It was late morning. He was fatigued. His feet found uncertain purchase on the loose rocks. Then he slipped. His body lurched to the outside. His hands flung out wildly, but there was nothing to grab. He twisted his body, trying to restore his balance, and then the travois slipped off the side of the trail yanking him over the edge. He fell down the hill bumping against rocks, grabbing desperately at bushes and limbs but the travois flung him downward without stopping. The fall seemed to go on forever in a blur of sky and hillside flashing in his face as he rolled.

Then it stopped. Jason was jammed up against a house sized boulder two hundred feet down the hillside. He slowly took stock of his situation. Every part of his body was bruised. Pain seared in his left side when he tried to move; he hoped only bruised ribs. He gingerly tried moving his arms; they weren't broken. Next he tried his legs. Aside from being bruised, they worked. No broken limbs. The backpack had saved him from a worse injury to his spine by cushioning him against the rocks on his way down. But between his pain and steepness of the hill, he was not just going to hike back up this slope.

He looked up at where the trail seemed to be. *Shit. What a mess.* The slope was steep. He struggled out of his backpack and unhitched the travois. After, he lay exhausted, unable to move.

Finally gathering his strength, he unwound a hundred feet of line from his travois. Next he tied a steel ring to the frame. He looped the line through the ring and tied both ends around his waist. This gave him almost fifty feet of room to climb. Further up the slope, he could tie one end of the line to a tree and pull the travois and pack up with a two to one advantage. After setting up his system, he started painfully crawling up the slope. He could only move about ten feet uphill without having to stop to wait for the pain to subside. When his line was close to running out he stopped where he could tie one end off and then laboriously pulled the pack and travois up. Without the two to one advantage it would have been impossible.

By late afternoon, Jason was half way up the hill. He secured the travois against some rocks and laid back to gather his strength. After resting for some time, he began climbing again. Each time he had to pull the travois the pain caused him to cry out, but he kept at it. He could not survive without the gear in the travois and pack. And so, painful foot after painful foot, Jason dragged the gear up the slope. Hour after hour he climbed and pulled.

Nearly delirious with pain now, Jason chugged down some water and lay back against the steep hillside. After a rest he forced himself to start again. He could not spend the night on the side of the slope. He might not be able to move by morning. He had to reach the trail.

The sun had set by the time he finally reached the top. He laid down on the trail like a wounded animal and waited through the pain for sleep to come. Dawn came and with it the pain. It took an hour to sit up and get some water and an MRE. His body was hurt all over, but the ribs were the worst. He spent the morning arranging a more comfortable place to lay down with his sleeping bag and ground cloth.

I'm not going anywhere soon. At this point, he couldn't imagine putting on his pack and harnessing himself to the travois. *Have to rest here even though it's on a trail.* He kept his 9mm close at hand and hoped no one would come along.

Jason stayed in that spot on the trail for another full day. He alternated between resting, eating and making his body move so he wouldn't become immobile. The next day he tied his backpack to the travois and put the harness around his waist. With this set up he could shuffle forward. It was painful and slow, but he was on the move again.

The forest strips one of pretension. It must be encountered on its own terms. Now injured, Jason had serious second thoughts. Could he make it in the wild? His struggling, now worse, kept him at odds with his environment. He was tempted to abandon his gear and lighten his load, but resisted; until he found other resources, the gear would be necessary to keep him alive. Shelter was now a serious concern. He was injured and exhausted. He needed a place to heal and recover his strength but there was nothing.

After the accident, he would wake at dawn, cold and sore, always favoring his left side. Water, and a power bar or MRE was his breakfast. It took maybe twenty minutes of moving around slowly before he was loose enough to pack his gear and get back into the harness. The travois was now damaged. The frame was bent and one of the wheels didn't turn. This made it all the harder to cover ground. On a good day he had a trail to follow, if not, he had to bushwhack his way, tripping over fallen logs and underbrush. The pain in his side remained. He would walk for two hours before his body demanded rest. After ten minutes he would force himself to get up, strap on the harness, and start out again. The pattern repeated with a longer stop around noon to eat. By four in the afternoon, he could go no more and looked for a flat area to camp. Some days Jason would stop with enough energy and force himself to set up his lean-to shelter over a pile of leaves to cushion his sore body. Occasionally he had enough energy to make a small camp fire and heat a meal. Then he would crawl into his sleeping bag and fall into an exhausted sleep. More often he ate cold rations and slumped exhausted into his sleeping bag and ground cloth.

Dreams were erratic and often frightening and he would awake, breathing hard. Only the night sounds of the forest broke the deep stillness—the hoot of an owl and, sometimes, the far off bark of a coyote. A sense of aloneness flowed over him like a dark wave. Some mornings he awoke in tears, having had tortured dreams of Maggie, trying to reach out to save her, unable to stop the terrible descent of the plane; its fiery explosion waking him.

Then the rains came, cold and harsh in the early spring. Jason would spend the night shivering under his tarp, getting little sleep as the rain found every crevice to drip down on him. He had learned how to build a fairly dry and comfortable shelter of branches and the forest ground cover, but he often had no energy to complete such a task. Daylight brought little relief. The wet woods dripped with water making it nearly impossible to light a fire. The result was camping cold most nights and no relief from the wet and cold in the morning.

As his strength diminished, he moved down to lower elevations—towards easier ground—to reduce the effort to move forward. This change brought him to the edges of the forest and the danger of meeting outlaws increased, but it was his only option if he wanted to keep going. Onward he trudged, ever more tired and sore. With the rain, small creek crossings now became dangerous obstacles.

He stopped at the edge of a narrow torrent of water. It was ten feet across. In a drier time he could hop across the water; now it was more threatening due to his injuries and the gear he carried. How deep was it? The water was moving fast enough to sweep him off his feet if he wasn't careful. Four feet of depth would be enough to drown him as it swept him downstream. What would not have given him much of a pause was now a dangerous obstacle.

He steeled himself as he studied the water. It was cold, ice cold this time of year. He looked for evidence of a shallow area as he planned his crossing. Finally he tied a line to the travois, leaving it on the bank and slipped down into the water. With a stick he cut to brace himself, Jason worked his way across, leaning into the current, careful to not let his feet be swept out from under him.

He scrambled up the bank on the far side. Now taking the line, he looped it around a small tree and began to pull the travois. It jerked in the current and he struggled to pull the gear across. Finally it reached the bank and the current lessened its grip. Jason reached down and pulled it up on the bank.

This pattern repeated itself with each crossing slowing his progress considerably. His ribs remained painful and his fatigue increased. Being constantly wet from the rain and the stream crossings sapped his strength. He did not have the energy to hunt or set snares. *This is bad*, he thought, grimly. *I need some shelter and time to heal.* He kept steering his course to flatter ground, increasing his odds of contact.

Chapter 7

One day, looking across the valley to the east, Jason spied a farm house with smoke coming from the chimney. *People!* The farm was situated on a finger of private property thrust into the folds of the national forest. *Maybe I could stop there for a few days to recover?* In his condition he had to take a chance. As Jason worked his way down to the valley, the weather began to close in; the wind picked up from the east, cold and damp, the sky thickened with clouds. As dusk approached he stopped. He did not want to approach the house in the dark so he set up his lean-to shelter as the rain began. That night it blew and rained harder than he could remember. There was no hope of a fire. His structure failed to keep out the driving rain. The hours of the night dragged on. Sleep wouldn't come. The rain penetrated his shelter and then his clothes. The cold seeped deep inside of him. He huddled under the tarp and shivered through the night.

His mind drifted to Maggie, remembering the warmth of her body in the morning when they would awake. Her scent had a sweet muskiness. He would bury his head against her body while she sleepily wrestled with him until they were both awake.

The grey morning brought no relief from the cold and wet. The rain was still coming down—this was going to be a multi-day storm. As soon as it was light enough, Jason forced his stiff body into action and gathered his dripping gear. He slowly made his way out of the bush and through the fields in the direction of the farm house.

The house was in good repair, no broken windows or half-open doors. The barn looked well maintained. The hedges were trimmed. The whole place spoke of order and productiveness. Whoever lived here took pride in their home. Before reaching the farm yard, he carefully circled to the front and limped up the drive. Would they let him stay? Would they shoot him on sight? Jason remembered that he had once rejected others from the safety of his house; now he was the petitioner. Caution called for him to just move on, but his injuries demanded he take a chance.

"Hello in the house!" He called out.

A moment later there was a shout from inside, "Stop!"

Jason did as he was told. He figured that command was accompanied by a weapon aimed at him. The rain continued to fall.

"What do you want," the voice from inside called out.

"Just some shelter until the storm passes, maybe in your barn?" Jason responded.

"Don't want any strangers around, you better go."

"Please, I know you're suspicious but I mean no harm. I just need a little shelter before I move on."

"Where do you come from?"

"Hillsboro. Things aren't good there, there's corruption and a shortage of food. That's why I left." Jason proceeded to give the voice in the house a short version of his trek to date, leaving out the encounter with the men in the underpass.

"I don't want anything from you but some shelter. I'm looking to find my own place to survive until things sort themselves out." He wondered how long that would be as he spoke the words.

There was some muffled conversation inside. Jason stood in the mud and rain and now began to shiver uncontrollably. He continued, hoping to strengthen the discussion in his favor, "I can help you with any repairs if I can stay a few days. I think I will prove to be helpful. Then I'll be on my way."

"You got any weapons on you?" The voice from inside called out.

"Of course. A rifle, pistol and bow and arrows for hunting," Jason replied.

"You'll have to turn them over if you want to stay," came the reply.

Jason looked down and thought for some moments. How could he get past that objection? He looked up at the house, "I can't give them up. They're the tools I need to survive. I've approached you openly, not like someone trying to steal from you or attack you. That should count for something. Look, it's raining hard, I'm cold and wet...and injured."

After a pause the man in the house replied, "Let me see that your weapons are empty, then you can hang them on the porch. I won't take them. They'll be out of the rain and in plain sight. You can take them back when you leave."

Jason thought for a moment. This was the best offer he was going to get. "Fair enough," he replied. Trying to ignore how cold and wet he was, he slowly unstrapped his rifle; it had no clip and he pulled the charging lever to show no chambered bullet. Next he did the same with the 9mm. Finally he laid the bow with its quiver of arrows on the ground next to the firearms. A man emerged on the porch from the house with a lever action rifle held at ready. He was stocky built, six feet tall, about 10 years older than Jason, but rough and fit, like a man who had farmed all his life. The rifle was probably a 30-30 thought Jason. "My name's Jason, what's yours?" he asked in an attempt to lower the tension.

"Sam," the man answered, the rifle still held at ready, not quite pointed at Jason. "Bring your weapons to the porch, then you can head over to the barn. The barn is dry and you can spread out your gear inside. The sleeping should be pretty good in there."

"I hate to ask, but is there any chance of getting something warm to drink? I'm really cold and I'm afraid I'm becoming hypothermic." He was starting to shiver uncontrollably.

"Stash your gear and then come back to the porch. I'll get you some hot tea. There's no coffee left."

"Hot tea would be great, especially the 'hot' part," replied Jason with an attempt to smile. It was a joy to talk to someone who seemed normal. Jason wasn't sure how many people were in the house, but suspected it was just Sam and his wife. He didn't inquire. Sam seemed to not want to give away much personal information.

He headed to the barn. Inside he spread out his wet gear to let it dry. Then he walked back to the porch. Sam must have been watching because he met Jason at the door and handed him a large mug of steaming hot tea along with some biscuits and jam. Jason sat down and devoured the biscuits and sipped the tea balancing his eagerness for its warmth against his desire to not burn his tongue. The large mug of hot liquid began to have its warming effect and Jason's shivers grew less intense.

"Sorry I don't have more to offer," said Sam.

"This is wonderful," replied Jason, "I wasn't expecting this much...biscuits and jam...wow."

"We've still got a good supply of jam left after the winter," said Sam. "Tell me more about what is going on in Hillsboro."

Jason filled him in with more details about the shortages, looting, martial law and the corruption he experienced.

"You had any problem with gangs up here?" Jason asked.

"Not so much, occasionally a few bad guys came around. I had to shoot at some of them, but they didn't have much fight in them. It got worse as winter approached and they got more desperate and hungry. Then they disappeared. Haven't seen anyone yet this spring. Not sure what's happened to them."

"What about your neighbors?" Jason had noticed some houses nearby.

"One widower died last winter; caught pneumonia. We took care of him but there was not much we could do to help" Sam replied. "The other two couples left for Hillsboro. Now that you tell me about things down there, it doesn't sound like that was a good move. I'm glad we didn't go with them." They were both silent for a moment.

"How did you fare through the winter?" he asked.

"We did alright. We regularly put food up—by canning—so we had supplies. We had to butcher a cow and bandits took the others. I couldn't stop all the rustling. We have some chickens that we keep. It was hard to save them over the winter but we managed to keep most alive."

"Can you still farm this spring?"

"Yep, wheat and corn," replied Sam. "With the harvest we keep some seed and keep the cycle going...wish we could get a couple of goats or sheep, but they've disappeared. But we'll be able to start a vegetable garden again, that helps a lot."

Jason decided to take a chance to learn more, "I'm guessing your wife is inside, are there more of you, or have the two of you done all this?"

Sam looked sharply at him, measuring him and his question. "Yes, I have a wife. It's just the two of us. Our kids moved away five years ago. We haven't heard from them since the power went out and don't know how they're doing. We pray for them and hope for the best. They were raised to be self sufficient—growing up on a farm." Sam paused for moment, then said, "Wife's name is Judy. You may as well meet her. Come on inside."

They went in the house and headed into the kitchen. The warmth enveloped him like a soft, cozy blanket. There was a wood stove in the kitchen and it was going strong, taking the damp out of the room. The smell of the day's cooking filled the air. Jason breathed in deeply, savoring the odors and memories that they triggered. Sam introduced Judy. She greeted Jason warmly, like a mother although she was only about 10 years older. Judy was a short but solid woman about five foot two or three. Jason immediately felt at home and welcome.

He recounted his trek from Hillsboro. "I fell off the side of the mountain...I know it sounds stupid. Anyway, I rolled about two hundred feet down and bruised or cracked a couple of ribs. I damaged the travois in the process. It sure has been painful."

"You have to stay until you're healed up." Judy said. Sam looked at her but said nothing.

"That's generous of you. I'll do what I can to help out. I don't think anything could be as hard as pulling that broken travois with these sore ribs."

Sitting down and relaxing in the kitchen, Jason began nodding off, overwhelmed by the warmth and his fatigue.

Sam smiled, "Maybe you should head out to the barn while you're still awake."

Judy started to say something, but Sam gave her a look to keep quiet. She disappeared for a few moments and returned with two wool blankets and a pillow. *A pillow!* Jason couldn't hold back the grin when he saw it.

"This should help you to get a good sleep," Judy said as she dumped the bedding in Jason's arms.

Sam added a poncho, "Cover the bedding, you don't want to get it wet."

Thanking them, Jason took the bedding and headed back to the barn. Once in the barn he scraped up some left over straw into a pile against an interior stall. Then he set up a lean-to from the top of the stall to the floor, laid down another tarp and covered that with the blankets and pillow. Then, taking off his clothes for the first time in more than a week, he stooped under the tarp and crawled into the nest he had created. Lying back with his head on the pillow, Jason sighed deeply as his aching muscles began to relax and fell into a deep sleep. Sam and Judy stayed up all night in shifts, keeping a watch on the barn, just to be sure.

Jason slept from that afternoon through the night until the next morning. He was awakened by the delicious smell of breakfast being cooked; fried ham, eggs and biscuits. His stomach growled and heaved as the quick pangs of hunger rose up. He dressed quickly and headed to the house, hoping he would be invited in. Sure enough, when he got to the porch, Judy called out for him to come into the kitchen. There on the table were biscuits with some canned meat and fresh eggs. *Eggs!* Jason couldn't believe it.

"How...?" he asked.

"Didn't Sam tell you? We saved some hens and a rooster," Judy replied. "They're worth more laying eggs than for us to eat them. It took some work to keep them from thieves and predators, but we modified the chicken coop to meet both challenges—lock 'em up at night." She said with a grin.

"We had to make a strong, lockable coop," said Sam, coming into the kitchen. "You should know these eggs are special, they're free range, very organic."

Jason smiled. "They could be any kind of range and I'd relish them. I never thought I would be sitting in a kitchen eating eggs after I left my house. When you mentioned saving some chickens over the winter, I didn't realize you had your own egg laying operation."

"All it takes is some hens and a randy rooster," Sam replied with a wink.

Judy put out the plates. Jason started to eat, then he stopped as Judy and Sam bowed their heads and gave thanks for the meal.

Judy noticed Jason's confusion and discomfort. "We give thanks for every meal we eat. We give thanks for our ability to provide for ourselves in this strange time. And now, we can give thanks for being able to help someone who came to us in need."

His mouth full, Jason just nodded, but he wondered how one could keep giving thanks to God after what had happened. "Don't you find it hard? I mean, life has changed, our society has been ripped apart. What about your sons? They may have not fared as well as you."

"All the more reason to pray...for them and for others. We're doing well. We've been used to living on our own for years, but we know that many people are not equipped so well as us. They need our prayers all the more."

Jason shook his head at their easy declaration of faith in the face of such a disruption in society. It continued to rain, so Jason and Sam spent the morning talking about the future, the farm and the work projects where he could use Jason's help. It was the first time since the EMP attack that Jason had heard positive talk about the future—something more than just survival. Later he went to the barn to rest and dry out his gear. That afternoon Judy scrounged up some foam padding and helped Jason sew some extra padding in strategic areas of his harness in an effort to reduce the abrasions.

The next day the weather broke. Jason's ribs were feeling better after two luxurious nights sleeping with a pillow and dry blankets. He was able to move better and be of some help to Sam. Sam drew up a list of repairs and the two men set out to work. As the days progressed and Jason healed, he was increasingly helpful. They settled into a routine of work, talk, and then eating in the kitchen. Jason offered to contribute some of his food, but Judy would not allow it. "We have enough and we'll be planting more soon."

They worked on getting a neighbor's old tractor, retired many years earlier, back to life. Since it was pre-electronic, Sam thought they could get it to run again. Sam's tractor had died with the EMP burst. They collected some diesel fuel and found a couple of batteries that weren't completely dead and wired them together. They removed and disassembled the injectors, cleaned and carefully reassembled them. After putting everything together they spent a painstaking hour priming the system and were rewarded when the engine finally coughed to life. They whooped it up and slapped high fives with each other like a couple of school boys.

Over the next week, Jason learned about plowing and disking the soil; and how to plant the corn and wheat. According to Sam, all the cereal grains could be done the same way. He stood in the field, inhaling the dark, musky scent of the tilled earth. It was soft and black. It spoke of a mystery. Put something in it, bury it and it will be returned a hundred-fold. Jason marveled at it all, how roots lived a hidden, subterranean life, pulling in nutrients from simple dirt and turning that into plant growth.

"It's not simple dirt," Sam said as Jason marveled out loud. "This soil is rich in chemicals and nutrients that plants need. The wonder is how the roots collect those nutrients so the plants can grow."

"Planting seems like such an act of faith," Jason said.

"It is in more ways than you can imagine. It's not just the wonder of plants emerging from seeds, but you have to have faith that the proper amount of rain will come, the bugs won't overwhelm the crops and you can get the harvest in without rain ruining it. Rain helps at one part of the process and then hurts at another part."

Jason also helped Sam with the vegetable garden which they planted by hand. They put in beans, onions, beets, carrots, kale and other greens. Jason was stunned at what Sam and Judy had available to them by carefully storing from each season's harvest. His mouth watered in anticipation of the bounty they would reap.

A warm glow kept coming over him as the days passed. Jason wondered about the feeling; there was an elusive quality about it. It was pleasant, but he couldn't readily find a name for it. Then one day it hit him; he was experiencing the joys of family; the warmth and bond between people who cared for one another mixed with the shared efforts of working towards common goals. It was a feeling he hadn't experienced since his childhood. Jason basked in the glow, soaking up its warmth and comfort.

This couple was self sufficient and thriving. Much of the country needed to know what Sam and Judy knew. The country was going to have to revert back to the family farm producing its excess for those in the cities.

Chapter 8

Planting and other work went on for two weeks. Jason's ribs healed and his strength returned. One morning after breakfast, he asked Sam about the possibility of staying on at the farm.

"I could help you with all the chores and more than make up for what I eat. I could also help in any defense of the farm...if that became necessary."

Sam looked at Jason. "Judy and I talked about you the last two nights. You've been a good work partner and I think we've helped each other, but I'm not sure we should add a third party to our home."

Jason looked at him in surprise. He thought his idea was perfect; at least it seemed so from his point of view. "Why? Don't I add to the farm? I work hard and I've got some useful skills."

"Yes you do..."

"Don't I fit in well with you and Judy?" He had been getting very comfortable. "I'd really like to stay."

Sam looked at the ground for a long moment, "Jason, you do carry your weight. We work well right now, but this is short term. Judy and I have been self sufficient since the last kid left five years ago and we like it that way. You're a good man," he continued, "but this is not our style of living. We felt called to help you...it's our Christian duty. And you've help us in return. But we're not that upset at what has happened. Like I said, we've lived alone for years.

I'm glad we could help you but you need to find your own place...or a place to make your own."

"What about an extra man for defense?"

"We can take care of ourselves. We have so far. And I think we'll see even fewer people this year. We're pretty far away from any big towns."

Jason sighed and nodded. "I guess I'll get my gear together. I'm feeling better and I probably should set out tomorrow."

"I don't want to hurry you out."

"It's better to go now rather than later." The dismay he felt was sharpened by his remembered sense of loss of family.

Sam helped Jason get his harness fine tuned. The addition of Judy's strategic padding made the travois feel much more comfortable. Jason had repaired the damage and felt confident it would work even better. Judy made him take two of the wool blankets knowing that Jason would find the wool useful. Sam also gave him one of the ponchos for the inevitable rainy days and nights.

The next morning, after an extra large breakfast and many hugs, Jason got himself into his harness and pulled on his backpack. Judy looked sad, as if she were seeing off one of her kids. Even Sam looked a little sad, but Jason smiled at them.

"You were a Godsend. I'll never forget you and your help. I'm so glad you didn't shoot me that rainy day when I showed up. I must have looked pretty bad."

"You did and I'm glad I didn't," Sam responded, grinning. "We'll always remember you, too. We wish you well in finding a place of your own."

"We'll be praying for you," Judy added.

Sam advised going north on the road for about a mile and he would find an old two-track trail, just after a little creek, heading west into the foothills. It was one of numerous old roads dating back to colonial times that cut into the mountains. They were used to access the forest for its timber, bark and minerals. These old two-track trails, often called bark roads, hundreds of years old, provided relatively easy travel into the mountains. Up on the ridge, which Sam expected Jason could reach by evening, he would find a hunting trail going north.

With a smile and wave, Jason set off down the drive. He hoped Sam and Judy would be all right. They had made it through the first winter just fine. But as he walked down the road, he could not shake a nagging worry about Sam's dismissal of threats from outlaw gangs. He hoped Sam was right.

Chapter 9

Jason hiked up the bark road. His travois worked so much better than before. The spring day was sunny and filled with promise. The trees were beginning to bud. The air was clear, the birds were singing. He could hear a Chickadee with its clear, three note whistle, and the staccato chirping of a purple finch. In spite of his sadness at leaving, it was a day that held the promise of new beginnings. This first day he stopped early to enjoy the weather and savor some of the food Judy packed for him. It wouldn't last long, so he decided to eat it right away. He set up camp just off the road, below the ridge. It had been a comfortable first day hiking and he was pleased that he and the harness were getting along better.

Shouldn't feel sad, he told himself, reflecting on Sam and Judy's decision, just grateful that he found them when he did. They allowed him a respite from his plunge into the deep end of wilderness living. They provided him a place and the time to heal and recover from being overwhelmed. Jason now felt much more ready for his odyssey. He was hardened and chastened from his initial experience and had learned some lessons about finding the rhythm of the forest.

He turned his thoughts from Sam and Judy to his own plans. It was still to find country that was remote and had game, and then find some shelter where he could establish a living situation that was a step up from camping. Long term camping was not a viable option. It would break his body down, especially through the winter. He would look to find or create more substantial shelter. He sensed he was getting closer to his goal. He could feel it as he went to sleep under his lean-to.

The next morning Jason lingered around his camp after breakfasting on Judy's biscuits, a hard-boiled egg and some herb tea. Judy had insisted on giving him some eggs, biscuits, canned meat and mint tea, and Jason wanted to enjoy them. Suddenly he heard what sounded like shots in the distance, down in the valley from where he had come. He stood and listened carefully; there were more sounds, definitely shots being fired.

He doused his campfire, unstrapped his rifle from his backpack, stuffed three extra loaded magazines in his pocket and strapped on his pistol holster. Grabbing his binoculars, he ran back down the two-track to a switchback where there was a break in the trees. The house was obscured but he could see two old pickup trucks in the front area. It was clear the gunfire was coming from the house.

He set out on a run down the road, hoping he would not be too late. He ran until his lungs gave out, walked until he recovered, and started running again. At the bottom of the slope, he cut through some fields using a swath of woods to shield him from the house. The gunfire ended and before he reached the house he heard the trucks leaving.

At the edge of the woods, Jason stopped and scanned the house; no sign of anyone. With great caution, he approached the rear corner and tried the back door. It was locked. He went around to the front. The windows were shot out and the door was broken and hanging open. Crouching, with his rifle at ready he slowly entered the house.

He listened. There was no sound from inside. The furniture was knocked about and overturned. Creeping further into the house, he found Sam's body in the hallway on the way to the kitchen. He had been shot multiple times. Blood was spattered everywhere. A pool of blood seeped out from under his body. Jason grimaced as his stomach heaved. It had been some years since he had seen a dead body, especially a friend. Tears welled up in his eyes. He brushed them away and ventured further into the house looking for Judy. The kitchen was ransacked, the table was overturned. Cabinets were torn open and emptied. He found a part of Judy's dress torn and lying on the floor but he could not find her.

They've taken her, she's alive! Then his face clouded as he thought about how they might treat her. The pantry was emptied. The basement where Judy kept the canned food had been discovered and stripped. The liquor cabinet, Sam's pride, was empty. Jason could not find any other sign of Judy in the house. He took a sheet from the bedroom and covered Sam.

I'll find her, Sam. I'll get her back and make them pay for...this. He couldn't find a word to describe it.

He had to try to catch up to them. How far had they gone? His mind was filled with grim thoughts of what was coming. He went to the well in the yard and pumped cold water over his head, took a long drink and shouldered his rifle. Then he set off at a trot on the road going south.

Jason ran for about an hour when he saw smoke ahead. He veered off the road and worked his way through the fields and hedge rows, moving more carefully as he got closer. Finally he stopped and lay down at the edge of an overgrown field. He was about 60 yards from the encampment, located in the yard of a partially burned farmhouse. Tents were spread around the yard. Some pickups and jeeps were parked in the grass, interspersed with a few motorcycles; all were older models that the gang had gotten running. The farm house still stood. The roof was intact. People—mostly men—were moving in and out of the house. Fires were being set in the yard and food being cooked. On the porch were some of the spoils from

Sam and Judy's house. From the looks of it, the group was getting ready to party and feast, enjoying what they had stolen from Sam and Judy.

Evening approached and Jason lay in his hide. *Got to wait till dark.* He had not located Judy. He hoped she was not in the house because he couldn't see how he could get her out with either of them surviving.

The drinking started. The sounds grew louder as more alcohol was consumed. Soon the scene became raucous and violent. Drunken scuffles broke out amongst the men. Jason heard the females scream as the men manhandled them. The screams and squeals became a background to the overall din of the encampment. Through his glasses, Jason finally located a tent at the edge of the yard with men steadily going in and out. The din continued well into the evening until around midnight when it started to gradually quiet down.

Over the next two hours, Jason slowly crawled through the high grass in the field. The dark hid his matted trail. He went carefully, not wanting to make his move until the group drank itself to sleep. He aimed for the tent where he had seen men going in and out, hoping Judy might be there and hoping at the same time that she wasn't. The reality, he guessed, was probably much worse. Even at 50, Judy was not an unattractive woman, and who knew what code of conduct ruled this group? The violence he had seen in the Miller's house was the equal of what he had read about in medieval times; even the equal of the barbarians who brought down the Roman Empire. They thought cruelty and violence towards the enemy was a virtue.

Jason reached the tent and listened for some time. The only sound he heard was a low moaning and whimpering. Very slowly he cut a small opening in the back of the tent. He put his eye to the small slit and tried to see inside. In the tent's darkness he could make out one small figure on one side, Judy? There was another, larger figure lying on the other side. Slowly Jason started to slice the tent open.

His heart was racing and his breathing became ragged. He stopped to calm his breathing lest it became too loud.

Be calm. Breathe steady.

He repeated this mantra over and over in his mind. When the figures in the tent did not move, he steadied himself and finished cutting the tent open. Then he slowly worked his way through the opening. As he was pulling himself through, the sleeping figure groggily mumbled something, hearing the brush of clothing and struggling to wake up. Without hesitation, Jason thrust his body over the man covering his mouth with one hand and with the other, shoved his knife into the man's neck. He jerked and flopped instinctively trying to get away from the attack. Jason worked the knife back and forth, slashing and cutting the life out of him. After a short struggle there was a gurgling sound and he went limp. Jason held on for a few seconds more and then pulled back; the man was dead. He turned quickly to other figure,

"Judy, is that you?" he whispered.

"Please, no," came her weak reply.

"It's me, Jason," he said as he went over to her, listening for sounds outside of the tent. All was quiet. Judy had a blanket thrown over her; under it she was naked and bound.

"Jason" she whispered, "it's you?"

"Don't talk. I'm getting you out of here." He whispered.

"They raped me. I hurt...I'm hurt...inside."

"Shhh. I'll get you out."

He cut her bonds. He could feel the cuts and bruising on her wrists and ankles from the ropes. He found a shirt and put it over her. Taking the blanket, he helped Judy crawl through the opening in the tent. Outside, Jason had Judy lie on the blanket which he dragged behind him as he crawled back along his path. This time he went faster and with less caution, taking a chance that everyone was asleep.

On reaching the tree line, Jason wrapped Judy in the blanket and picked her up in his arms.

"Hold on, it will be a bumpy trip. I've got to get us away from here as fast as possible."

"Don't let them catch us. They hurt me," Judy said again. "Over and over, they wouldn't stop."

Then she started moaning. Jason gritted his teeth against her sounds of pain and set out. It was hard going, in spite of Judy's not being very big. Jason drove himself on and on, stopping only to adjust how he carried her; in his arms, piggy back style and over his shoulders. But always he kept moving, whether a walk, a shuffle or a slow jog, he would not stop.

Two hours later they arrived at the farm house. He gently laid Judy down in the yard and went into the barn to retrieve a two wheeled cart he had seen. Next he ran into the house and collected pillows and blankets. He made a padded bed in the cart and set Judy in it. Jason knew she had been bleeding during the past two hours while he carried her. He laid her in the cart and put a pillow between her legs. He told her to push it up tight to stem the bleeding. Judy was so weak that Jason had to help. Apologizing for the bumpiness, he told her he was going to take her to his camp where the gang would not be able to find them.

"I'll keep you safe, Judy. They won't hurt you again."

"Sam?" she asked. "They shot him over and over. They laughed and shot him, again and again." Then she collapsed in the cart and Jason set out, now running, towing the cart behind him. He left muddy footprints on the road, but he didn't care.

I hope they come after me, he thought, grimly. His mind was growing darker as he ran on, hearing Judy's moaning in the cart, getting weaker and weaker.

He turned up the bark road, running, shuffling, stumbling, not stopping. As the grade got steeper, his legs got heavier, but he kept going. It was like the worst army training run he had ever experienced. His lungs were on fire, his breath came in ragged gasps and still he went on, even at a shuffle. He couldn't stop until he got to his camp and tended to Judy. Her soft cries drove him on and on. At last he arrived. His camp was on top of the steep bank that had been created when a flat area or 'bench' was cut into the hillside to make the narrow shelf for the road bed.

Jason laid Judy gently down on the blankets from the cart. As he lifted her, he felt how wet the pillow was from her blood. He wrapped Judy in the extra blankets she had given him the day before. Their worlds had disintegrated since that bittersweet goodbye. He roused Judy enough to get her to drink some water.

"Don't let me go," she said. "Hold me." He took her in his arms, wrapped tight in the blankets. "They hurt me deep inside," she mumbled. "I'm hurt bad."

"You'll be all right. I'll take care of you".

"I'm cold," she said softly. She was shivering. Jason pulled his extra parka out of his pack with one hand and draped it over her while he kept her tight in his arms. Gently he rocked back and forth. The shivering decreased and she seemed to relax more.

"Don't leave me up here in the hills...for the animals." He could barely hear her voice.

"I won't leave you, you'll be okay, you're going to be okay," he said, he hoped, with conviction. "I'll take care of you."

"Sam...Sam," she said. "Why did they have to keep shooting Sam?" Jason just kept rocking her gently. Judy slipped into unconsciousness. He kept holding her and rocking her for the next two hours as her life slowly slipped away.

David Nees

Chapter 10

The dark of the night gave way to a dim blue pre-dawn sky. The sun seemed reluctant to light this sad day. With tears in his eyes, in the half light, Jason gently carried Judy to a rock outcropping and nestled her body there. He sat down and cried, for Judy, for Sam, for Maggie, for himself and for all the people he knew who had lost their lives from the EMP attack. He cried for the loss of civil society in Hillsboro and for shooting people in ambush. And when he had cried all the tears he could cry, his mind went cold and hard. He gathered his gear and stashed it in the rocks near where he had laid Judy. He drank some water and ate some food. Next he checked his rifle, the extra magazines, and his 9mm. Then he set up his firing positions; one forward, with two retreat positions along the top of the bank cut into the hillside. They covered the road and anyone climbing up the slope. His last position would be in the rocks with Judy.

He expected the gang to come after him, or at least a part of them. He had killed one member and taken their captive; they could not let his actions pass without a response. This would be a fight to the death. Jason was not going anywhere, and he was going to take out as many as he could. His anger dissolved any reservations about killing. If he was fortunate, he would survive, but he didn't care if the outcome was his death. He was not going to be stupid—no suicide charges—he was going to be methodical. Take the sniper's approach. As he readied himself, the brightening day did not disperse the darkness in Jason's heart and mind. Fatigue left him as anger energized his body.

Come on, you can track me, you can find me. Come on and taste my vengeance.

Within an hour of it getting light, Jason heard motors in the distance. *They'll go to the farmhouse first then they'll find my tracks. Don't miss the trail. I'm waiting for you.*

Jason was about fifty yards from the switchback where he had first spied the attack on Sam and Judy. As he waited, Jason thought about his fascination with stalking, even as a kid. He would spend hours with friends or by himself in the woods playing Indians. He learned to walk quietly on the leaf bed of the forest. With a pretend rifle, he would try to sneak up on prey. When he got old enough to hunt by himself, he practiced the same technique.

He joined the army after high school. His marksmanship skills soon came to the attention of his officers, who encouraged him to try out for sniper school. There his childhood skills were developed until Jason became a deadly sniper. He was going to use all his skills today to wreak havoc on those who had violated Sam and Judy.

The gang found the road and headed up into the mountains towards Jason. His plan was simple. Stop the trucks by shooting the lead driver, keep shooting as many as possible, do not let them get organized and pinpoint his location. If he was pinned down he would crawl back to his next shooting position and start over until they pinned him down again. He could repeat the pattern one more time. He had some hollow point ammunition for his rifle which he loaded into his magazines. He loaded four 20 round magazines, one in the rifle and three in his jacket. At the relatively short distance from which he was shooting, Jason needed only to hit a target and the person would go down.

The morning air was cool and still, but Jason began sweating as adrenalin surged through him. The rumble of the engines grew closer.

Sounds like two trucks. Probably ten to twelve men.

He waited until both trucks had negotiated the switchback then opened fire on the lead truck. The first shot went through the windshield and hit the driver. Jason quickly shot the second truck's driver as well. Men began jumping out of the back. Jason shot as fast as he could acquire a target. The lead truck rolled back against the other and they jammed in the trail. The gang members hid behind the trucks searching for the source of the shooting.

The firing from the trucks was wild and not well aimed. Jason would see a rifle, often an AK47 or an AR15 variant, just held up over the fender and fired in his general direction. Still some of the bullets began to whistle close by. When he saw a rifle above the bed of one of the pickups, Jason shot, rapid fire, at the wall of the bed, hoping to penetrate the sheet metal and hit the shooter. Occasionally he heard a scream indicating he was successful. After a few minutes, Jason slowed his rate of fire to ensure he didn't overheat the barrel of his rifle. One of the men made a run for the slope on Jason's side of the road. His shot caught him in the hip, twisting him to the ground. His rifle flung out of his hands as he landed screaming in pain. He tried to crawl back to cover. Jason ignored him. Two more made it to the base of the slope where they were protected from Jason's fire.

Can't let any more get up against the cliff.

He paused to replace his magazine. One of the men crawled up over the cliff, stood up and started firing in his direction. Jason, lying in a prone position, quickly sighted him and shot him in the chest. The force of the shot knocked him backwards to the ground with his rifle flying away from him. The next man peered cautiously over the lip while Jason was still aiming in that direction. Jason's shot hit him in the face. The back of his head exploded and he toppled back down the cliff.

Some of the gang moved out from the pickups to the woods to their right, down-slope and across the road from Jason. They were now firing from tree cover and had zeroed in on his location. Jason backed away from the lip of the cliff and quickly crawled back to his second firing position. From this new position, he could see up against the cliff on his side and confirm that no one was attempting to climb it. There were still some men back at the pickups, the rest were in the woods on the other side. Jason waited, motionless with his rifle at ready. He could hear some discussion coming from the woods but could not make out what was being said.

Patience, he who moves first gets killed.

He waited. Sure enough a figure darted from one tree to another nearby, heading in his direction. The move was too quick for Jason to get off a shot. He waited. He did not want to expose his new position. The next tree was farther away. *Patience.*

Then gunfire erupted from the other trees—*cover fire!* Jason kept his sights on the gap between the trees. The figure leapt out, crouching and running; Jason squeezed off three rapid shots, the last caught the man in the leg just as he reached the tree. He was knocked down from the shot but managed to get behind the tree. The gunfire now turned his way, but the shooters still did not have a good fix on him. Jason saw movement in the brush as one of the shooters attempted to get into a better position. He fired a burst of rounds into the brush and heard screams. A third gunman in the woods melted back further into the trees and headed for the trucks.

While Jason was concentrating on the gunmen in the woods, two men back at the pickups crawled into the cab of the rearmost truck and got it started. They backed it up in a flurry of dirt. Jason fired off some rounds at the retreating vehicle, but then stopped. He did not want to waste ammunition. The man in the woods screamed for the truck, running through the trees to intercept it as it headed down the mountain.

Jason rolled over on his back; it was over. He was drenched in sweat. He had fired forty-five to fifty rounds; his rifle was very hot. He could hear the sounds of the wounded at the truck and in the road. He breathed deeply, waiting for his heart to stop racing. The acrid smell of gunpowder floated in the air.

Gathering himself together, he crawled back from the edge of the cliff. *Got to find that guy in the woods. He's shot in the leg but still dangerous.*

Jason crawled away from the battle, parallel to the road, until it wound around the shoulder of the slope, giving him cover. He dropped down onto the road and, after listening for some time, took a deep breath and sprinted across it, diving into the ditch on the other side. Protecting his rifle from the ground meant Jason had to land on his forearms when diving for cover.

He grunted loudly as he hit the hard dirt. "Damn, that hurts."

Better skinned up than shot.

Now that the main battle was over and Jason's rage spent, he realized he wanted to live and was determined to not get killed by being careless. He put all his woodsman skills to work as he crept and crawled towards the shooter. After gaining the downhill side of the road, he moved further downhill, deeper into the woods, heading back towards the wounded man. It was not the most advantageous position—down slope from your enemy— but he guessed the shooter would expect him to approach closer to the road. He had certainly heard Jason cross the road, whether or not he had seen him. Jason was banking on the injured man not being able to keep silent.

As he got closer to where he thought the man was hiding, he moved ever more slowly. What he learned as a young boy playing in the woods was that patience won out. Do not move unless you know it will be completely silent and you cannot be seen from a forward position. That lesson paid off as he heard a stifled groan and a rustle. The injured man adjusted his position and the pain caused him to make a sound. Now Jason had an approximate fix on the enemy. He was forward and to his right, close to the road.

He adjusted his position to look uphill towards the road. He waited and watched; there would be more sounds, he was sure. Time was not on the other man's side. After five minutes of waiting, as expected, he heard, and this time saw movement, as the man adjusted his position again. He was aiming past Jason, looking closer to the road. Slowly, slowly Jason brought his rifle to bear on the target. It took him some careful minutes to adjust his position and make sure he had a clear shot through the underbrush. He was not worried about small leaves and twigs, but he did not want any saplings to make his shot go astray. He zeroed in on his target, adjusted by inches at a time, until he felt confident of his shot. Then he fired three quick rounds, the second and third bracketing his first. As best he could see, through the brush, the figure slumped to the ground.

Jason rolled back down slope and then ran crouching past the man's position to approach him from behind. He moved more quickly this time, though still using the trees for cover. At last he could see the man slumped over his rifle. Two of Jason's shots had hit him, one below his face and one in his upper side. He was dead and never saw his executioner.

Now he went back into stealth mode, moving towards the truck, looking for the second shooter in the woods. He found him gravely wounded and very weak. The bullet had torn into his shoulder and he was bleeding profusely. His weapon was five feet away from him but he made no attempt to reach for it as Jason approached. Jason looked at the rifle. It was Sam's 30-30.

He picked it up and pointed it at the man, "this is for Sam," he said, and he shot him in the other shoulder. At this close range the bullet tore into his shoulder, dislocating it and ripping it open.

The man cried out. "Just wanted you to feel the bite from the gun of the man you killed." Jason said. The man glowered at Jason, unable to move with both arms torn. "You did evil things to my friends and now it's time for you to pay." Jason's next shot was between the eyes.

He found two more men alive near the truck and dispatched them with their own weapons. Then he collected the weapons and ammunition from the bodies before searching the truck where he found more. Along with Sam's 30-30, Jason kept two AR15 rifles and all the ammunition. They fired a .223 round, the same as his Ruger. They were good rifles. He thought it a good idea to have the back-up weapons and the ammunition was priceless. He also took a couple of 9mm pistols and all the 9mm ammunition he could find. Next, Jason maneuvered the truck crosswise in the roadbed to create a roadblock for any other vehicles trying to drive further up the mountain.

If they come back, this will slow or stop them. He opened the hood and took out the distributor cap and rotor and flung them into the woods. Jason had no use for a pickup truck where he was going. He paused to survey the scene. There were bodies around the truck, against the cliff and in the woods. There was no breeze; the strong smell of gunpowder still hung in the air between the trees.

It will smell worse later. Jason, drenched in sweat, walked back to where he had laid Judy. He still couldn't think of her as 'Judy's body'. *I made them pay for what they did, Judy. Not all of them but as many as I could.* He sat down next to her. As the adrenaline left his system his body began to relax.

Chapter 11

Sometime later Jason awoke with a start. He listened carefully but heard no unusual sounds. He drank the last of his water. He knew now what he had to do; take Judy to her husband. He gently tied some cords around the blankets wrapped around her. After reloading the magazines, he shouldered his rifle, picked Judy up and set out again towards the farmhouse. Jason cut across the fields making a direct line towards the house. In about three hours he was at the last tree line, where he had waited the prior day. It seemed incredible that it had only been yesterday. There was no sign of anyone at the farm and after watching for some long minutes, he approached the farmhouse. He went in the back door and laid Judy on the kitchen table. Then he dragged Sam's body into the kitchen and, with some effort, hoisted him onto the kitchen table.

At first Jason didn't know what else to do. After thinking a bit, he went upstairs and found the linen closet and took two sheets. Then he went to work wrapping the bodies. He carefully crossed their hands on their breasts and folded the sheets over them, with their heads exposed. Then he went back upstairs to look for some personal items. It seemed fitting to place them with their bodies. A Bible, a wedding picture, Sam's hunting knife, some jewelry and a cross; Jason placed them on the table with the bodies.

This is their house, this is their burial place, let this be their funeral pyre.

His earlier thoughts about staying on the farm were driven by Sam and Judy—the sense of family he found with them. Now without them, it was just another abandoned and looted farmhouse. He needed to find something more remote. He went about collecting tinder and placed piles of it throughout the house, starting under the kitchen table.

Goodbye Sam and Judy. You were good people. You gave me shelter, encouragement and guidance and sent me out with kindness to follow my own path. He reflected on the time he spent with them. They were people who could have made this new reality more civilized, maybe better than before. They were brought down by the forces of barbarism that had been unleashed and it was such a loss...tears, again, came to Jason's eyes.

When the power went out, the world as everyone knew it, interdependent with few people self-reliant, or even knowing what it meant to be self-reliant, changed. And three types of people emerged. First were the outlaws and barbarians, who society had always kept in check, if not fully under control. They emerged with power because they were used to living outside the law and exploiting opportunities. They were not going to build anything good, being focused on exploitation and greed. They were the predators. They were the power manipulators; those who had some of the same drives as the outlaws, but worked within the system. This group organized the citizenry and, with no authority to restrain them, tended towards dictatorial control. Jason had seen this happening in Hillsboro in an alliance of the police leadership, some politicians and the criminal elements. Then there were the citizens; the mass of the people who just wanted order and would support anyone who brought order and took care of them—the sheep.

But Sam and Judy didn't seem to fit into any of these groups and neither did he, Jason thought. Maybe that was why they had to separate themselves from the rest. Sam and Judy didn't make it, but Jason vowed he would, for himself and for his two friends. Maybe someday like-minded, self-reliant people, the protectors, would come together and demand a better future...maybe.

He took some diesel fuel and doused the tinder and went through the house lighting it. When the piles were all lit, he left the house and started back through the fields to his camp near the ridge. After gaining some elevation, he turned to look back and saw, with satisfaction, the house, now fully ablaze. It was a magnificent funeral pyre for a magnificent couple. Then he turned and set his face to the north and began hiking.

Book II: The Family
Chapter 1

Jason hiked for two weeks, putting multiple ridges and miles between him and the Miller farm. The travois was working better, though still with some difficulty when the path got too rocky. The extra weapons and ammunition slowed him, but he hiked on, committed to not abandoning those precious assets. He settled into a routine of hiking until the afternoon and then stopping with enough time to eat and make a shelter to sleep.

He now felt more in tune with the forest, making good miles when he was on a trail. And when he didn't have a good trail, he accepted his situation and moved more slowly. He stopped resisting the forest, but adjusted to whatever it presented. This acclimation enabled Jason to see more detail in his surroundings; the hints of game trails where one could set snares, the larger openings that aided one's passage through underbrush, the best way around rock fields. He was now expending his energy in a more efficient manner, not trying to force himself through every obstacle. He had a map of the region and tried to keep his position marked. The further he went, the less accurate this became, but the map still gave him an overall indication of his progression into the remote parts of the forest.

He took more time to make a shelter when he stopped. He would cut a straight pole, lay one end in a tree notch four or five feet up and the other on the ground. Next he would create a tent shape with branches from the ridge pole to the ground. He would pile leaves and debris from the forest floor on the sides and then weave in more branches to hold the filler. All sides would be enclosed except for a small opening at one end. He insulated the floor with leaves. On top of everything he would lay his tarp and the shelter would then be ready for sleeping. It was quite cozy and, when properly constructed, surprisingly rain proof. If he stopped where a campfire could not easily be seen, he would start one in the evening and enjoy a warm meal and the cheer a fire brings to the dark solitude. On many warmer nights, he would string his cover tarp from a ridge pole, lay down a ground cloth, and put out his sleeping bag. Every few days he stayed encamped and hunted for food, setting snares and gathering what edible plants he could find. His plant guide book got a lot of use; he didn't want to poison himself.

When he reached open fields, natural or left over from earlier farming, he stopped to harvest the wood sorrel, kudzu, dandelion and chicory plants he could find. The wood sorrel could be eaten raw. The entire kudzu plant was edible and he would make hot drinks later that evening from the dandelion or chicory he found. Occasionally he would come across clusters of ramps or wild onions and collect as many as he could carry. Marshy areas provided a treasure store of plants to harvest; cattails, the katniss plant and sometimes water lilies.

Since it was still early in the season, Jason could feast on the fiddle head shoots of ferns which he found in the shadier parts of the forest. The berries would have to wait until high summer, but Jason noted their abundance, along with wild grapes, at the edges of fields. For one who knew where to look, the forests and fields provided a rich store of food to balance a diet of game meat.

Jason generally awoke with the birds, just before first light. He would lie still and listen, sniffing the air, testing to see what the day might offer. Then, stretching and limbering his stiff muscles, he slowly got going. If he had made a fire the night before it was a simple task to restart it, putting tinder on the banked embers. Sometimes he treated himself to a warm wash before breaking camp and loading his gear for the day's trek. Jason felt more at home now, but the solitude bore down on him relentlessly. Often he noticed that he was talking to himself.

His numbed state of mind gradually eased through the routine of hiking and camping. Nights, though, often found him in agony. He began to blame himself for Sam and Judy's deaths.

If I had left one day later they might still be alive.

He couldn't shake the thought. The raiding gang would have found themselves in a crossfire between Sam in the house and Jason in the barn. They might have won the battle. The thought became ever more firm in Jason's mind, increasing his guilt about leaving. Again, the memory of his dad leaving came back to him. He had left Hillsboro and now Sam and Judy. Had he become that kind of a man...like his dad? The question ate away at him. Tears came as the human loss pressed down on him—Maggie, and Sam and Judy.

To counter his sadness, he focused more and more on imagining what he was searching for—shelter, permanent shelter—trying to visualize it. But something else was needed. After Sam and Judy, Jason understood how hard it was going to be to live alone until society got sorted out, if ever. He felt confident that he could master food and shelter, but the companionship and satisfaction he had experienced working with the Millers—being helpful, being part of a team—made him realize how precious that relationship was—like family in so many ways.

Can't dwell on that. It'll only make it harder. I've made my bed. Now I must lie in it. He knew he wouldn't have lasted in town. He had seen the militia taking everyone's freedom away in the name of order and safety. It was inevitable that he would have clashed with them. There was order in town, but with strict control. Those in charge wanted to know where you lived, what you did to survive, where you found food. The questions had grown increasingly aggressive and came from the assumption that, nine months after the EMP attack, you were either under the town's jurisdiction and control or you were an outlaw, scavenging and looting. The concept of a self-sufficient person was not part of the thinking.

But this being alone part is going to be damned hard. He couldn't shake feelings of dread about the loneliness that haunted him, feelings that were outside of his woodsman skills, untouched by his ability to survive in the woods.

One day Jason came across a small deer herd. They had not been hunted, this far into the mountains, so they were not skittish. Killing a deer could give him a good meat supply. It would free him for a few weeks of setting snares. The extra time could be spent locating long term shelter. He'd have to smoke the meat to use it over time which worried him. Smoking meant fire, smoke and smell, all of which would advertise his location, to predators as well as humans. But it was a chance he felt he had to take.

In preparation he built a smoker. Away from his camp, he made a tall cone of straight poles surrounding a fire pit. He tied cross poles on which to hang the meat and covered the structure with branches to keep in the smoke. Then he was ready to hunt. Two days passed and the deer didn't show.

Did they read his thoughts? What the hell?

But on the third day, the deer showed up and Jason took one. He field dressed it well away from his camp and smoking area, then, back at the smoker he quickly butchered the carcass, cutting the meat into strips and setting them on the poles. The smoke was filled with a rich aroma, inviting and stimulating. It was quite a signal to all the animals in the forest. Jason stayed on high alert, hoping he would not have to defend his catch from bears or worse.

He kept the meat smoking for twelve hours, feeding the fire with wet wood and leaves. Then he cut the meat into smaller pieces and carefully wrapped them in ramp leaves he had collected. It was not ideal, but it was the best he could do. While the smoking was going on, Jason feasted on venison steaks. He ate heavily for a couple of days, then wrapped the leaf packages in a tarp, stuffed them into his pack and headed off again.

He was now going to explore the valleys that spread out from the side of the ridge he was on. It was time to find a permanent place to stay. It was the beginning of summer and he had much to do to get ready for winter. With his smoked meat and his gear packed, he set out.

Chapter 2

By the third day, Jason had worked his way further north and then crossed over a ridge to the west of his smoking camp. From this ridge he spied a fort shaped valley through his binoculars. The valley was enclosed by ridges on all sides. To the south the rise was gentler. The floor of the valley was marked by fields, now lying fallow. Numerous small creeks meandered through the valley floor, draining the ridges and feeding into a stream that had cut its way through the southern wall of the valley to join a larger river. A narrow macadam road followed the path of the valley stream through the southern embankment, ending in a single lane, iron truss bridge. From the narrow gorge to the south, the road wound up the valley. There were no signs of movement on it. The roofs of the few farm houses he could see were set quite apart from one another. From his vantage point, Jason could not tell if they were inhabited or not. He moved north, on the eastern side of the valley, keeping to higher elevations.

He worked his way past two farmhouses near the valley entrance. The grounds looked overgrown, the barn doors were open, there seemed to be no signs of habitation. They offered possibilities for shelter, but were too close to the road and bridge for Jason's comfort. Half way up the valley he spied a farmhouse that looked promising. It was set back further from the valley road on a cleared shoulder of the hill. A strip of woods screened the house from the road. Below the woods the slope flattened into fields bordering the road. The driveway went gently uphill before a making a switchback to cross a steeper grade then arriving at the flat area in front of the house. The house was on the eastern slope, facing south, looking down the valley, with a view across the valley to the western ridge. There was a barn on the west side of the house, closer to the tree line. Two fields stretched out behind the house to the north separated by a row of brush and trees. East of the yard stood the overgrown remains of an old apple orchard. It ran uphill towards the forest; the trees looked to be dying and probably bore little fruit.

The house and its position in the valley seemed ideal. It was shielded from the road, yet with a good view of the valley. It was late and the house was still quite far so he camped on the ridge that night. He lit no fire.

The next morning Jason found a closer vantage point providing a good view of the farmhouse. He wanted to observe it before approaching. A stand of rhododendron bushes shielded him. Lying there undetected, he settled down to watch.

It wasn't long before he saw a woman emerge from the house. Jason experienced a confusing surge of emotions. The house was not empty and that was a problem for him to use the place for shelter. But seeing another person made him realized how much he missed human company. The memories from his time with Sam and Judy came rushing back. A moment later two more figures emerged from the house. Through his field glasses, Jason could see they were girls in their teenage years. His mind raced; were they alone?

He watched; no one else emerged. The three females went out into the field. They looked like they were gathering what they could from the growth left over from last year's planting. They moved slowly and after an hour, drifted, one by one, back into the house with what they had collected. Later the woman went out to the well pump in the front yard and pumped some water into a jug. She pumped slowly, tiredly it seemed to Jason. Then she went back in. Soon smoke arose from the chimney.

They must be cooking what they've gathered.

Jason crawled back into the trees and sat quietly for a long time to think.

This won't work. There has to be a man somewhere and he'll shoot without warning to protect his family. I've got to move on.

But he couldn't leave. Something kept him there. It was more than the valley. It was certainly well set up in its geography. Memories of the violent encounters he experienced flooded back. This valley looked promising with its isolation and protection by the ridges. But something more drew him. He decided to take some time to watch and see what else happened at the farmhouse before moving on.

There was a broken window on the first floor. Someone had just tacked a sheet up from the inside to cover the opening. The front porch was beginning to sag. With a support post broken at one corner, it was yielding to the inexorable pull of gravity. Below the house, the barn door stood ajar, grounded from a missing hinge, it would no longer close.

Jason patiently watched for two more days and the routine stayed similar, the woman getting water from the pump in the yard, foraging for food, always moving slowly, almost listlessly. Occasionally the metal chimney would smoke, indicating a fire, probably from a wood stove in the kitchen. There were no lights at night. He was oddly reluctant to leave and push further north. He told himself that he needed to be sure about this family before committing himself to another place.

He began to question what he was seeing at the farm. Their gleaning of last year's planting didn't result in much to eat. He wondered if they were slowly starving, while he had enough to eat, even in his temporary camp. Should he get them some food? Jason was surprised at this thought. He toyed with it for a whole day.

"What are you trying to do? You'll scare them and blow your cover," he said. He had begun talking to himself more and more. He was pacing back and forth around his camp area. "You set out to be on your own. Don't change the plan. Just move on and let these people be." Memories of how he had declined to help the group of young people came flooding back. That decision felt more painful now after his experience with Sam and Judy. He tried to talk himself out of helping, but to no avail; he had declined to help one time and later had been helped. He could not avoid helping this time. That night he set out multiple snares.

The next morning Jason checked the snares—they were empty.

Crap! Now I'm trying to help someone, I come up empty.

The valley to the east had a stream in it. Jason had crossed it further south on his way to this ridge. He remembered how thick the cover was, not good for hiking. Perhaps it held a pond or marshy area? It certainly looked that way when he crossed it south of his current position. The creek came from somewhere. It was worth a hike down the east slope of the ridge to investigate. A marsh or pond would hold the promise of more game.

Maybe there are ducks down there. He set off with his rifle. Once committed to the idea, he found himself energized by his new mission. *The sheepdog,* he thought with a grin.

It was early afternoon when he got to the valley. There was a pond, as he had hoped. He noticed the soft ground around it was disturbed; dug up and muddied. Pigs. The mountains contained feral pigs. Their numbers may have been augmented by domestic stock that had escaped being eaten. The phrase "pigs gone wild" came to mind and brought a smile to his face.

They've gone hog wild! He sat down chuckling to himself at the silliness of it all. It was the first real laugh he had since Sam and Judy.

Pigs were a good sign. They were a valuable resource; every part of them could be used. Now since some were near, it made this area all the more attractive to Jason.

There would be time enough to get them after a permanent camp had been established. *"I'll get you, you little piggies."* He started to chuckle again. The laughter felt good. It had been a long time.

"Get back to work," he admonished himself.

Jason quietly approached the pond and sure enough, there was a small group of ducks floating at the far end. The pond was an irregular oval about eighty yards long and 50 yards wide. Jason hid in the brush at its edge. He would try for two but without a shotgun only one was a sure bet. He studied the group, working out which one he would shoot and which direction the others would move to take off. If he planned his second shot, he might be able to get the second duck as it struggled to get airborne. Take one shot and quickly point to where he expected the second duck to be.

He fired and then quickly got off two rounds at the second duck he had targeted. Luck was on his side and it fell into the water. The rest of the group took to the air in a cacophony of squawking and flapping wings. Jason quickly ran towards where the ducks were floating, and just like a good retriever, plunged into the lake. It was only chest deep but he swam instead of wading. Swimming was faster than sinking his feet in the soft bottom with each step. He got the ducks before they could sink and made his way back out to his rifle. Sitting on the ground with his prizes, he felt pretty good about his shooting, but in his haste to retrieve the ducks before they sank he had not taken off any clothing.

"Crap, now I've got to hike back up over the ridge with wet boots and clothes," he said out loud.

It was late that evening when Jason reached his camp above the farmhouse. His clothes had pretty much dried during the hike back up the ridge, but his socks were still wet. He spread everything out to dry and prepared the ducks for delivery.

Jason decided against the direct approach, going up to the farm house and trying to meet the woman and her girls without panicking them. He probably looked dangerous and frightening. He would have to use a different tactic.

Late that night he set out for the house. He would leave the ducks on the porch to be found in the morning. He tied them together with some of his line and hung them from one of the porch beams, keeping them safe from raccoons until morning. With his mission accomplished, Jason hiked back to his camp and settled into a deep and satisfied sleep.

Back down in the valley to the east four men paused as they heard the faint report of three shots. "We're not alone," one of them said, almost to himself.

"Shut up," another replied, as they continued to listen. They were camped along the creek that came down from the pond where Jason shot the ducks. They were hiking up the valley with a growing disinterest, still a couple of days hike away from the pond. The increasing density of foliage and lack of signs of habitation were dampening their enthusiasm. This group was not interested in wilderness camping. Now they paused to reconsider their plans.

Three of them, Nate, Randy and Zack, were friends from Ashland, a small town one hundred miles east of Hillsboro. They were in their twenties and had been involved in petty crimes from their teenage years. After the EMP attack, they began looting. There was a shootout with the local police, from which they barely escaped. Leaving town seemed like a good idea, looters were being executed on sight.

They picked up Bud shortly after departing. Bud and a friend had been wandering, looking for food and other resources. Bud's friend had been killed in a run-in with a small gang. The encounter scared Bud. He was an easy going eighteen year old who tried to get along with everyone. But without a good moral compass he was often willing to do whatever was expedient. Generally he avoided the worst people and made his way looking for the easy path in life. His one notable asset was his marksmanship. He had a good eye for shooting and carried a 30-06 rifle. He quickly proved his worth by his ability to shoot game.

The problem for these young men was that they were all city bred. They did not know how to live without the systems a city provided. Communities now could not provide the infrastructure on which they depended, so they were struggling to function until the power came back. The towns that had not descended into chaos were under tight control to allocate the scarce resources. These men rejected that control and were constantly on the move, becoming opportunistic scavengers, trying to find food and shelter for the winter.

Chapter 3

Jason awoke early the next morning with great excitement and immediately went to his lookout position to see how his gift would be received. Just like the other mornings, the mother came out first. She saw the ducks hanging on the line and looked quickly around in all directions. She went back into the house and came out a few moments later with a shotgun at the ready. She scanned the woods at the edge of the yard directly in front of the house, the strip of trees down slope towards the road, and the forest line uphill, to her left beyond the orchard. After some time, seeing nothing, she called inside and the taller girl came out and took down the ducks. They both went inside, and a half hour later, smoke rose from the chimney.

Jason smiled and went back to his camp. He ate some smoked venison and greens he had collected and then went to check his snares. Two of them paid off, rewarding him with a pair of rabbits. He moved away from camp to clean and skin them. His anticipation grew again with the thought of another meal to give to the family.

Much later that night, Jason settled in at the edge of the woods to watch the house. With his binoculars, he could make out someone at the window watching for hours. Finally they disappeared from the window. Two hours later Jason crept out to hang his gift of the rabbits on the porch. Dawn found him napping at his observation position. This time the mother came out earlier and she came with the shotgun at ready. Again she spent some time studying the woods around the house and then took down the rabbits.

"So what do you do next?" he asked himself aloud. "You going to keep sending them food? What's your goal?" The question hung before Jason. He shied away from it not wanting to examine his motives or address his actions.

The snares remained empty. A second day went by. After the third day Jason wrapped up a large portion of his smoked venison and hung it on the porch that night, then retreated to his lookout position.

This time when the mother came out and saw the package of venison she began shouting something towards the woods. Jason couldn't hear what she was saying from the ridge. With no answer coming, the woman took down the venison and went back into the house. Jason sat back to think about the situation.

Maybe this is getting too creepy. Should I introduce myself? The thought both excited and scared him. He kept a dialogue going in his head throughout the day. Asking questions about his motives, whether he should move on, the potential of the valley, his memory of that time he didn't help and what may have happened to that group. The answers came as the day wore on. He was looking for shelter, a place to stay, but now, there was something more. The unanswered question rose up again. *What do I want out of this?* The answer was companionship— someone to help and take care of.

The thought startled him even as it came to mind. It had been hiding in his thoughts ever since his experience with Sam and Judy. He recognized his enjoyment in the tasks he had now taken on for this family. He was invigorated by a new sense of purpose. He had even begun cataloging some repairs he could see that were needed around the farmhouse and yard. It was time to meet this family, and with that realization, came a sense of dread. *What if they reject me?*

He would not force himself on them. *Did I show I can be a provider?* "Suck it up, tough guy. You're more nervous than you were in the gun fight with the gang." He told himself.

The decision made, Jason tried to clean himself up, but there was little prospect of helping his tangled hair and beard. Still he washed his face, trimmed his hair as best he could with his knife and straightened out his camp clothes before heading down to the farmhouse. He carefully approached the house, and found a good hiding position where he could wait. His heart was racing. He felt lightheaded.

Why am I so nervous? The possibility of rejection certainly loomed large, perhaps larger than it had with Sam and Judy, but he couldn't shake the realization that, somehow, this was more important than Sam and Judy. This family needed his help. There was no movement so he called out to the house.

"Hello in the house!" He shouted; and then repeated himself.

From the house, came "Who are you? Where are you?"

"I'm just one person, and I'm in the woods, across from your front yard," he replied. "I'm the one who's been bringing you the food."

The door opened and the mother came out with her shotgun raised. She was looking in Jason's general direction but could not pinpoint him. She was tall, around five feet nine inches and looked to be in her late thirties, possibly forty. She was thin and plainly dressed in shirt and jeans. She stood confidently on the porch, her straight posture accentuating her height. She wore her hair, light brown in shade, shoulder length, framing a finely proportioned face with full lips, strong chin and clear eyes. Even seen from a distance, there was an air of dignity about her. She was taking a risk to show herself in spite of Jason's presents to demonstrate his good intentions. She stood poised and ready with her shotgun on the porch.

"Come out and show yourself."

"Promise you won't shoot?"

"No promises. So you are the one bringing the food?"

"Yes."

"Why?"

"Cause you looked like you needed it."

"I am not going to keep shouting to the woods like this, show yourself," she said with all the authority she could muster.

"I don't want you to shoot me."

"I know you are armed," she called back, "so I need to see you."

"How about I empty my pistol, it's all I have on me, and throw it out into the yard? Then I'll come out and sit on the ground. I don't want to alarm you. Then will you not shoot me?" This was similar to the difficulty he had in connecting with Sam and Judy—a sign of the times, he thought ruefully.

"Go ahead."

Jason pocketed the magazine, cleared the chamber and tossed the 9mm into the yard. He took a deep breath, then stepped out from the covering brush and walked slowly into the middle of the yard, near the pump and sat down.

"My name is Jason."

"What are you doing here?" she asked, ignoring his introduction.

Jason gave her a condensed narrative of his odyssey since the EMP attack. He emphasized the growing corruption he had observed in Hillsboro and how he thought he would be better off away from large groups of people until this disaster sorted itself out—if it ever did.

"I'm grateful for the food, but you will have to move on, my husband is coming home soon." The woman declared.

"I'm sorry," he replied, "I've been watching for a number of days and I don't think your husband has been around for some time."

Her eyes flashed.

"Think you are so smart? How about I shoot you right now?" she said. Her eyes flashed in anger; the shotgun now pointed at his chest. "He *is* coming back…soon."

"No, I don't think I'm so smart, and please don't shoot. I just noticed the house needs repairs and you don't seem to have had much to eat. That's why I went hunting for you. I guessed your husband got caught away when the power went out last year, and you've been making it on your own since then." He was trying to calm her down. "As I told you, I lost my wife. Her plane crashed when the power went out. I know what you've experienced. Many people have experienced separation and loss of loved ones like we have. Everything is shut down. Our world has changed." Her face remained inscrutable; he couldn't tell how she was taking this in.

Finally he added, "Could you sit down and not point your shotgun at me? It might go off and that wouldn't be good for me."

The woman's eyes softened slightly as she digested what Jason had said. "I'm sorry. It sounds like you have had a difficult time as well. It's been hard, but we have survived to this point. I still believe my husband is coming back." The last said with extra emphasis as if to reinforce her conviction. As she finished she carefully sat down on the top step of the porch, resting the shotgun in her lap, keeping it pointed at Jason. Her body remained tense, alert, as she stared at him with a still-wary look in her eyes.

Chapter 4

This is strange. This man shows up and he provides food for us. When that starts getting too weird he shows himself. Anne pondered the situation thoughtfully, not sure what her next move could...or should be.

Her husband, Ron, was not coming back soon. She had been bluffing. He had left last year two months before the EMP attack. Ron had become disenchanted with their experiment in country living. Seven years ago they had decided to live in the country; Anne came from a small town and was enthusiastic about the plan, Ron less so. He was a salesman for a manufacturer of industrial machine tools. The job didn't require him to go into an office on a regular basis. He spent much of his days traveling to small factories around the Carolinas, showing his products and checking up on prior sales and installations. In addition, much of his work could be done on the phone or computer so living in the country was possible.

When they discovered this remote valley and the farm for sale, they both became enthusiastic about the romance of an idyllic, bucolic lifestyle. The farmhouse was old, but in good condition when they purchased it; two stories with a porch and tin roof. It was located up from the valley floor and provided long, peaceful vistas of the valley. They would often sit on the porch in the evenings, just drinking in the views.

They were not farmers. They leased out their fields for hay production, as did some of the other newer valley residents. When they moved in, it took some time to get to know the other families in the valley. There was a mix of multi-generational families and newer owners, like Ron and Anne, who wanted to experience rural living.

A year before the EMP attack, Ron began showing signs of discontent. They had been living in the valley for six years. Getting to and from the farm had become an ever increasing irritant as Ron's career advanced. He was moving up in the company and worked more frequently at headquarters. He kept telling Anne that his career was suffering and the girls were not getting nurtured by all society had to offer. Anne argued that quality of life was most important, not career advancement. She insisted that life was better, saner, in the country than in a big city like Charlotte. She relished the simplicity of life growing up and wanted that for her girls, almost as much as a college education. Sure, they would probably not stay in the country, but Anne was also sure, that country values would stay with them throughout their lives.

Their conversations did not progress and Ron's position hardened. He began to stay overnight at the office more frequently. Anne missed him and tried to make Ron's time at home as pleasant as possible, working hard to reinforce what had attracted them to their experiment in country living, but it became increasingly clear that Ron was not happy. He grew distant. A coldness settled into their marriage, which Anne and the girls could not thaw.

The dying of their relationship was a process, not an event. Ron became more distant and removed, even from the girls. The end was finally marked when he called her from work and said he was accepting a promotion that required him to relocate to the company's Indianapolis office. With that announcement came the statement that he was in love with another woman and was planning to seek a divorce. There was no discussion or consultation with the family. Over the phone he agreed to send a monthly check to support them. Anne worked in the local school system, but her salary was not enough to sustain the family. Ron acted as though his offer was a gallant gesture. Anne, in her shock, could not respond.

She had clung to the slim hope that Ron would come to his senses. That the woman would not prove to be of good character and he would realize how rich he was with his family, but nothing had happened before the EMP attack. After that it was too late.

When the power went out, she had not thought much about it. That happened often in the country. Only this time it did not come back. Days went by and there was no way of getting any information. The car didn't work, so she could not go to town. After a week, she and the girls visited their neighbors to the south, but they were also in the dark. The school bus stopped coming through the valley when the power went out, and with the car not working, there was no way to get the girls to the regional school located near Clifton Furnace, the nearest small town. Anne and the girls hiked into the town, a picturesque place now catering to drive-through tourists, looking for country-store experiences. In town she heard that the power seemed to be out all over the state, but people didn't know what had actually happened. The school was closed and no vehicles worked except some older ones. Anne purchased what food she could with the cash she had, no credit cards were being accepted, and walked back to the farm with the girls.

The weeks passed. Their neighbors to the south of them packed up and headed into Clifton Furnace; from there they were going to try to get to Hillsboro, nearly a day's drive away. Anne talked about the move with them, but her instinct was to stay. Caution overrode any desire to relocate. Since the power stayed out, Anne guessed it might not be better anywhere else. The departing family gave Anne the excess food they couldn't pack; mostly dried and canned goods. She and the girls then hunkered down to ride out the situation at home, hoping the power would come back soon.

Now, nearly a year later easy access to food had run out. Anne and the girls had hiked north to the other farms in the valley. They were struggling like her, but they were all determined to remain rather than relocate to a town. Anne was able to collect some additional food from another neighbor who decided to leave the valley, which helped, but by now they had run out of most of their resources. Anne had almost reached the point of giving up and going to town to beg for help when this stranger showed up and brought them food to eat. But what did he want?

"I could be helpful; I'm a good hunter and I can fix things." Jason broke into her reverie.

Anne's attention shifted back to the moment. His tone sounded a little desperate. *So, he wants to stay here...with us.* Her mind froze at the thought. She needed help, but it seemed reckless, dangerous to accept help from a stranger. There had been no violence in the valley, but how could she invite a complete stranger into her household? She understood that she and the girls were not doing well and she saw no relief on the horizon. Help was needed; but from a stranger?

Anne's options were limited. Reject this offer and the family would have to make the trek to Clifton Furnace or even Hillsboro to find help. She suppressed a shudder at the thought of bringing her daughters into such an uncertain situation. Or she could accept this offer and open her family to some possible danger from this stranger. He seemed polite and well mannered, but still, she knew nothing about him.

Anne made Jason recite his story again, looking for clues to evaluate him. Was his story consistent? If it wasn't, then she could assume it was a fabrication. If it was consistent, what did it tell her about this man's character? She needed time to consider her position and alternatives.

This morning she had resigned herself to becoming a refugee. Now there was the possibility of remaining here in the valley until the power came back on. But with that option came the acceptance of a stranger into the lives of her and her daughters. As Jason recounted his tale, Anne listened and pondered her choice. It was in her nature to be direct. She did not like subtle gamesmanship, so after Jason finished, she went right to the heart of her concern.

"I'm sure you can help..." she paused, looking straight at him with piercing eyes, "but what do you want?" Her question hung in the air between them and now that she voiced the question, she was suddenly afraid of the answer she might get.

Chapter 5

J ason stared straight back at her, stopped still by her question. His mind raced. *What do I want? Why is it so important to connect with this woman and her children? Why don't I just move on?* The memory of the warmth he felt with Sam and Judy came rushing back to him. This family needed someone to help them. Is that what he wanted? To be that someone?

The woman waited as Jason pondered his response. He wasn't sure what he should say and the very thing that came to him sounded so odd, he was not sure he should say it.

"Well?"

The answer welled up in Jason, a powerful emotion, a need he had long suppressed. He blurted out, "a family...to not live alone." A great choking sound came up from his throat as he suppressed a sob. "I'm sorry, that must sound weird."

"It's okay." She studied him for some time as Jason struggled to get his emotions under control.

He looked at her, wondering how his answer had been received. Her face gave no indication. *Did I go too far?*

"My name is Anne," she said finally.

"Hi, I'm Jason. I'm a good hunter—"

"You already told me that, and I think you have proven your claim."

"Well, I can fix things." Plowing on gamely, he continued, "I can fix the broken window on the house. And your porch needs its support replaced. I can fix that as well. I notice that you get water from this pump in the yard. If there's an indoor pump, perhaps I can get that to work. It would be nice not to have to go outside in bad weather." He went on, expanding his sales pitch, "I also have a complete field guide to edible plants found in the mountains. I've been eating them for months and I'm still alive, so the guide must be pretty reliable." She smiled.

"On a serious note," he was taking a risk, but this could be the closing argument, "there are some very bad people out there. I've run into them already. I can protect you and your girls if they ever come into this valley. I hope they never do, but if it happens, I will defend you and your family with all my ability."

Her smile faded and she looked serious again—not mad, but serious. "These are hard times...difficult and strange. I don't think I could have ever imagined such a situation as I find myself and my girls in. I wonder at times if life will ever go back to normal. I wish it, but it hasn't happened yet. Being isolated up here in this valley we don't know what has become of the rest of the state, let alone the rest of the country."

Anne's eyes wandered as she spoke, as if lost in her own words. Jason sat very still...*was she talking herself into a 'yes'?*

Anne continued, "I have been expecting the power to come on for almost a year, but...nothing. Now you come along offering to help and telling me how it may never come back. And on top of that you seem to think society is breaking down." She shuddered visibly. "You've acted respectful, even if a bit odd..." She paused. Jason sensed she was making a decision. Would she take the risk and accept the help he offered?

"You can stay." Her voice was firm, her decision made. "Here are the rules. You stay in the barn at night. The house will be locked. You can eat with us, but you sleep in the barn. I am not part of the deal and when my husband comes back, you will have to leave. And you must leave my girls alone. If you make a pass at one of them, I will shoot you without a word of warning."

Jason let out an almost audible sigh, "Thank you," he said with relief in his voice. "Thank you. I'll be a good helper. We'll make a good team and I won't cross the boundaries you set."

"See that you don't and I do not think we need to talk about a team." She paused. "I won't guarantee how long you can stay. Time will tell how this arrangement works out." Another pause, "I guess you should meet the girls." She turned and called out to the house, telling them to come out.

The girls stepped out and walked up to their mother, who stood up. "This is Catherine, my oldest daughter," she said touching the taller of the two. "And this is Sarah."

Jason remained sitting and nodded to each girl, saying how glad he was to make their acquaintance, trying to be polite but not ridiculous. Catherine was about 16 or 17 Jason guessed and already taller than her mother. She looked a lot like her mother, but darker in hair and complexion and with the advantage of natural youthful beauty. She had dark, penetrating eyes that bored into you with a direct look. Sarah was shorter. She had a lighter complexion than her mother or Catherine with hair more blond than brown. Her face was more rounded than Catherine's. There was a sparkle and lightness about her that was distinct from her older sister's more serious countenance. Jason could see that she was going to be a beauty.

Catherine gave Jason a long, studied look, much like her mother; measuring him in a critical way. *She's a cool one and won't be won over easily by anyone.*

Sarah also studied Jason but more the way a woman might if she were interested in him. It was a bit unnerving in light of her young age and Anne's threat. On the whole, Sarah seemed more open and friendly than Catherine.

Got to be on my best behavior. His heart flooded with joy at the prospect of becoming, even temporarily, a part of this family.

Chapter 6

The four men hiking up the valley to the east had stopped when they heard Jason's shots at the pond. The gunfire sounded far off and the bush was getting thicker. They didn't hear any more shooting, but after some discussion they decided that it was not worth hacking their way through the dense cover only to find a hunter shooting at them. Instead, they retraced their path south. A few days later they came back to an old two track heading west onto the ridge. They decided to follow it. There was not much reason to go further south. That area was picked over and infested with dangerous gangs. They were looking for houses and farms to loot. Their problem was the pickings were slim. Pushed further out by the larger gangs, they were losing momentum in their bid for survival and getting more desperate and more dangerous. They struck out west towards the ridge. A few days later, they reached the pass.

Jason was a flurry of activity. There was so much he wanted to do it was hard to focus on where to start. He first set out to teach Anne and the girls what foods they could gather in the woods and fields. They used the edible plant guide and, after some study, they all went out on gathering trips. After a few outings, the girls continued foraging on their own with Jason's admonishment to not eat anything until he had inspected it. The edges of the fields provided a rich assortment of plants. The black and raspberry bushes were abundant, promising much fruit as the summer deepened. There were some marshy areas in the lower creek and fields that yielded ramps and wild onions. Wood sorrel grew in abundance as did chickweed, so there was no shortage of salad greens.

As he had promised, Jason replaced the broken window with one from the barn and shored up the front porch roof with a post. Each night he retired to the barn, whose door he had repaired. The foraging lessons and the work on the repair projects eased Jason's assimilation into the family structure. All of them working together, with Anne and the girls learning new things, energized them and they began to bond. It didn't hurt Jason's approval rating that they were eating better. Anne became less guarded as the days passed.

Jason asked Anne about the other residents of the valley. She told him about the four other inhabited farms, noting that, except for one family, there were no other children her girls' ages. "I guess living here hasn't been so good for them in some ways...since the power went out." She paused, lost in her thoughts.

"The girls seem fine to me. They're bright and learn quickly. But what do I know?"

Anne smiled. "Well you're doing pretty well dealing with them...for a novice that is."

"I grew up with an older brother...no girls in our family, so sometimes I'm at a loss about how to respond to Sarah or Catherine. It certainly is different."

With Jason's explanation of what had happened the girls began to understand their dad would not be coming home. They had held out hope that he would return someday. Now his departure seemed final. As mad as they were about his abandoning them, the finality of never seeing him again was sobering.

Catherine remained cool and distant, though polite. She was attentive, wanting to learn all Jason had to teach her. He could see that she respected what he knew and how he wanted to not only survive, but thrive in this new reality, but she kept her distance emotionally. Sarah, on the other hand, quickly warmed up to him. She still missed her dad, but delighted in having Jason around as a substitute father figure. As she grew more comfortable with him, she would flirt and tease him endlessly. Jason, not having spent much time around thirteen year old girls, was not sure how to react and retreated to maintaining a friendly distance from her attention. Often he would look to Anne for help when he didn't quite know how to handle Sarah. His discomfort, obvious at times, seemed to delight Sarah all the more.

One evening after getting the kitchen pump working, Anne and Jason were sitting on the porch as the sun began its descent over the western ridge. The early evening sunlight lit up the trees on the eastern side of the valley in a flood of light. They watched the sun's lighting shining on the mountain slope, sitting in silence, taking in the beauty of the evening.

Finally Anne asked, "What about your family?"

"My mother is retired and living in Florida. I don't know what has become of her and can't really find out. My brother is in California. He works in the computer industry. You could say we are a well spread out family. Now we're totally out of touch with one another," he paused for a moment. "Before we could all be connected...with phone and the internet. Now it seems like complete separation, living in different worlds—worlds I can't reach. And with Maggie gone I'm pretty much alone. I can only hope that my mother and brother are fine...there's really no way of knowing." His voice trailed off, as he got lost in thoughts of them.

After some moments, Anne broke the silence, "So now you have an adopted family, it seems."

Jason turned and smiled at her. "Yes...I guess I do." Their eyes locked together for a moment; then Anne turned away, breaking the connection. Jason changed the subject. "Have you ever talked to the others about joining together, to pool resources or set up joint defense?"

"There was some talk, but we're so isolated. We didn't see any evidence of violence and didn't expect any, certainly not from Clifton Furnace. So everyone decided that it would be an unnecessary, a waste of resources. We have a few weapons, mostly shotguns and hunting rifles." She shifted in her chair to look directly at Jason, "These are independent people in this valley. We look after ourselves. Except for the three families who left to go to Clifton Furnace, the rest of us just want to stay here and wait things out."

"It probably would have been a good idea to get more organized."

"Do you think that's so important? It's not people's style in the valley."

"It could be." He went on, "I'm concerned about safety, about our defenses."

"But is there a real danger to worry about?"

"This is a secluded valley, but I found it. And there are some evil people out there who have joined up into gangs. I'd hate to think of them coming here with us unprepared...I guess I worry a lot about that."

"I know...Sam and Judy," she said quietly. "Do you think that could happen to us?" She paused, then added, "How would we defend against such an attack?"

"There are a lot of burlap and plastic bags in the barn—"

"Old seed bags. They go back to the previous owners and Ron kept them as well. I'm not sure if he ever planned to do anything with them, but he didn't want to throw them out."

Jason paused for a moment to let Anne's thoughts clear then continued, "Well, they'll be very handy now. We need to set up some shooting positions in the house and protect them with sandbags. I'd like to fill them with sand from the creek bed and place them upstairs, not necessarily at the windows, which is where everyone would shoot, but at shooting holes I'll make in the walls."

"You want to cut holes in the walls?"

"I know. It's not the typical handy man fix-up project." He faked a deep voice, "Ma'am, I'm here to cut holes in your walls, it's the latest in home remodeling."

Anne gave a short laugh and smiled, "you'll have a hard time selling me on that one. And please include how we'll fare during the winter with holes in our walls, Mr. Handyman."

"Seriously, Anne, we need to be able to shoot from the house at anyone trying to get to us. I can cover the holes from the inside when the cold weather comes. I'll make sure you're warm in the house."

Jason worried he might be moving too fast; they were still figuring each other out. Or, as he thought, Anne was trying to figure *him* out. Jason already knew he was attracted to her but kept himself in check, giving her time to sort out their relationship.

"As part of my remodeling scheme, I also want to cut a hole in your roof," he continued.

"What? Are you kidding?" she asked in surprise. Jason just looked at her. "You're not kidding. Please tell me why," she continued.

"It's to give us a lookout position and a dominant firing platform. Think of it as a widow's walk." As soon as he used the phrase, he was sorry.

Anne looked at him sharply. "What exactly is a 'widow's walk'?" she said with an edge in her voice.

"It's a high parapet or standing space on a house, sometimes up on the roof. It was the place where wives looked out to sea, watching for their sailing husbands to return from their voyages. It's a bad choice of words; I'm sorry."

"It's all right," Anne replied. "I shouldn't be so sensitive."

The evening grew still and the light faded on the eastern slopes as they continued to talk quietly about changes to the farm.

"I know you are serious about protecting us," Anne said, "and I appreciate it. Thank you." She stood up, then bent down to give him a kiss on his forehead and went inside.

Jason sat for some time as the evening darkened savoring the kiss, digesting it, his mind swirling around it, replaying the moment over and over. A rush of happiness began to flow over him. Finally he stood up.

Get a grip. You've got work to do. Get some sleep. He opened the door to the house and shouted out, "Good night everyone!" The good nights came back from various parts of the house and Jason walked off to the barn smiling.

Chapter 7

Two days later he hiked over the ridge and down to the pond where he had previously taken the ducks. On the way he heard a shot from the valley floor. He changed direction and approached from the south end of the pond, keeping to the willows and brush bordering the water. The shot came from the other end of the pond. He worked his way through the dense cover, moving towards the source of the report. He was careful, not hurrying; there was cover in the willow thicket, but no protection from gunfire. Near the head of the pond he saw an old man in the clearing bent over, gutting a pig. He was intensely focused on his work. When Jason stepped from the thicket, the old man jerked his head up and turned towards him, his face set in an angry scowl, his eyes fierce. He started toward his rifle lying in the grass.

"Don't." Jason said. He had his rifle at the ready.

The man stopped. He slowly straightened up. After a moment of studying Jason, he demanded, "Who are you and what're you doin' here?"

"I could ask you the same," Jason responded. He couldn't tell how old the man was. He was thin with stooped shoulders, but his body exuded a wiry strength. He wore loose, rough work clothes and his hands were large and calloused, telling of a life of hard, physical work. From under a mop of graying hair he eyed Jason with dark, suspicious eyes set in a leathery face marked in a permanent scowl.

"I asked you a question. You're trespassin'," he said in a gravelly voice.

"What do you mean trespassing? The national forest starts on the ridge above us and runs through this valley."

"You can call it what you want. These are my woods, have been for generations."

"Who the hell are you?" Jason asked.

"You're the trespasser. Who are you?" The old man was now shouting.

The conversation was not going anywhere so he answered, "My name is Jason. I'm staying at the Whitman's farm in the valley to the west." He nodded towards the ridge.

"So you're the new man she's got. I heard about you. Well, you're not welcome here. This is my pond, my pigs, my woods."

"Again, these woods don't belong to you."

The old man continued as if not hearing, "I figure you're here to poach my game. This is how I feed my family. You could be shot for poaching."

"There's plenty of game to go around, and it doesn't all belong to you."

"There ain't with strangers like you coming into the valley. Go back where you came from. You don't belong here." The man's anger seemed to be rising again.

Jason's mind raced. *Got to calm things down.* "Look, I don't want to go to war with you. I'm trying to help the family survive. I need to hunt, same as you."

"Where'd you come from?" the man asked.

"Hillsboro."

"Why'd you leave?"

"It's corrupt in Hillsboro. And they don't have enough food. I figured I'd strike out on my own."

"So you going to come out to my woods and think you'll be just fine?"

"Didn't plan on being here, but when I came to the Whitman farm I realized they needed help...and I needed a roof over my head."

"We don't take to strangers coming into the valley, especially city people from Hillsboro. We take care of ourselves here."

"I'm not like others in Hillsboro. And it didn't seem like the Whitmans were getting much help when I came along."

The old man stared at him for some time, measuring him.

"What's your name?" Jason asked again.

"Name's Turner."

"Mr. Turner, it's good to meet another person from the valley."

"I'm warning you to stay out of my way. I don't want to ever see you on the ridge above my farm. Don't want anyone spying on me. You hear me?"

"I hear you. I'll stay away from your farm and the ridge."

"See that you do. And stay away from my pigs." And with that he turned back to gutting the pig.

Jason said goodbye and set off for the ridge. There would be no pigs today. He resolved to be more careful when hunting in the woods. On returning to the farm, he related the incident to Anne.

"He's pretty much a recluse. I'm surprised he spoke that many words to you." She said.

"Better than shooting me."

As they were talking, Catherine came in. "Who are you talking about?"

"Mr. Turner. Jason ran into him at the pond over the ridge," Anne said.

"I'll bet that didn't go well," Catherine said.

"It went well enough that we didn't try to shoot each other. He seems to think the whole ridge and pond in the valley to the east belong to him. He said it's been in his family for generations."

"I think it was, years ago," replied Anne. "He's complained about the government taking it away to create the national forest for years."

"I don't think he's ever gotten over it," Catherine said.

"Well, he doesn't like me being here. He thinks I'm poaching his game."

"That could be a problem," Anne said.

"I think we reached an agreement. Nothing was said, but he seemed to drop the issue after telling me to stay off the ridge behind his house. Maybe he realizes that we all need to eat."

"That's probably as close to acceptance as you will get," Anne said.

"If he's typical, no wonder the valley has never organized," Jason said.

"He's more reclusive than the others. The rest are more polite, but just as independent."

"Just be careful of him...and Billy. They both have a mean streak in them," Catherine said.

Anne then spoke up. "I think it is time for you to meet everyone in the valley since you have already met the most reclusive resident."

Everyone turned to her. "So how do we do that?" Sarah asked.

"Why, we just pack some food and hike to the neighbors."

"We can't do that in one day," Catherine said.

"We'll rely on other's hospitality to put us up for the night. I'm guessing we can do the trip in two days. It will be a fun outing. Let's go tomorrow. It's time we introduced Jason to the valley." Anne's excited tone left no room for discussion.

The next morning, they set out with backpacks full. Jason carried his 9mm and his Ruger carbine. They walked past the Turner farm. The morning was cool and everyone wore a jacket or sweater. The next farm was abandoned, its owners having gone to Clifton Furnace, hoping to get to Wilmington where they had relatives. The property beyond it belonged to Tom and Betty Walsh. They moved into the valley fifteen years ago. Tom was a Vietnam veteran. When he retired from his company in Charlotte, he and Betty moved into the valley. Their kids were grown and had left years ago. Tom was built like a fire plug, strong and solid. He had a ruddy complexion and an open, friendly face. Betty was a big boned woman who like the outdoors and enjoyed the farming and hunting with her husband. They were down to earth. You knew right away where you stood with them.

They were greeted as they approached the front porch. After introductions everyone sat down outside. The sweaters and jackets were shed as the day warmed.

"So you were out on your own, in the forest for weeks?" Tom asked after hearing Jason's story about how he came to the valley. "Anne, what possessed you to take a chance on him? I imagine he was not a pretty sight when he showed up."

Betty jabbed her husband in the ribs. "That's not very polite. And, besides, it's none of our business."

"Tom is right. His appearance did give me some reservation. But we were out of food and my instinct told me he was a good man, which, thankfully, turned out to be the case." She smiled at Jason.

"I was actually on my own for about four months total. I ran into some bad people along the way. That's what I was getting away from." He paused, then continued, "Anne tells me that no one in the valley is interested in forming a group for protection." Jason said.

"Against who or what?" Betty asked.

"Well, against the kind of people I ran into." Jason replied.

"We talked about it, but we're so remote, we figure the odds are pretty low and didn't warrant the work. Besides, how would we protect the valley against gangs?" Tom responded.

"I'm not sure, but Anne's farm is the first one you come to as you go up the valley, so I figure we need to be ready. We don't have the luxury of any occupied farms between us and the valley entrance."

Tom thought about that comment for a moment, then replied, "I don't think the rest of us are relying on Anne's place to be our buffer. We just don't see the threat being significant."

"Maybe not, but the downside could be fatal. I've seen it in action. Even with a low probability, I want to be prepared."

Tom shrugged as if to indicate they would agree to disagree. The conversation meandered for another hour when Anne said, "We should get moving, I want Jason to meet everyone and there is a lot of walking left to do."

An hour later they were at the house belonging to Andy and Claire Nolan. Andy was a round, pudgy man with a cautious face. His face had the look of a person evaluating something and trying to make up his mind. Clair looked like a grandmother. If you imagined one, she would be what came to your mind's eye. They were polite but quiet. They wanted to know all about Jason's adventures and what was going on in Hillsboro but didn't say much about themselves and how they were managing after the EMP attack. They seemed to be getting along just fine, looking well kept and well fed. The conversation was polite, friendly, but didn't seem to penetrate the polite screen put up by the couple. Their visit was shorter than at the Walsh's and so Jason and the family said goodbye and set out to reach the last farm before evening.

Anne hoped that John and Natalie Sands would invite them stay the night. John was an architect and had moved into the valley five years ago. He had renovated the old farmhouse, making it a showcase of his skills. As they approached the farm, Jason saw the results of John's design and renovation work on the building. A new wing had been added with large glass windows. It formed the base of an upper deck that gave a stunning view of the valley from where the house sat. All the windows had been upgraded, some standing six feet tall, mirroring the windows of the last century before air conditioning. The front porch was wrapped around the left side of the house to counter balance the wing on the other side. The changes gave the old farmhouse a dramatic look without completely abandoning its classic roots.

John and Natalie were in their late thirties, similar in age to Jason and Anne. They had one daughter, Lisa, who was seven years old. Both adults were excited to receive them and, like the others, interested in Jason's story—his trek and how he had arrived in the valley. They were a handsome couple. John had a full beard, neatly trimmed and Natalie had long, dark hair framing a thin, regal face. He looked almost professorial and Natalie glowed with a dark, exotic beauty. They would have looked at home on the cover of a magazine: the perfect professional couple with a lovely daughter and an award-winning house in the country.

"What brought you all the way out here?" Jason asked after they settled down in the living room. Lisa had taken the girls to show them her room and all her toys.

"With my work, I can live about anywhere. When we found this place we fell in love with it...and I saw what could be done with the house. It became my calling card. I put all the images of its renovation and re-design on my website."

"How are you getting along now, after the EMP attack?" Jason asked.

"We always kept a large supply of dry and canned goods, since we live so far out. And Natalie loves to garden. The vegetable garden was a hobby, now it's an important part of our daily routine." John said. "Neither of us shoots but Tom showed me how to set snares and traps...and we catch fish from the stream. We'll trade vegetables for some meat occasionally."

Jason sensed that John and Natalie expected the power to come back on soon even though it had been almost a year.

"We have solar to power our water pump and lights and we heat the house with passive solar and a wood stove."

The visit was comfortable; one almost could forget that the EMP attack had happened and that life had changed in a fundamental way. The electric lights, though few in number, were a delight to Sarah and Catherine. They ate a modest dinner of vegetable soup and corn bread and later, bedded down in the guest room.

Early the next morning, after some tea and more corn bread, they started the long hike home. The return hike was easier, all slightly downhill; they walked in the growing heat of the day. Distracted by small discoveries along the road, the girls sometimes ran ahead or lagged behind the steady pace of Jason and Anne. The two spoke infrequently, enjoying the silence and peace of the day together. Occasionally Anne would grab Jason's arm to point out a bird or some other item of beauty that caught her eye. Jason soaked up the pleasure of the day: the sun shining; this woman beside him, full of her enthusiasm for the beauty around them; the girls playing with one another, enjoying this simple outing. He hoped it could continue forever.

Chapter 8

The four men hiking west on the bark road made it over the mountain ridge and into the valley. They stopped at the first farmhouse, abandoned for almost a year now. The beds were a pleasant change from sleeping on the ground, but there was little else for them to find.

After a rest and scouring the house for supplies, they hiked north to the next farm. This one was also long abandoned. They proceeded to scavenge for what little there was left. When that meager supply ran out, they got ready to hike north and explore more of the valley. They had seen smoke in that direction. It held the promise of food and other resources. They were all armed and figured if they didn't get handouts, they could take what they wanted. They were willing to steal as well as scavenge.

The next day Jason was on the roof planning the shooting platform. Being up high, he took time to carefully scan his surroundings, and spied some smoke to the south seeming to come from one of the abandoned farms. He watched for some time until Anne called out, "what are you doing?"

"Anne, didn't you tell me the two farms to the south were abandoned?"

"Yes, they've been empty for almost a year now. We saw them leave to go to Clifton Furnace."

"Well, there's smoke, and it seems to be coming from one of those farms." Dead silence below. "I'm watching to see what else I can figure out."

After another ten minutes, he came down. Anne and the girls were waiting for him with anxious looks on their faces. Jason explained again about roving gangs, especially in the more populated areas, leaving out the more gruesome descriptions of their behavior.

"One of these gangs may have entered the valley. We have to assume they are dangerous and up to no good. We also have to assume they will come this way so we need to get ready for them."

"What do we do?" Sarah asked, in a frightened voice.

"First, be brave. We'll be ready and they won't expect that, so it gives us an advantage—an advantage I will use to our benefit. When they get here, all three of you will stay inside. Do not go outside of the house. Anne, you take the 12 gauge pump and shoot anyone coming into the house. Catherine, you take the 20 gauge and use it as back up, and Sarah, you'll have the .22 caliber rifle." Jason proceeded to show Anne and the girls how to use the weapons in close quarters. "When they arrive I'm going to be outside so I can ambush them before they rush the house."

"Why do we have to fight them? Can't we just give them some food and tell them to go away? Let them know we're armed?" Sarah asked.

"I wish that would work," replied Jason. "They're going to assume we have lots of resources to protect. They might leave, but they would come back, forewarned and more dangerous. Believe me I've had experience with this type. We don't want to give them a chance." Sarah looked doubtful. "If it will make you feel better, they will probably show their true intentions before we have to act. Now let's get ready."

"When will they come?" Catherine asked.

"Not sure, but if there was not much in those farmhouses they won't be long in coming. We'll set up watch from the roof. They'll either come up the road or through the fields. They won't come from the ridge above us. The going is too rough there. That will be good for us. We'll either have equal ground or the high ground."

"What do we do if we see them? Should we sound an alarm?" Anne asked.

"No, we keep quiet. We'll have some time to prepare after we see them. Maybe an hour if we're lucky. We have to stay close today, not even go down to the barn. Anne, make sure we eat early and have some quick food ready."

Jason showed the family where to position themselves, keeping as far as they could from any glass flying if the windows were shattered. He realized that he was taking this fight on alone; Anne and her daughters were the last point of defense.

If they have to shoot, I'll probably be dead.

He could feel the anger building as he talked with Anne and the girls about how the action would take place. His fears were coming true and the valley's peace was going to be violated. But the gang could not win. This gang, or one like it, had destroyed Sam and Judy. They would not destroy Anne, Catherine and Sarah. Jason was going to be the destroyer, like he had been on the trail up in the mountains. That was his role now. A deadly coldness came over him as he instructed the girls and their mother.

Chapter 9

The small gang headed out for the farmhouse to the north from where they had seen the smoke. Nate, their leader, decided they should go through the fields, not along the road; that way he figured they would reach the farmhouse from uphill, assuming most of the houses were close to the road. It was not easy going, and they grumbled as they trudged through overgrown fields and pushed through the thick hedgerows. It took the better part of the day. Along the way they stopped to talk about what they would do when they came to the farmhouse. Zack suggested that they wait until the next day, but that meant sleeping in the open and no one liked that idea. In the end they decided to attack at night, when everyone was asleep. From the last field they could see the top of the farmhouse, brightly lit in the late afternoon sun. They moved on to the tree line and stopped. The house was well up from the road, not downhill from where they were positioned, but that did not alter their plans. They could tell the house was inhabited. They stopped in the cover of the trees to wait for the dark.

Catherine was up on the roof keeping lookout, and she saw the figures—four of them—a half mile away, crossing a field. The sight startled her and her stomach tightened with dread. She quickly came down the ladder to tell Jason.

He immediately set out the weapons and made sure each one was loaded with extra ammunition close at hand.

"They probably won't attack until night," he said. "My guess is that they're surprised to find the house directly in their path. They were coming through the fields because they expected to attack the house from uphill with more cover."

"Why do you think they'll attack? How can you be sure?" Anne asked.

"They're not approaching openly, are they? They've seen the house. They know it's inhabited, and now they're hiding, waiting, for what? It doesn't look friendly to me."

He went on to explain his strategy. "I'll take my bow out along with my rifle. The bow is silent and if they fan out to attack, I can get one of them before they know I'm out there. After that it's all rifle work." He tried to sound matter of fact, but nothing he said could ease the tension. Everyone stared at him wide-eyed.

"I don't want you to leave us," Sarah said after a pause. The others nodded in agreement.

"I'll be more effective outside where I can attack from their flank. They won't expect it and it will upset any plans they made."

"Can't we just lock our doors and keep them out?" Sarah asked.

"For how long? What if they just wait around for us to come out? What if they shoot at us through the windows? We'd be prisoners in our own home. They might decide to rush the house. They may think they can overwhelm anyone inside. If I stay inside, I may not be able to take everyone out if they rush us." He finished with the thought uppermost in his mind, "I'm not going to let anything bad happen to you."

Jason set up a lookout spot in the house on the second floor. His binoculars worked well in low light. He was hoping to pinpoint their location in the woods as they waited for dark.

Catherine took the first watch. She was working hard to be calm and cool. Sarah stuck close to Jason as he moved around the house, checking the doors and windows. He made sure he had a silent exit out of the back door.

Anne took Jason aside, "do you think we'll be safe here in the house alone?"

"Yes. I'm going to make the fight happen outside, away from the house, where they won't expect it."

Something in his voice and the look in his eyes convinced Anne. She nodded. "I'll go up and take over from Catherine," she said finally.

Catherine came down the stairs and quietly told Jason that the men were still waiting in the woods to the south of them, beyond the front yard.

"They're waiting until dark," he confirmed as everyone gathered around him. "They'll want to get into position and get to the house before the moon comes up." There was a quarter moon that night. "No one go near a window. Keep your weapon where I told you to position yourselves." They all nodded. "We'll use the oil lamps and act normal, then pretend we've gone to sleep. You'll have to be very quiet and remember, don't go near the windows, and wait until someone comes in before shooting."

As night fell, they lit a lamp, tried to eat something, however no one had an appetite, and then finally put out the light. They took their positions as Jason slipped out of the back door. He paused to listen. The night was quiet. His heart raced and his breathing was ragged. He started shaking.

He worked to quell the rising tension inside. He had left Sam and Judy and they had been killed. He was not leaving now. He would face this threat, no running; no leaving. He would defeat them like he had defeated the gang that followed him after he rescued Judy. However, the last time he hadn't cared about the outcome. Back then there was a nihilistic rage in him to exact revenge for his friends' killing. There was no rage this night, only a cold

fear of what would be lost if he didn't prevail. In an
attempt to calm down, he went over his plan for a surprise
attack, his best hope of victory.

Finally calmer, he left the house and worked his way
uphill, crawling through the grass to reach the edge of the
old orchard stretching towards the forest line. The orchard
provided some cover, especially with the knee-high grass
that had grown up. Jason figured that the gang would use
the orchard as cover to get closer before making a final
rush on the house. He scanned the woods with his
binoculars. His tension slowly built again as he waited.
Down at the creek the night's stillness was broken by the
frogs starting their multi-voiced croaking. A gentle night
breeze flowed over the grass where he lay hidden as the
cooler air settled in the valley.

The last fight had been in the heat of anger. Tonight
everything was colder, more calculated. There was more
to fight for now, but the same outcome presented itself:
they die or I die.

Be effective, make the shots count. Don't hold back. He
repeated the mantra over and over in his mind. A
calculated ferocity was needed this night.

Jason wasn't sure the bow would be effective, but he
held it ready along with his rifle as he waited, keeping still
as he had been trained. The hours passed. The house was
silent. Finally he saw the men come over the fence at the
edge of the woods and fan out into the orchard. They were
spreading out in advance of attacking the house. The lead
man moved towards Jason using the cover of the trees.
The last one in line stopped in front of the house. Jason
lost sight of the two in the middle but still could see the
first man in line as they fanned out. *That's my first
target—with the bow.*

They were spread out now, which played into Jason's
hands. *If I can take one out without them realizing what's
going on, I've got a chance.*

He could hear the men calling to each other in whispers. They were going to creep up to the house, separated from each other, making them harder to hit. As they were checking in along their line, Jason drew his bow on the shadow figure nearest him. He could see him well enough to shoot 'center mass', in his chest. After the last man checked in, Jason let his arrow fly. The man screamed. Jason's arrow had found its mark, hitting him in his left chest, but not killing him. He screamed in pain. One of the other men called out in confusion.

The first man yelled, "Help! Ambush!" Then collapsed, coughing and moaning.

Attention turned towards Jason, not the house. They could not see him, but he knew his element of surprise was now gone.

He discarded the bow and took up his rifle. He could barely see the last man in the line. The two in the middle could not be seen at all. The gang was searching in his direction, looking for his position. Jason took aim at the last man in the line, Nate, and fired. The man fell. He could not tell whether or not he was hit or had dropped for cover. The middle two began firing shots in Jason's direction. He saw the gun flashes out of the corner of his eye as he flattened to the ground behind one of the trees. After the volley, Jason rose and fired off five quick rounds in the direction of the closest flash. A cry indicated that one of his shots had struck its target. The other man shouted and fired at Jason. The shots were now close; the shooter had zeroed in on him. He rolled over and crawled away as bullets flew past the spot he had just abandoned. He could hear their sharp, short whistle as they passed overhead. From a new position he fired off five more rounds at the flashes. This time there was no return fire. When he looked around the tree, he couldn't see anyone. Finally he caught sight of a shadow throwing itself over the fence and disappearing into the woods beyond.

Was it over? Jason started towards the fleeing shadow and then caught himself. He could be shot by one of the wounded men. Then he heard Anne call out his name from the house. Stepping behind a tree for shelter, he shouted back, "I'm all right. It's over. Don't come out."

Then he worked his way towards the attackers. The first man he came to was the closest one, shot with the arrow. He was laboring for breath. The arrow had pierced his lung, which was filling with blood. Jason took his pistol and shot him in the head. Then he carefully approached the second one. The man was badly wounded, but still alive. Jason could see him well enough in the light of the moon that had started to come up. He glared at Jason as he gasped for breath.

"How many of you are there?" Jason demanded. "Are you part of a larger group?" He only got glares and raspy breathing back. Jason waited for a few more moments and then shot him in the head. Without remorse, he headed to the third gang member. He was not sure of his position. Crouching, he worked his way forward, moving carefully. The man could be waiting in ambush.

There was a rustling sound ahead and to his right. Jason wheeled, bringing his rifle to bear on the sound when a shot rang out. The bullet tore through the meat of his shoulder, spinning him around and to the ground. Two more shots flew over where his head had been. Ignoring the pain in his shoulder he brought his rifle to bear on the flashes. He fired off five closely spaced rounds and collapsed down tight to the ground. The pain in his shoulder nearly made him cry out. This time there was no return fire. He waited silently for a few minutes. Then he began to crawl towards the direction of the shots.

"Jason, are you all right?" Anne called from the house.

He didn't answer. Finally he reached the attacker. Jason's shots had hit him in the abdomen and leg. He was doubled over in pain, the gun lying beside him. Jason slowly stood up and kicked it aside.

"Jason," Anne called again.

"I'm okay," he replied, not taking his eyes off of the wounded man. "Stay inside." Blood started coming from the man's mouth; he would get no information from him. He just glared at Jason as he shot him in the head.

With his good arm, he collected the guns from the men: two 9mm pistols, a .45 automatic, one AR15, another .223 carbine and one 30-30 Marlin lever action. Now he needed to find the ammunition. That was a prize the fleeing man might dare to return for. Blood was running down his arm, dripping off his hand from his wound. He tried to ignore it and painfully climbed over the fence to hunt for the backpacks which he figured might have ammunition in them. Jason found where the group had come over the fence. From there he walked a zigzag pattern back and forth going further into the tree line until he came to the place where they had waited. As he hoped, four backpacks were lying in the matted undergrowth. He was getting dizzy, but forced himself to continue. He tied the packs together and, dragging them behind him, slowly made his way back to the house.

On entering the house, Jason found the girls and Anne hunkered down in a safe spot, away from windows, all their weapons at ready. They all looked scared.

"What were you doing?" Anne said in a sharp tone. "We've been sitting here pretty much scared to death. We don't know what is going on and what you are doing and then we hear more shots outside..." Her words tumbled out over each other in her frightened state. "You're hurt!" She suddenly exclaimed and ran to him.

"Oh no," Sarah cried out. Catherine stared at him wide eyed.

"Fighting for your life is not a pretty thing," Jason said. "I had things to finish things out there to make sure we were safe." Anne had her arm around him as he stumbled to a chair. "One of the gang got away. I was going to chase him, but decided it wasn't a good idea...being night and being injured." He nodded to the packs on the floor. "I collected the weapons and backpacks. Figured they would have ammunition in them." The girls recoiled in horror from them.

"I don't want them anywhere near me," said Sarah firmly.

"Forget about the packs," said Anne. We have to look at your shoulder." She moved to take Jason's shirt off.

Catherine stood up. "I'll help," she said.

Anne nodded. Sarah just stood there wide eyed, afraid to look at his wound. Anne helped Jason into the kitchen. She and Catherine finished removing his shirt. Jason asked for a mirror so he could see the wound. The bullet had gone through the muscle, but had not shattered any bone. He was lucky.

"Sarah, get a lamp lit so we can see the wound," Anne said. "It has to be cleaned. I can wash around it with soap and water," she looked at Jason, "but I should probably pour some alcohol or whisky directly in it."

Jason grimaced, but nodded in agreement. "Give me a clean towel to press on the wound while you get ready. It'll help to stop the bleeding."

After cleaning the entrance and exit wound, Anne to Jason, "We have to sew the exit wound at least partially closed. It's too ragged and open."

Catherine looked at her, "Will that be all right? There is no anesthesia for the pain."

"If you do it now, my shoulder is still partially numb. I'm not looking forward to it, but it's best done quickly." He smiled wanly.

"I'll get needle and thread," Catherine said.

"Get white thread," Anne responded.

"Sarah, stoke up the fire in the stove and get some water boiling to sterilize the needle and thread," Anne directed.

"Then keep watch from the window," Jason added.

"Can I watch from here?" she asked. "I don't want to go upstairs by myself."

Anne looked at Jason and he nodded in assent.

With a wash cloth rolled up for him to bite down on, Anne proceeded to sew up as best she could the ragged parts of the exit wound. Catherine helped keep the pieces of flesh in place for sewing. Jason grunted and growled at the pain and Anne kept saying she was sorry. Soon the ordeal was over. Anne tore up a clean sheet for bandages and tied them tightly to Jason's shoulder.

Finally Jason staggered to the couch with a sigh, his arm in a sling. Anne stared at him with an unfathomable look on her face. The girls were still wide eyed. Anne gave Jason a glass of the whisky she used to clean his wound. He sipped the whisky along with a glass of water.

"We should go through the backpacks. We want to keep anything of value, especially all the ammunition."

"I don't want anything in them," Sarah announced. "I don't want to touch them."

"I'll go through them," Anne said quietly, "But not tonight. They'll keep until morning." The tension in the room was still palpable.

"Everyone should drink some water, not just me," Jason said. "The stress can make you dehydrated."

"I don't want to drink. It'll just make me have to pee. I'm not going outside tonight...or any night from now on," said Sarah in reference to using the outhouse.

"We can use chamber pots like they did in the 1800s," replied Jason. "Your mom can pick out the proper bowl or pot."

"Gross!" exclaimed Sarah, but she condescended to Anne picking out a pot.

"If it's okay with everyone, I'd like to sleep in the house tonight," Jason said.

Everyone was fine with that idea. After some discussion about where to sleep the girls voted for all of them to sleep together. Anne, Sarah and Catherine went upstairs to retrieve mattresses and bring them down to the living room. Catherine then checked all the locks on the doors and windows.

Although wounded, Jason was not sure he would get much sleep this night. The fourth man was armed, but he probably didn't know whether it was one person who ambushed him and his pals or multiple people. While there wasn't much likelihood he would be back, Jason still felt he should keep watch. As the girls got the mattresses set up, they began to relax and get sleepy.

Catherine asked, "What will you do with the bodies of those men outside?" She had been thinking and digesting things for most of the evening.

"I'll take care of that by myself in the morning," replied Jason.

"Will any animals come tonight?" she asked.

"Maybe, but there's nothing I can do about it tonight."

"What will you do tomorrow?" she persisted.

"I'm not sure, but don't worry, I'll get them away from the house."

"Will you bury them?" Sarah asked.

"That's a lot of work for a one armed man. I can't think about that tonight," Jason said, trying to dodge the issue.

"Enough," said Anne. "You girls settle down and get some sleep. This has been a...a... scary, unpleasant day."

She was hunting for the words but couldn't find the right ones to describe how her world had changed with this attack on their house. There had been six months of dealing with her husband's abandonment and nearly a year of isolation after the power went out. Then Jason showed up and thank God he was here, as the outside world in its worst form came crashing in on their isolated valley. Little did Anne realize there were worse groups out there since law and order had broken down. For now though, this was bad enough. She motioned for Jason to follow her into the kitchen.

"What did you do out there? Those shots at the end, did you shoot them again?" she whispered to him.

Jason whispered back, "I had to finish things. Please don't press me for the details, but it had to be done."

Anne thought about that for a moment, turning it over in her mind. Then, just like the first day they met, Jason could see her make a decision—a choice. She was facing something she had never faced before. She was being forced to accept something new, something foreign, but necessary to survive.

"All right, I won't ask again. In the morning I'll help you dispose of the bodies. You're injured and need help but I do not want the girls to have to deal with that. And I want you to teach us how to shoot. Not just be able to shoot a weapon, but to load it, clean it, be familiar with it and to...to...kill with it."

Jason realized that Anne had crossed some sort of frontier. In that crossing she stepped forward into something new, something she was unsure of, but something that Jason realized he would play a part in. He touched her shoulder gently. "Yes, I will. Now I need to sit down. I'm ready to collapse."

Anne could see he was exhausted. "I'll watch through the night," she said.

Chapter 10

The next morning, after checking Jason's wound Anne helped him drag the bodies away from the house and into the woods. She dug a shallow hole into which they dragged the bodies. After covering them with dirt, she gathered some rocks and piled them on top of the graves. They left no marker. Then Anne took the backpacks, now emptied of ammunition, and set them out in the field to the south. If the other attacker wanted to return for them, he would find them long before he came near the farmhouse.

The captured weapons and ammunition, added to what Jason had brought with him, made a sizeable cache. He assigned each of the women an AR15 or one of its variants. They all shot the .223 round, the same as his Ruger carbine. For training, Jason selected the two 30-30 rifles and the .22 from the house. He would use up that ammunition for training, limiting the use of the semi-automatics for actual defense. The 30-30s and a 30-06 would also be used for hunting, again saving the .223 rounds.

Anne's acceptance of their situation helped convince the girls of the need for firearms training. They were not completely inexperienced with guns, but had done only a little shooting with the 20 gauge shotgun and the .22 rifle—mostly cans on a fence post.

As Jason's shoulder healed he became more active in instructing the family on with the weapons. He spent each day working with them on the concept of quickly acquiring a target and then hitting it. He rigged the clothesline to hold a chest sized target and had it pulled across the shooting range. The girls would start with their backs to the target and have to turn around and quickly sight and shoot it. As they progressed further into their training, Jason devised ways to add in levels of stress and intensity.

After some discussion with Anne, he set Catherine up. She carried a 30-30 with her back to the target, as usual. This time Anne was moving the target back and forth on the line. As the target began to move, Jason began throwing sticks at Catherine. She reacted in shock.

"What are you doing?" she cried out, offended and confused. Jason continued to throw the sticks which Catherine was trying to dodge.

He yelled at her, "You're in a fight for your life! No one cares how you feel! They want you dead—or worse! What are you going to do about it, cry?" With the sticks still flying he yelled, "Shoot!" She turned and sought out the targets, her eyes blurred with tears. The rifle fired five times before she hit the two targets.

Then Catherine turned back to Jason, her eyes blazing, "You jerk! What did you do that for?"

Jason didn't reply, but motioned her to one side and gestured for Sarah to come forward. She hesitated, her eyes wide with dread.

"Mom, what's Jason doing?" she asked.

Anne only motioned for her to step up. The results were similar, even though Sarah knew it was coming, and her reaction was the same. They repeated the drill for the rest of the afternoon, including Anne, who also found it distasteful. But as the day went on, they became more immune to the sticks, and sometimes stones, flying through the air along with Jason's shouting at them. They were able to hit their targets more quickly and with fewer shots. At the end of the day, they understood.

"If we have to defend ourselves there will be bullets flying and wood splintering. It will be noisy, furious and scary. You must be able to maintain a sense of calm in the midst of that chaos and make your shots count." He paced like a drill sergeant, back and forth. "This is serious and you need to be tough to survive it. If enough bad guys come, I can't do it all on my own, like the last time." They were all somber as they digested what Jason had said. His rough actions were forgiven, but the fact that he had done that to them in training drove home the seriousness of their preparation.

The drills continued with Jason inventing other novel ways to simulate the pressure and noise of a fire fight: pots banged next to the shooter's ear, pushing and shoving the shooter before telling her to fire. Catherine quickly became a top shot. Her serious demeanor stood her well in learning the skills Jason was hurriedly trying to impart. Like her mother, she realized that she needed this extra ability to not feel terrorized by this new reality.

Sarah did well but didn't come to the training with the same seriousness. She realized the world was different and more dangerous, but she looked to Jason to protect her and the family while her mother and Catherine worked to shoulder some of that burden for themselves.

Sarah excelled at flirting and getting Jason to acknowledge her attractiveness. It wasn't long before she had established herself as Jason's favorite—at least in her mind. Anne and Catherine, understanding her need for attention, went along with it.

Jason kept up the intensity of the training, concentrating on fighting strategies and shooting practice. There were also lessons in loading and unloading the weapons, cleaning and sighting them. During this time, Jason also worked on setting up shooting positions from the second floor of the house. Then there was the back breaking work of hauling the sand from the creek up the hill to the house. The heat of the summer made this task all the more difficult. The black flies especially liked to swarm around them as they sweated under the heavy loads with hands full. The torment drove Jason to substitute bags of dirt for much of the protection.

The barn held plenty of resources in the workshop area; lumber, hand tools, nails, screws, nuts and bolts, so he was able to build sliding panels that closed the shooting holes to keep out the bugs and wind. The holes were concealed on the outside by a grid of lattice and branches nailed to the wall. Branches were strung on wires in front of the lattice to conceal the shooting holes. The wires were held by removable pegs so they could be dropped if the branches caught fire.

Only if you directly observed a muzzle flash would you know exactly where a shot came from. With this camouflage the house took on an organic look, seeming to be growing branches from the upper story. The dirt and sand bags protected each shooter from a direct hit.

The girls had gone back upstairs to sleep after a few days, but they moved themselves into one bedroom for a greater feeling of security. Jason's days of sleeping in the barn were over after the night attack. Neither the girls nor Anne would consider having him go back there. He slept on the living room couch, which was quite an improvement over the barn's floor. His sleep was now sounder. The nightmares faded as did dreams of Maggie.

Jason kept working like a madman through the summer to make the house safer. There were only a few complaints from the girls, which Anne handled for him. She was in the best condition of her life and the girls were now stronger as well, their bodies taut with muscles from the work and training.

Over the weeks of work, Jason began to assume more and more leadership with the girls, often taking them to task for doing things poorly or shirking from their fair share of work. Anne did not intervene, allowing him to assume some level of parenting authority. The girls took it reasonably well. Sarah fully accepted Jason's increased role as the man of the house. As always, Catherine came along more slowly, but her growing admiration for Jason was deeper than Sarah's flirtatious infatuation.

Chapter 11

The family grew closer as they progressed through the summer, making the house safer, practicing shooting and fighting tactics, and hunting and gathering. Jason often noticed Anne studying him closely as they worked. She warmed to him, growing more comfortable and relaxed as they worked together. She finally told him about Ron, a little chagrined about her bluff when they first met. The circumstances surrounding Ron's absence were more painful than Jason realized. He was embarrassed to find himself encouraged by Anne's story; it indicated a more final separation from her husband.

Jason's attraction to Anne steadily grew over the summer, even as he worked to keep his imagination in check. He knew she was comfortable with him and they had developed a solid partnering relationship, but beyond that, he dared not let himself think too much. Still he reveled in his adoption into the family. His sense of purpose and a need to be useful found ample expression in his new role.

One summer day Anne sent the girls out to gather black berries and raspberries from the bushes that grew along the field's hedgerows. She helped them pack some food and water as they would be out for at least half the day. Off they went with their pistols on their belts and their rifles slung over their shoulders. Watching them set out, Jason felt proud of their increased self confidence. They were certainly safer for the training, but the remoteness of the valley was their best protection. They had seen no evidence of any larger gangs in the area and Jason concluded that the four attackers had been an isolated group.

Later that morning Jason was down in the workshop assembling some frame pieces for his rooftop shooting station. Anne came in to help wrestle the pieces of wood in place for bolting. Anne and the girls mostly wore jeans, shirts and boots for all the work they were involved in, but occasionally they wore dresses, as a defiant feminine statement it seemed to Jason. It was a delightful change of look which he enjoyed.

Today Anne came down to the workshop in a skirt and tee shirt; not unusual, but not typical when doing shop work. As they worked, Jason realized that Anne was not wearing a bra. During the work, she brushed against him when the opportunity presented. Her breasts swelled against her shirt so their full outline showed. As the work continued, Anne found more opportunities to press ever closer to Jason. The slight touches and brushes he had experienced over the past months, coming accidently, always excited him, but he knew they were completely accidental—without hidden meaning. Now her body touched him with intent. At first she brushed lightly against him, then more intensely. As she pressed against him, Jason heard her breathing becoming heavier. He lost track of his work as his excitement rose.

He stopped and turned to her and she pressed against him. Jason had never before embraced Anne and now she was pressing up close against him, not holding back. His body tingled with thousands of electric shocks at her touch. He trembled; she felt the pressure of him through his pants. She looked directly up at him and pulled his head down to her. They kissed, tentative for a moment, and then fiercely. The months of tension, of holding himself back were loosed in the energy of their kiss. Anne responded with an intensity of her own. She had held her growing desire for Jason in check for so long. Now she exhilarated in the rush of releasing it. Jason reached under her shirt and ran his hands over her strong back. She pulled him tighter to her.

Their lips parted, "Are you sure?" Jason asked.

In answer, Anne quickly took him over to the corner of the floor where Jason had kept his mattress and dragged him down. She lay back as he pushed up her shirt, sighing deeply as he stroked her breasts. Anne pulled his shirt over his head and tore open his belt buckle, hurriedly trying to get his pants unzipped. Her breathing was labored, her body eager for him.

"Let me take my boots off," he said.

"Hurry," she replied as she tried to push his pants down, her breath now coming in gasps. He slid her skirt up and she pulled him on to her. They both let out gasps. Jason pressed in gently as Anne opened to him. She moved her hips, adjusting herself to his rhythm. In only a few short minutes, a deep rumble came from the back of his throat and he thrust harder and sharper. Anne responded to his excitement. Then she wrapped her legs over him, pulling him tighter to her as his whole body shuddered in release.

"Yeeesss!" She called out.

The aftermath of what felt like a tsunami had them panting and gently moving together.

Jason rolled off to one side and let out a long sigh. Anne kissed him long and full. "It was wonderful, to feel you bursting inside me."

They lay together silently for some time. Jason marveled at his good fortune to find this woman. He bent over Anne, kissing her face and breasts. Anne could feel her abdomen tingling again. She wrapped a leg over him and pulled him on to her. They joined again, this time longer, savoring each other and the delicious feelings, long dormant and now let loose.

After, Anne lay in his arms with a satisfied smile. He studied her; she was so beautiful, not delicate and slim like Maggie, but a solid, beautiful woman. And now one who showed him so much passion.

Anne looked at him. She could read a question forming that he didn't want to ask, for fear of breaking the moment's spell. "After the power went out I didn't want to accept that it would change our lives—our society," she said in a soft voice. "I kept telling myself the power would come back on and Ron would come back to us. When you arrived, I was confronted by the fact that things had changed, maybe forever. I still wanted to hope that it hadn't, that maybe everything would become normal again. But it hasn't. And after the attack, I realized that I had to deal with this new reality—to accept it—if the girls and I were going to survive. You gave me the courage to do that."

She didn't know if she was making sense, but Jason continued to look at her affectionately. "You lost your wife and I know it must have been traumatic," Anne continued. "You didn't pressure me for affection. That gave me time to come to terms with the changes in our lives. Time to accept these changes. You waited for me to come to you...and now I have."

"Anne," he said softly, "Early on I knew I could fall in love with you. I tried not to think about it, to build up any expectations. I didn't want to ruin our tenuous relationship. I tried to be satisfied with being an adopted member of the family, like an uncle. But in spite of myself, I fell in love. And now you've returned that to me. I never expected all this when I set out. I just wanted to survive while the world was going crazy."

Jason got choked up as he finished and Anne's eyes filled with tears as she listened. She kissed him long and full and pulled him back down to her. Their bodies melted together in a long embrace, drinking in one another through their physical contact. Work put aside for the day, they went up to the house afterward and made themselves something to eat.

Chapter 12

Anne planned to talk with the girls when they came home. "I'm going to tell them that we are now a couple," she explained. "We have to face the reality that our spouses are gone and we have to move on with our lives. This may not be easy, but I'm not going to sneak around with my girls, and you certainly are not going to sleep on the couch anymore."

"I rather like the couch, now that I've gotten use to it," Jason replied.

"I think you'll find my bed more pleasant than the couch," she said with a wink.

The girls came back loaded with berries that were divided up for eating fresh and cooking into a sauce, sweetened with honey, for canning. Anne talked with the girls while they cooked.

"You know your dad has been gone now for two years."

"Yes," said Catherine.

"And you know Jason's wife died in a plane crash when the power went out," she continued. "We've talked about losing our spouses and how we are now working together to make it in this new world."

"I hate the new world," Sarah said.

"But you have learned to adjust to it," Anne replied. "And, admit it, some of it has been okay, especially since Jason joined us."

"If you count shooting and killing okay," Sarah shot back.

"I didn't say it was all good, but we have done more than survive, we are beginning to live again. You girls are so much more self-sufficient and able to take care of yourselves. I can see you're stronger and more assured. Yes, it's tough and hard and, yes, your father left us to fend for ourselves. We can't undo that, just like Jason can't undo losing his wife. But the important thing for me is to see you girls not only survive but thrive."

"What's your point, Mom?" Catherine asked. "Are things ever going to return to normal?"

"I honestly don't know, honey," Anne replied. "You've heard Jason talk about what he saw happening in the city, and you've experienced some of the bad types that are now on the loose. Is the country still in existence? Who knows? All I know is that we can build something here while we wait to see what happens out there."

"So, what's your point?" Catherine repeated.

"Well," Anne said slowly, "Jason and I have grown close together over the months he has been with us. We all have grown closer. Jason is good for us as a family. We have come to realize that we both have a lot of affection for one another, so we have decided to become a couple."

"Like, being married?" Sarah asked.

"Yes dear. We can't get married, there's no one around to do the ceremony, but that's how we feel about each other. We want to join our lives." Anne paused to let her words sink in.

Finally Catherine spoke, "I figured this would happen."

"Are you okay with it?" Anne asked.

"Jason is a good man and we've learned a lot from him. I think he's good for us and good for you. So, I'm okay with it." Catherine seemed a bit sad with her reply.

"Sarah?" Anne asked, turning to her younger daughter.

"It's good, Mom, I want Jason to stay with us forever." Anne breathed a sigh of relief.

The family continued to grow closer. Catherine took responsibility for many of the tasks. She was a good worker and organizer and took a great deal of weight from Jason's shoulders.

"I'll finish the camouflage for the shooting holes," Catherine said one evening.

"That would be great," responded Jason. "I can start on the rooftop shooting platform. That's going to be a lot of work, but worth it."

"It will make the house look funny, the way you describe it," Sarah said.

"It might. Maybe you can figure out how to make it look better," he replied.

"I could hang potted plants on the walls," she said, only half seriously. "You know you need a feminine touch in this rooftop project." She gave him her most grownup look. "Without me helping you, it will look like a bridge construction, or part of the barn."

Before Jason could reply, Anne broke in, "Sarah, you'll get to help keep Jason from making it look too much like a barn project, but I need your help in the food gathering."

"Not fun," Sarah said.

"Don't complain," Jason offered, "I do want your help in making things look good. It may even help disguise the purpose of the platform." Sarah smiled triumphantly at this acknowledgment of her importance.

Book III: The Gang
Chapter 1

Bud survived the attack on the farm by fleeing over the fence. He ran for an hour before stopping, thoroughly winded. Crouching in a hedgerow and listening, he could hear no pursuit and breathed a sigh of relief. Later that night he came to a ridge line where the land sloped down to a river. He nestled himself in the bushes and fell into an exhausted sleep. In the morning he could see a town to his right, on the other side of the river. There were people about, so he dropped down and waded across the stream, hoping to find some food. A lookout spotted him and saw that he was armed. A shout went out and he was ordered to drop his weapon and get on the ground. As guns were leveled at him, Bud turned and ran. He didn't know if word of the fight at the farm had reached town and he would be arrested, but he didn't want to wait to find out. When he was out of site, he turned south, skirting the town and rejoining the road when he was past it.

He kept wandering south, barely surviving on scraps he found at abandoned farms and houses. He was good at looking in all the hidden corners. Often there were scraps of grain, an overlooked box of dry goods or, if it was a good day, a can of beans. Hunger was his constant companion, driving him to keep moving, keep looking for food. At night he dreamed of extravagant meals that left him feeling even more hungry and desolate in the morning.

Alone and struggling, he didn't know where he was going to wind up, but kept moving south. He had no desire to go north; that had almost cost him his life. He saw more signs of human activity the further south he went. He tried getting into some small towns but was challenged and clearly told he wasn't welcomed. After a couple of aggressive rejections he gave the settlements a wide berth. Yet he was clever enough to note their defenses as he passed by. That information might be helpful to him one day. With very little ammunition left, threadbare and foot sore, he came upon a gang encampment.

Bud spent some time carefully studying the gang before he approached them. It was a large group, maybe fifty or more members, large enough to dominate any of the towns he had passed. They looked wild but Bud had few options by then. With much trepidation, he approached the lookouts. When spotted he was ordered to stop and lay down his rifle. After doing as he was told, the guards asked him what he was doing around the camp. Bud replied that he wanted to join them.

"We don't need you," came the reply. "If you know what's good for you, you'll get out of here."

"But I can help you out," Bud responded. "I've come from up north and know about some of the communities up there."

"I'm telling you, you should just keep going."

"I got no options, and I can help," Bud replied despondently. He didn't relish going it alone any more.

The two guards looked at each other, then the kid. "You're taking your life in your hands," one said.

"Yeah," the other chimed in. "You'll be safer getting out of here. If you want to stay, it's your ass."

"I want to join up."

"Take him to Big Jacks," the other guard ordered.

With a shrug, he took Bud and headed into the camp. By the time they reached the center of the camp, many of the gang members were tagging along. Bud got more and more nervous. Was the rest of the gang expecting some kind of show, at his expense? They were camped around a small group of houses at a rural intersection with tents and a few pickups spread around. At the front of one of the houses, the guard spoke to an armed man on the steps.

"This guy wants to join up."

"We don't need another mouth to feed. Get him out of here," the guard replied after giving Bud a disdainful looking over. "He's too skinny to eat," he said with a grin.

Bud's heart jumped. The rumors of cannibalism were true! It was too late to turn around; he would have to play out what he started. The leader of the gang, Big Jacks, emerged from the house. He stood about six feet eight inches tall and weighed close to three hundred pounds.

"What's this?" he asked in a deep voice.

"It's a kid who showed up and wants to join. Say's he has info on towns to the north."

"And for that we should let you join us?" Big Jacks looked at Bud. Bud could not even nod his head in response. "Maybe we just squeeze the information out of you and then carve you up and eat you?"

Bud just stood there trembling. His bowels felt like they would let loose any moment. His brain finally engaged and he took a chance.

"I'm a good shot." It was true. Bud had a knack for aiming well. Now his knack might save his life. Big Jacks just stared at him, so Bud pressed on. "I'll bet I can outshoot most of your gang."

Big Jacks laughed, "That's a big brag, runt. I've got some sharpshooters." He paused for a moment, then said, "If you can outshoot one of them, maybe I'll let you in. If not, we'll be eating you for dinner."

Big Jacks called for two Coke bottles to be set out on a table at fifty yards, and summoned one of the gang. The man came forward with a wicked looking military rifle. He glanced at Bud with disdain and got into a prone firing position. He took a long minute to sight his target. The rifle fired with a loud report and shattered one of the bottles. They handed Bud his rifle and he lay down on the ground. His heart was racing and his breathing was too rapid. He took some deep breaths and tried to calm himself.

"Shoot already," one of the gang shouted.

"Maybe he don't know where the trigger is," offered another.

Bud settled himself down, steadied the rifle on the bottle and squeezed off a shot. The bottle shattered.

The gang erupted, shouting insults at the gang's marksman whom Bud had equaled. Big Jacks looked like he was enjoying the show.

"Put out two more bottles, only further away," he commanded. This time the bottles were set at around seventy yards. The gang's shooter told Bud to go first. Bud got on the ground again, now more confident since he had made the last shot. He was smart enough to know that he needed only a very slight adjustment to hit this bottle only another twenty yards away. He calmed his breathing again and squeezed off his second shot. The bullet hit the top of the bottle, shattering the neck and sending it tumbling to the ground. The gang started whooping it up again. Now the pressure was on the gang's marksman. He got on the ground and slowly took aim on the bottle. His shot rang out and the bottle shattered. Everyone erupted in cheers; the game was going to continue.

"Move 'em further away." Big Jacks ordered. Two new bottles were now placed about a hundred yards away. Bud was ordered to shoot first again. He quieted himself. He closed his mind to everything but the bottle. He knew his rifle, a 30-06, was good for the distance, he just had to aim correctly. He adjusted, raising his aim slightly to compensate for the distance, and squeezed off a shot. The bullet smashed through the edge of the table, caught the bottom of the bottle and shattered it. The gang erupted in hooting and hollering, exhorting their man to meet the challenge of Bud's shot. Bud sighed audibly; he might have just saved his life.

The gang's shooter lay down and quietly took aim. After a long moment he took his shot. The bullet whistled past the bottle which remained standing. There was silence for a moment as he got up cursing and making excuses about someone stamping their feet. Then the group erupted in laughter and ribbing, with the shooter cursing them all in return.

Big Jacks looked at Bud, "This seems to be your lucky day, runt. I'll let you join us for now. But you'll still have to prove your worth if you're gonna stay." He pointed to one of the gang. "Go with him to get you one of our sniper rifles. Looks like you know how to use one." Pointing to his captain, Big Jacks said, "He'll tell you the rules. Follow'em and you'll be okay; don't follow them and you'll be in trouble with me."

Chapter 2

B y late summer, Jason, Anne and the girls had made much progress. The house was set up with concealed and sandbagged firing positions on the second floor. The rooftop observation and firing platform were completed and sandbagged. They had hauled sand and dirt until they were totally sick of the task. They had trekked over the ridge to shoot pigs down at the pond. The pigs proved to be a great resource, not only providing meat to smoke and cook, but fat to use for making soap. They now had a homemade version, scented with crushed flowers they gathered from the fields. It was crude, but it worked. Life was not easy, but it was improving. Jason often thought about what else he and Anne could do to return more normality to their lives. They talked about traveling to the school to scrounge up some books for home tutoring, but the day to day needs of gathering food, preserving what they gathered, and repairing their equipment and clothes seemed to take up all their time and energy.

"No wonder kids dropped out of school early on the frontier," remarked Jason one day.

"And I can now see why, in spite of the dangers, women had lots of kids," she replied. "It certainly helps with the work."

Their day would start at first light. Anne or Jason would get the wood stove in the kitchen going to boil water, while the other would harangue the girls until they got out of bed. After a breakfast of herb tea, some fruit and left-over meat or grains, they would all set about doing their chores. Some days would be spent on the house defenses; some days would be spent with the girls going hunting, either alone or with Jason. Anne spent much of her time gathering food and repairing clothing.

Part of the day was always allocated to gathering and splitting wood. They needed a constant supply, not only for each day's cooking, but to build up a winter reserve. And there were always repairs to be made—windows, door latches, roof leaks and the continuing work on the rooftop shooting platform. Every five or six days, Anne insisted they all take the day off. Sometimes they went on a picnic, sometimes they hiked down to the pond to swim and collect marsh plants and sometimes they just relaxed at the house with the girls taking long baths in the tub outside.

No one stayed up very long after the sun went down. They had kerosene oil lamps that still worked but they didn't provide good light for reading. And by the evening the family was generally spent from the day's activities. Before retiring to bed, they always went through a routine of locking down the house.

Jason's work on defenses now focused outside. He had dug a ditch in the front yard partially circling the house. On the house side of the ditch he put up a chest high barbed wire fence from the supplies he found in the barn. As he explained, the point was not to stop, but to slow down any rush on the house, giving the defenders more time to fire.

Catherine was the best shot besides Jason. She even took up the bow, practicing every time she could. Jason encouraged her, as hunting with the bow saved ammunition and was quieter. Her skill developed to the point she could bring down a deer. Even though Jason and Anne were a bit nervous, Catherine would take Sarah out to hunt, sometimes leaving before dawn. They no longer feared the woods like they had when Jason arrived. They moved with quietness and confidence, often bringing back substantial game. If they bagged a deer, they were not squeamish about field dressing it. After the gutting, they would tie the carcass to a pole and carry it back to the farmhouse.

No one left the house without being armed. When the girls went hunting, they took the appropriate weapon for the game they were after, and always carried 9mm pistols on their belts.

Jason had not grown up with sisters. Some days he learned that he had to just take it easy as task master. The girls wanted to dress up, to do domestic things with their mother and to not concern themselves about guns or house defense, or splitting firewood. On those days, Jason learned to give in and work on projects alone or go hunting.

At other times the girls, especially Sarah, would flirt with him. They would make him the center of attention, practicing their skills on the only male around. Even Catherine flirted with Jason at those times. She was certainly more reserved than Sarah, but more mature in her approach. Anne watched as these scenes played out, intervening when she sensed Jason needed help.

Nights were for sleeping. Jason and Anne rarely indulged in making love at night, preferring the privacy during the day, when they could be apart from the girls. It didn't help that most nights everyone was spent from the day's activities. Life had its routine and that mostly consisted of manual labor. Jason often worried if their idyllic situation would continue. He knew gangs like the one that had attacked Sam and Judy were still out there.

Chapter 3

One morning Sarah came running down the stairs and breathlessly reported that there was some smoke way to the south. They all ran to the roof lookout. Jason studied the smoke through his binoculars. It seemed too large for a campfire, but he couldn't tell much else. It was fairly far away, but very disturbing.

"What do you think it is?" asked Anne.

"Not sure. It seems to be more than just a campfire."

"Clifton Furnace is in that direction," Catherine said. "Could a fire have started in the town?"

"I doubt a fire could have started spontaneously," Jason replied. "We haven't had any storms with lightning. Something's up."

"Could it be a gang?" Sarah said with tension in her voice.

"Maybe." Jason hoped she was wrong, but he had a growing knot in his stomach: *this could be trouble.*

The family went down to the kitchen to discuss the situation. "I could go and scout what this is. It looks like it's a ways off, so I might—"

"No way!" Sarah said. "You can't leave us alone...tell him, Mom."

"I agree," said Anne. We have to stick together, if anything happened to you, we'd be in a terrible spot."

"Let's talk about the worse case and prepare for that," Catherine said.

"Okay," Jason abandoned his idea. "We won't have as much information, but Catherine's right, we can figure out the worse scenario and plan for that."

"So what is that?" asked Anne.

He paused, then said, "Possibly a large gang like the one that attacked Sam and Judy's place. That is what I've worried about all along as we've worked on the defenses for the house. They're dangerous, but on the positive side, these groups aren't well organized. It's not in their nature. They don't fight in a disciplined way and we're probably all better shots than they are."

"Do you really think so?" Catherine asked.

"Yes, you especially, you're a good marksman."

"You mean markswoman," corrected Sarah.

"If you say so. The point is, not only is Catherine a better shot, you and your mom probably are also. We represent a formidable team if we don't fall apart in the noise and pressure of a battle." In spite of their concern, everyone looked proud of themselves.

"The key is being able to function in the heat of a firefight. It's loud and dangerous. I've made you practice with a lot of noise and distractions, but that is nothing like what we will experience if a gang attacks us."

Jason talked about whether or not they could shoot another person. He knew that Anne and the girls could not afford to hesitate. "If we are attacked, you must be able to aim your rifle at someone and pull the trigger. I know you can do that with a target. You're all comfortable with your weapons, but this time you won't be shooting at targets."

Sarah looked doubtful. There was a long silence. Catherine finally asked, "When that small group attacked us, you fired some shots after it was all over. You've never talked about that. What were you doing?"

Jason decided it was time to put all the cards on the table.

"I went carefully up to each person that I had shot, in case they still had their weapon and could use it. I didn't want them to shoot me. The two that were alive, I shot...and killed. The third one was already dead." There was silence in the kitchen.

Finally Sarah asked, "Could they have lived...if you hadn't shot them?" Her voice was timorous and tentative.

"Probably not," he replied. She began to look relieved, "But if they could have lived, I would probably still have shot them." Sarah now gave Jason a concerned look, as if seeing him anew and not sure of what she was seeing.

"Sarah...everyone...these are very bad men. The ones that attacked us meant us harm. If they could have killed me they would have and then probably raped and killed all of you. I wasn't interested in rehabilitating them or giving them another chance." He paused to look at each girl. "The normal rules about how we behave have gone out the window. This is anarchy and barbarism. There's no authority to stop these people. And the group coming may be worse than the last one."

Jason continued, "I'm not trying to rationalize my behavior, but I want each of you," he looked directly at Sarah, "to have no hesitation about shooting these savages. Do not hesitate!" She started at his intensity. "We're not pursuing them, Sarah. If they went another way and never came here, we would be happiest. But if they come here, we'll probably see right away that it is not an innocent visit but an attack."

"And we need to be ready to surprise them. We do not need to be like the other farms they've raided and whose owners they've killed." Anne added to the point.

At last Sarah responded, "Okay, I get it. Don't think about them as people we can reason with, just targets to shoot." Jason nodded. She got it better than he hoped, maybe better than she realized.

From that moment on, they focused their activities on battle preparation. There was no more cooking or shooting and when night came they didn't light any of the oil lanterns. Jason hoped whoever was in the town would not notice the valley and not venture into it. Thankfully most of the work on the house was completed as they didn't dare risk doing any more hammering. Water was gathered and stored, blankets arranged to wet down and suppress fires.

Jason went over and over how they probably would arrive—by the road this time, maybe even in pickup trucks, if they had gotten older ones running—and how the family would fight them. The battle plan was that Catherine and Anne would aim their fire at each edge of the area in front of the house. It was critical to keep the group from surrounding the house. Sarah and Jason would concentrate their firing on the center of the attack. Jason would operate from the roof position and Anne and the girls would shoot from separate positions on the second floor. Sarah would be called to help with either side if Anne or Catherine felt they needed additional firepower. Jason slipped some drainage pipe through holes in the attic floor so he could communicate with the girls from his rooftop position. He didn't know if it would work, but they all felt better to be connected in some fashion.

Now they watched and waited. Was it a gang? Would it show up? The smoke had gone away. Maybe whoever had made it had gone as well and not noticed this valley. Jason wondered how long they would have to remain in stealth mode, before he could declare an "all clear".

Chapter 4

Bud's career as a sniper consisted mostly of shooting game for the gang. At times when he shot a deer he would enjoy a brief moment of popularity. Big Jacks, the leader, had run a biker gang. They were involved in drug running through the Carolinas and southern Virginia, mostly crystal meth and weed. When the power went out, they discovered that many of their bikes still ran. They were older models without electronics. With this mobility, Big Jacks immediately set out on a looting spree. He gathered fuel, guns and ammunition first, food second. Smaller gangs, some with motorcycles, some with older pickup trucks began to attach themselves to Big Jacks. To them he represented the strongest force in a time of increasing anarchy. Jacks' brute force stood out, even amidst the lawlessness. He attracted men who disdained order and obeying rules; men who functioned outside the law and were comfortable there. They took pride in their outlaw status and now, with civic order breaking down, their lawless behavior only increased.

When things got too hot in the Charlotte area, Jacks set out on the road to find easier pickings in the smaller towns. The countryside was disorganized. State government was non-existent and federal authority had limited reach. It was left to each town, large or small, to organize themselves. Getting organized meant gathering resources and protecting them from gangs like the one Big Jacks ran. His plan was to take over a town large enough to support him and his gang although exactly how he would do that remained unclear. If his gang became large enough, he figured he could overpower local resistance and put a town under his control. The town's resources would then be his. He could live grandly as a kingpin and add to his domain with raids on other towns. The leaders of smaller gangs that joined him shared his plan and provided assistance in keeping his growing band of outlaws in line. They would prove helpful in controlling a larger town after his conquest. Visions of power, wealth and women drove him and the gang. Loyalty was maintained by keeping the group fed and holding out the hope that they were not just on an endless cycle of raiding and starving.

Another method of creating loyalty was more personal. Each new member pledged themselves to Big Jacks. He told them that, even though they swore allegiance to him, they were free to leave. Then after a pause he would add that after they walked out of camp, they would be considered food and hunted down. That message created a strong deterrent.

Big Jacks kept his gang on the move raiding, killing, and engaging in cannibalism when hunger drove them to it. The gang was growing and looking for larger communities to raid for the food, women and any other comforts the towns could provide.

Bud was able to detail the defenses of the communities they came upon as they slowly worked their way north. He and the other snipers would shoot the guards, softening their defenses for the rest of the gang to overrun. He never quite got used to the cannibalism, but did not abstain. He rationalized his actions by telling himself that he would become suspect with the others for holding back. Engaging in this horrific practice kept the gang bound together—numbing their sense of humanity and compassion, making them more merciless.

They numbered around seventy when they arrived at Clifton Furnace. The town was a small cluster of buildings and side streets at the intersection of two county roads. One road from the south met another at a "T" junction with the other running east to west beside a river. The town had formed around an iron smelting furnace that processed the local iron ore found in the hills. Over time as more people settled there a diverse economy grew, providing goods to the surrounding farms. The town was a practical collection of businesses that had morphed into quaint, country establishments. It became one of those hidden country gems that city people flocked to. There was a general store with a wooden floor, reminiscent of a century ago. The remains of the smelting furnace were preserved and shown off to tourists.

There were few people left in Clifton Furnace when the gang arrived. A dozen residents hung on, gardening and harvesting what they could, taking comfort in each other's company. When the people in the village saw the gang coming, many ran off in a panic, leaving their possessions behind. The few that didn't escape were rounded up. Three women and two men were caught. After scavenging the town for its remaining food and liquor, the gang began to party. In the midst of the celebration Big Jacks grabbed one of the women and the other two were given to the gang. The men were tied up and later killed, as food ran low. When the gang grew tired of the women, they, too, were killed and eaten.

The village provided few other resources. Some mechanical gear was found in the local garage which the gang used to service their pickups. While they were there, Big Jacks decided to send small groups out to gather what they could from local farms while the main group remained in the village. Bud told Big Jacks about a valley to the north that was very secluded and probably had some good resources.

"The valley is well hidden with only one way in as far as I could tell."

"Why do you think it's worth goin' there?" Big Jacks asked.

"Well, if it's hidden, it may not have been raided." Whenever they came upon a farm or small town that had been raided, very little remained to be scavenged. He continued, "I was up there. We found two farms empty but the third had people in it and was well defended. I figure they had a lot of stuff to protect. I bet it's good pickings."

"So, just because someone ran you off, you think there's a goldmine of stuff to raid? And that's supposed to be worth my while to go up there?"

"There are more farms further up the valley. If they all have food, it could add up to a good haul."

"So how many of you was there?"

"Just four of us. We were ambushed as we snuck up on the house. They knew we were coming. If you sent more men they wouldn't stand a chance."

"Okay, we'll see if you're right. But you better hope I'm not sending men out for nothing."

The senior members of the gang assembled to decide who would go out to raid. Big Jacks relayed Bud's story.

"Bud says there's some farms north of here that haven't been raided. Easy pickings he thinks. I'm going to send a couple of pickups to run through the valley and see what they can collect."

"You need to send two? How far is it?" one of the men asked.

"It ain't far. I'm sending two 'cause one of the farms fought back. Bud got run off from there."

"Bud gettin' run off...that don't mean much," someone said. The others laughed.

"Maybe not, but I'm going to send the pickup with the M60 on it. Bud's going as well."

Everyone agreed with Big Jacks' decision since there was evidence of armed resistance. Most farms put up little to no resistance when they arrived. The smart or lucky ones simply fled at the arrival of the gang.

The M60 was a light machine gun with a bipod support that the gang had adapted to be mounted to the roof of the cab. It created a solid platform from which to fire in a wide arc. The weapon was belt-fed and shot a powerful 7.62mm NATO round. With the gun's rapid rate of fire, Big Jacks figured his men could quickly overcome any resistance.

He had stolen the gun from a National Guard armory. With that raid he had also acquired a .50 caliber M2 machine gun, but with limited ammunition. It was a massively lethal weapon which he planned to use in taking over a large town.

The next morning the raiding party set out for the valley. They made their way ten miles up the county road that followed a stream, then turned right over the narrow iron truss bridge onto the local road leading into the valley where Jason, Anne and the girls waited.

Chapter 5

They heard the pickups before they could see them. From the rooftop, Jason spotted two trucks. Through his binoculars he saw what looked like a machine gun mounted on the roof of the lead truck.

Oh my God! That can make splinters of our walls! The machine gun had to be taken out of action right away.

Jason assembled the family. "There are ten to twelve men in two pickups. We can defeat them. They won't expect the firepower we can bring to bear." Everyone listened carefully. They had their shooting positions assigned, stocked with ammunition, and everyone had water to drink. They had rehearsed the firing instructions, their clips were loaded and ready to change out quickly.

"No one shoots until I shoot. We must let them get into the yard—that's our killing zone. If we shoot too early, they'll spread out into the woods and be more dangerous. I'll shoot at the truck with a gun mounted on its roof." He didn't mention that it was a machine gun. "When you hear me fire, start shooting at the other truck. Aim at the targets in the cab first and then in the back. Remember what I taught you about acquiring a target, shooting and, if you hit it, move on. You don't have to shoot perfectly, just keep hitting the targets. That will take them out of the fight. And don't all stop to reload at the same time. Someone always has to be firing from the second floor."

Everyone looked at Jason wide eyed. "They are coming to take everything from us. To kill us. Don't doubt that," he said. They all nodded. There were no questions now, only the looks. Anne and Catherine appeared resolved. Sarah seemed more doubtful. Anxiety showed in her face. Jason hoped she wouldn't lock up when the shooting started.

It wasn't long before the two trucks turned onto the drive leading to the house. The pickup with the machine gun took the lead as they slowly drove up the long entrance road. Before reaching the relatively flat area at the front of the house, the road took a sharp turn and headed steeply uphill.

I'll stop them after they get over the top of the rise.

As the lead pickup ascended the steep area, Jason sighted the driver through the windshield. *This is it.*

The truck cleared the steep part and entered the flat area of the farm yard. Jason opened fire and the house erupted with gunfire from the rest of the family. The first truck was caught at the start of the front yard area and the second on the steep part of the drive. The men in the bed of both pickups jumped out and ducked behind the trucks for cover. Jason kept firing at the lead truck while the family fired at the other. The machine gunner tried to bring the gun to bear on the house. As he swung the gun, the driver slumped over and the truck started rolling back toward the steep slope and slewed sharply to the right. The machine gun let out a ripping burst of fire into the air as the truck tipped over spilling the gunner out of the bed.

Thank God! That takes out the machine gun.

Everyone ran for cover, some towards the rock outcroppings near the front of the house, some towards the few trees in front, and some tucked down behind the trucks. The second truck had stopped on the steeper part of the slope and everyone jumped for cover. The noise was deafening. The gang was firing at the house indiscriminately as Jason had hoped. The smell of the gunpowder grew thick in the air. There was shouting as the raiders tried to coordinate their response. There were also cries from those hit by the shooting from the house. As he had predicted, the gang poured a lot of gunfire at the house without much effectiveness. Bullets were flying everywhere. Then he noticed the return fire from the house was diminishing.

"Keep shooting!" he shouted down the tube. "Don't let them organize and charge!"

Catherine was the first to respond and she started placing her shots with great effectiveness, aware of her job to keep the attackers from fanning out. Attempts to move laterally were met with her effective fire. Anne and Sarah soon joined in. Everyone was risking their life to look up from the sandbags and shoot, but they realized that the attacker's shots were very random and their lives depended on their ability to return fire.

The attackers homed in on Jason's rooftop firing position and it quickly became very hot. Jason had about twelve feet that he could crawl along on the platform. It was limited movement, but it allowed him to get off some shots through notches in the platform before triggering a fusillade of return fire which forced him to just crouch and wait behind the sand bags.

The overturned truck faced the house and offered minimal cover. As the girls concentrated their fire there, it got too hot for the men crowded behind it. Three of them ran forward, trying to gain the rock outcropping in the yard. Two made it and the third was hit in the chest and fell in the open. He was not killed, but lay in a gathering pool of his blood, coming out from under his prone body as he writhed on the ground. The girls shifted their fire to the other attackers.

When Jason drew fire to the roof, Anne and the girls got off more shots. And they made them count. As the battle went on Anne and the girls became more effective. When attention turned back to them, Jason was able to increase his rate of fire. It went back and forth like that for some time. The effect was a steady volley of deadly shooting coming from the house.

The attackers could not get a good aim at exactly where the girls were firing from on the second floor. There was a continued randomness to their shots but with the volume of shots fired it was lethal to move around in the rooms. The bullets burst through the walls and scattered splinters throughout the rooms. If you stood up and didn't get hit by a bullet you could be lacerated by splinters, some large enough to be lethal. But everyone stayed behind their sandbags and kept firing. The heat became intense inside and the smoke from the shooting thickened.

Jason could see that one of the girls, probably Catherine, was chipping away at a boulder behind which a couple of raiders were taking cover. With each well placed shot she chipped away more stone and panicked the attackers. Finally one jumped to run for a nearby tree. This drew fire from everyone in the house and the man crumpled to the ground. Some of the attackers worked their way around the second truck and made a dash for the barn. They reached some trees and rocks just short it.

Jason yelled down through the tube, "Catherine, the barn side! Don't let them get into the barn!"

Shots started to pepper the rocks and the two trees, keeping the men pinned down. Jason turned his fire back to the center of the attack.

The shooting went on for many minutes—Jason couldn't guess how long. There were short lulls to reload on both sides. The family had gone through many of their clips and, as admonished by Jason, they staggered their reloads so they didn't completely lose the ability to keep up some level of firing. At times everyone could hear the raiders trying to direct each other, but no one seemed to be able to take command; just as Jason had hoped.

What no one noticed was that one of attackers had left the group. Bud had his camouflage ghillie suit on which allowed him to blend into the tall grass at the back of the battle area. He slowly crawled towards a depression in the grass, where he hoped he would be protected from the fire coming from the house. He was scared silly by the ferocity of the battle and quickly realized that he was better off playing the sniper role or, better yet, just hiding. On reaching the low area he lay flat and still. He was afraid to risk crawling further. Shooting would expose his position but not doing so might lead to the gang's defeat. If the gang realized he hadn't taken part in the battle, they would kill him. So he took some shots at the rooftop position. They were accurate, but he didn't have an exposed target to aim at. He could keep a shooter pinned down if he fired enough rounds, but that risked drawing counter fire from the rest of the house. He took only a few shots so he wouldn't expose his position.

Finally the attackers worked themselves up for a charge on the house. The ones still in the fight realized that they couldn't surround it and they were going to get picked off one by one if they stayed pinned down in their present positions. They were not able to shut down the firing from either the rooftop or the house.

They increased the intensity of their shooting to suppress the return fire. Jason and the girls just hunkered down to wait out the onslaught of bullets smashing through the walls. Then, with shouts the gang charged.

When the charge began, Jason and the girls could finally shoot back. They opened up relentlessly, ignoring the now wilder shots coming from the attackers as they ran forward. They could not let the gang reach the house. The deadly fire took its toll and the attack stalled at the fence. Seven men had charged; four were cut down and the remaining three turned and ran, dodging around to the cover of the trucks. They crawled into the cab of the remaining truck and let it roll down hill until they got behind the tree line. At that point, they started it, backed wildly down the drive, and headed off in a roar towards the village.

Jason watched to make sure they all had left. Then he joined the family on the second floor. He found Anne and Catherine bent over Sarah. She was gasping for breath. Blood was pouring all over her face and down her front.

"Sarah," Anne said, "Speak to me." Looking up at Jason, she said, "Jason, help her, she's been shot. She's hurt."

He looked closely at Sarah, "Get me a rag to wipe the blood." Catherine brought him a rag wetted from her water bottle. He gently wiped Sarah's face and head. "She's been hit with wood shrapnel, not shot. There's a lot of bleeding but it's not life threatening."

"Will she be all right?" Catherine asked.

"Yes. Anne, take her down to the kitchen and get some cold, wet cloths to clean her. Don't wipe, the wounds may be deep and we don't want to tear them." Turning to Catherine he said, "We have to secure the battle field. Go up to the roof and spot for me. They may have left someone behind or some of the wounded could still be dangerous."

Catherine grabbed her rifle, checked the magazine and turned to leave.

"If you see someone, give out a shout and point me in the right direction."

"Be careful," Catherine called back to him as she headed to the attic.

Wounded men were groaning in the front yard, lying alongside of the dead. Jason grabbed his rifle and went out the back door. He dropped into a crawl as he worked himself through the tall grass. Reaching the edge of the orchard, he turned and worked his way towards the front, using the trees as additional cover

Chapter 6

Bud was now alone; the pickup had left. He was frozen, afraid to move, not knowing what was going on in the house. He had no illusions about what could happen to him.

In his last encounter with Jason, he knew what the outcome for his buddies had been when he ran away. He had heard the shots. That would be his fate unless he could do something. Very slowly he raised his head. He could barely see through the grass, but that was good. It would be hard for anyone to see him. As he studied the house, he saw the grass move on the uphill side. Someone was crawling towards the orchard. It was like the last time. He watched and then glimpsed briefly someone rising and disappearing behind a tree. That someone was headed Bud's way. It was too late to run. He would have to fight. He had flattened himself to the ground during the last round of intense fire from the house. Now his rifle was laying there, not shouldered and ready to fire. He had to move his body to get into a firing position. He had to get up on his elbows with his left hand under the barrel and his right hand on the trigger with the stock pulled tightly into his right shoulder, all without being seen. It took a minute of careful movement to get his rifle to the ready. As he began to tuck it into his shoulder, his elbow slipped and the barrel tipped up in the air. He quickly lowered it just below the level of the grass and froze.

Catherine carefully scanned the grass. She was looking for something out of the ordinary. Many lectures by Jason had reinforced that there were no straight lines or perfect circles in nature. When she saw something straight and rod-like in the grass, she knew. It was there for a moment and then disappeared into the grass. She could not see anything else. She stared and didn't blink or turn her gaze away for a moment. She knew that if she did, she would never find that spot again. Finally she could discern parts of a solid, straight shaft, horizontal in the grass. She could only see a couple of segments of it but it didn't look natural.

Deciding that it was a rifle barrel, she carefully calculated where the body of the shooter would be in relation to it. Catherine then took aim at the spot she had chosen and sent six shots in a tight pattern along the length of where she thought the shooter might be.

The second shot hit Bud in the shoulder, flipping him on his side and the third hit him in his abdomen, turning him on his back. He cried out in pain as the bullets tore into him, throwing him back on his rifle. His shoulder was torn by the first shot and bleeding profusely. The shot to the abdomen tore through part of his stomach, destroyed his liver, and nicked a kidney before exiting out of his lower back. Numerous blood vessels were torn and bleeding inside Bud, bleeding that would not be stopped by external compression.

"What is it?" shouted Jason.

"A sniper...to your right, towards the fence. I hit him. He's lying on his back," Catherine called back.

Jason crouched and ran towards the position Catherine indicated. He quickly found Bud. He pulled the rifle away as Bud stared up at him.

"Don't shoot me, please," Bud said in a weak voice.

Jason stared back at him. There was no need to shoot him; there was an entrance wound in his abdomen with probably a larger exit wound in his back. Internal injuries were not something he could help, even if he wanted to.

Bud continued, "I'm hurt bad, please don't leave me."

Jason squatted down next to him. "Tell me about your gang."

"Should I come out there?" Catherine called out.

"No!" he shouted back. "Keep watch for anyone else."

"I should never have come back here," Bud said.

"What do you mean?" Jason responded.

"I was with the guys you ambushed months ago; I got away."

"What about this gang?" Jason asked.

"It's run by a scary guy named Big Jacks." Bud paused, grimaced in pain. "Can you help me? I don't want to die."

"I'll try, if you help me. How many are in your gang?"

"Fifty, seventy, didn't count them. I didn't want to...to...eat people. That's what they do." His words were becoming more difficult to form, but he wanted to get them out. "They kill people and...and eat them...they take the women...I didn't want to do things like that. I just wanted to survive."

Jason's stomach turned and he fought to control the revulsion rising inside.

"They'll be back," Bud continued laboriously. "Big Jacks can't have someone beat him...and you got his machine gun. He's coming back."

A plan was forming in Jason's mind, even as he heard Bud's warning. He looked closely at Bud's rifle; it was an M110 sniper/assault rifle. The weapon was similar to the AR15/16 but shot a larger 7.62mm round. It was set up for sniping with a variable power scope, a bipod and a 20 round clip. This would be a more powerful, more lethal weapon than his .223. "Do you have any more ammunition for this?" he asked.

"In the truck, the machine gun truck," Bud responded more weakly. "Please don't leave me. Am I going to hell?" he asked plaintively.

"I don't know about heaven or hell," Jason responded, "but I do know that you'll find out soon enough. 'Course you won't be able to tell anyone so we'll never know."

"I'm sorry for attacking you."

I'll bet you are. And now you are worried about it since you're dying.

Still, Jason felt the urge to comfort this scrawny kid who had attacked him twice and was now paying the price. "I'll stay with you."

As he waited with Bud a dark, black resolve grew inside of Jason. It almost frightened him. He knew he was going on a killing spree. He was going to take this gang apart. It was the only way. He couldn't wait for them. His resolve drove out fear. It left him focused on how to most efficiently kill these savages. The label was accurate. They had become predators, and they needed to be eradicated. He was determined to get the rest of the valley involved. They had to come together now.

Bud lapsed into unconsciousness. Jason went to the pickup and found the ammunition for the M110. Then he quickly dispatched the rest of the wounded and went back into the house.

The family was huddled in the kitchen around Sarah. The windows were shot out with glass everywhere. Jason went over to Sarah.

"How are you doing?" he asked.

She looked at him. She had a clean cloth wrapped around her forehead and others draped along the side of her face. "Am I going to be all right?" she asked.

Jason gently took the cloths from her face. He remained passive as he surveyed her injuries. She had multiple cuts across her face, one even on her eyelid. There were two that he could see would require stitching. One across her left forehead, just above her eyebrow and one down the side of her left cheek, thankfully back towards her hair line. She would be scarred but, he hoped, the scars would not damage her beauty.

"Yes, you're going to be all right. You're lucky that no splinters entered your eyes."

"I did what you said, not move around, but when I got up to shoot I got hit in the face."

"It's okay. You didn't do anything wrong. You were a good fighter. This could have happened to anyone in the room. I'm glad it wasn't worse."

Jason laid the cloths back on Sarah's face to control the bleeding. He motioned Anne to follow him out of the kitchen. "We'll have to sew two of those wounds."

"I know. This will be hard without anesthesia. I'm afraid it'll be harder for her than the battle."

"There's something more. I got some information from one of the gang."

Anne looked at him with concern.

"The main body is in Clifton Furnace. This group was just a raiding party. Some of them escaped and they'll head back to the village. I think the main part of the gang is going to return."

"Oh my God," Anne exclaimed. "Why would they want to return?"

"We beat them...and we have their machine gun—the gun on the truck. They'll be back for the gun and to defeat us. I don't think whoever is leading the gang can allow himself to lose this battle."

"But that's insane. There will be more killing. We may be killed. What do they get out of that?"

"I can't think like them, but they probably expect to get food and weapons if they can defeat us. It's motivation enough for barbarians like them." He held Anne by her shoulders. "Anne, they are cannibals as well. It's one of the ways they have survived."

She pulled back in shock. "That can't be true."

"I can't just dismiss what I was told. I don't want to tell the girls. I'm telling you only to reinforce how desperate our situation is. These people are beyond the bounds of civilized behavior. We have to expect anything."

"Well, what must we do? We have to tend to Sarah. What else can we do?"

"You're right. We have to stabilize her wounds. But Catherine and I have to go to the other farms in the valley, quickly. We've got to get their help. The next battle is for the survival of the whole valley."

Anne looked at him long and hard. "When will they be back?"

"I don't know. I hope we have a day at least. They may need time to organize and pack up for their raid. But there is no time to lose. I have to prepare for a battle and you must tend to Sarah. We can stitch her wounds later."

"It scares me to have you leave this house."

"I know. But it's necessary for me to do so. I'll be quick...I must be quick."

They went back into the kitchen.

Anne said, "Sarah, Jason has to contact the rest of the farms in the valley right away. We have to get their help in case any gang members come back."

"Why would they come back?" Catherine asked. "We beat them, didn't we?" She turned to Jason.

"Yes, but some got away and I learned there are more in the village. They may or may not return, but we have to get the others to help in case they do," he said.

"What about Sarah? She needs help," Catherine persisted.

"I'll take care of Sarah's wounds for now. She'll be alright." Anne stroked Sarah's hair. Turning to Catherine, "You must go with Jason. You know everyone better than him. It will help if you're there."

"Am I going to need stitches?" Sarah asked with some dread.

"Possibly," Jason replied. "We can't do it now. The wait will give us time to see if the wounds close well enough by themselves." He wanted to downplay the need for stitches at the moment.

"I don't want you to leave. We need you. I need you," Sarah said.

"Your mom will be here. I don't want to leave either, but this has to be done. Our lives may depend on getting extra help if this gang comes back."

"Why? We beat them once. We can do it again," Sarah said.

"I like your confidence, but now you're injured and we won't have the element of surprise on our side. If they come back, we'll need help."

Chapter 7

Catherine and Jason went out into the yard. Both avoided looking at the dead. He retrieved a come-along and some rope from the barn.

"We have to take the truck, it'll be faster than walking," Jason said.

"Won't everyone freak out with that machine gun on top?" Catherine asked.

"We'll take that chance. Speed is critical," he replied.

With a rope, he attached the come-along to a tree, then hooked the other end to the cab of the overturned pickup and winched it upright. It had a flat front tire. After changing the tire they rolled the truck down the hill to jump start it and drove up the valley road. They were dirty, their clothes torn, hair matted with sweat, cuts and scratches on their arms and faces. Shortly they encountered Tom Walsh trotting on the road towards them and stopped.

"What happened?" Tom asked. "I heard the shooting." He looked in the cab in amazement, "You two look a mess!"

"We were attacked by a gang—a raiding party." Jason responded.

"Did anyone get hurt? How are Anne and Sarah?"

"Sarah got cut up from flying splinters but she'll be okay. Mom is okay," Catherine responded. "You remember Jason, he's staying with us?"

Tom nodded to Jason. "Of course. Is this their truck?"

"Yeah. They were part of a larger gang and I think they may be coming back."

"Where'd they come from?"

"Clifton Furnace. I think they killed the remaining people in town then they set out to raid this valley," Jason said.

"So you think they're coming back?"

Jason nodded, "For food, supplies...and I have their machine gun. They'll be back. We need your help to round up everyone in the valley. We don't have much time."

"How soon?"

"If we're lucky not till tomorrow or the next day. There's no time to lose."

"Okay. What can I do?"

"We need to get everyone together. I'm going to skip the Turner farm. I don't think the old man will talk to me," Jason said. "Can you get him to come?"

"Yeah, I think so. He'd likely try to shoot you, especially driving up in this truck. He fusses at me, but I don't take his crap. I think he respects me. Where do you want to meet?"

"I don't know where."

"Let's meet at my house. Drive me up to the Turners and drop me off. You and Catherine go to the others and bring them back to my place. It'll take a while for me to convince the old man, but I'll get him to the meeting." Tom climbed in the cab. "That's an M60 on the roof. These guys were well armed."

"You must have been in the military," Jason said.

"Vietnam. We used them over there."

They dropped Tom off at the Turner's farm and drove on up the valley in silence. Jason felt the press of time. He didn't know how soon the gang might return and the worst scenario would be Anne and Sarah caught alone when they did. He shuddered at the thought.

Catherine seemed to sense his tension. "Having Mr. Walsh talk to Mr. Turner will help. The others will be easier to talk to."

They drove in silence. Then Jason said, "Catherine, you showed a lot of ability in the fight today. You not only shot well, you showed good judgment and you kept calm. Not many can do that in such an intense situation." Catherine looked at him as Jason continued, "I'd like to confide in you, but I don't want to frighten you."

"What are you talking about?"

"I want you to fully understand what we're up against. I'm going to have to explain it to the others in the valley, so I want you to hear it first. It's something I couldn't tell Sarah."

Catherine waited in silence.

"This gang that attacked us, they killed everyone left in Clifton Furnace. The kid in the tall grass filled me in. They raid farms and small villages. They rape, kill...and they eat the people they capture. That's what we're up against."

Catherine looked at him in horror. Jason wondered if he had said too much. "I guessed they were very bad," she said, "killing and raping. But I never guessed they would be cannibals. That's disgusting. You're right, you can't tell Sarah."

"That's why we have to win."

An hour later they were headed back to the Walsh farm with Andy Nolan and Clair, his wife, and John Sands. John's wife, Natalie, stayed back with their daughter. The group entered the living room. Ray Turner was already there sitting off to one side with his son, Billy. The others took seats that had been set out for the meeting. Betty, Tom's wife, directed Jason and Catherine to the couch which was the focus of the circle. They sank back ragged and exhausted from the gun fight.

Immediately the questions began. They came faster than could be answered. Betty went to get them some water. When she returned from the kitchen she stepped to the middle of the room, "All right. Everyone quiet down! We need to let these two tell us what happened. Let them talk, please."

The commotion stopped. Everyone stared at the two veterans of the morning's battle. Their eyes never left them as Jason recounted the day's events. They were all dumbfounded at hearing the details of the ferocity of that morning.

"I'm amazed you could return fire fast enough to keep them from rushing the house," Tom commented when Jason had finished his tale.

"The shooting positions on the second floor and the roof made all the difference. They were sandbagged and gave us protection. We'd have died without that."

Tom shook his head, "That's quite a feat," he said.

"It wouldn't have done any good except that Anne and the girls have gotten to be very good shots. It took all of us to hold them off."

All eyes turned to Catherine who did her best not to look awkward.

"Why do you think they'll come back?" Andy asked. "My God, from what you've told us it seems you dealt them a real blow." Andy Nolan and his wife, Claire, were a comfortable couple who seemed to get along just fine, even after the power went out.

"There were about fourteen in the attack, from a gang of fifty to seventy. They've already killed everyone in Clifton Furnace. This was a raiding party targeting this valley. Some of them escaped and they'll take the story back to the others. I don't think the gang leader can let us have our victory. And we have his machine gun."

"If it's a matter of the machine gun, couldn't you just drop the pickup off at the bridge? Let him have his truck and machine gun, like a peace offering? Then he wouldn't have a reason to come back into the valley," John suggested. John was the architect who had worked out of his remodeled farmhouse.

Jason looked at him in surprise. *Was he serious?*

Tom spoke up, "John, that gives the gang back a very dangerous weapon, one they could use on us."

John turned to Tom, "So you agree we should go to war with these people?"

"It seems like they're already are at war with us. If what Jason says is true about Clifton Furnace, why should we think they'll bypass us?"

"What do we have to offer? There's nothing here for them. I don't see it," John said.

Andy spoke up. "Maybe we could construct a road block at the bridge, something that would keep the gang out. Then we could give them back their machine gun without worrying about it being used on us."

"That's a great idea," John added.

"That might work," Jason said, "but how do we do that? And, more to the point, how do we do that in the next twelve hours?

"Why so quickly?" John asked.

"We don't know when they might come back—" Jason began.

"If they come back at all," John said.

"That's not an 'if' I'm willing to bet on," Tom said.

Jason continued, "*If* they come back, we don't know when it might be. But I can guarantee you that it won't be long in coming. They only have to gather their men and weapons before they set out to avenge the defeat we gave them today. If we act too late, we are wide open with no defense."

Tom spoke again, "We don't have any dynamite to create a landslide and we don't have the heavy equipment to dismantle the bridge. And if we did, how do we get out later? We can't be locked in this valley forever. Sure we've made it on our own so far, but if we need to leave, we must have a way out without backpacking over the mountains.

And anyway, what's to stop them from removing any barricade we could set up? From what Jason says, they have a lot of man power. Sorry, Andy, I don't think it's a workable plan."

"But how can we beat them? It's just the few of us against...how many did you say...fifty of them? I don't see how we win that battle," John declared.

Jason thought for a moment. "There aren't any good choices, the way I see it. I've survived, my family has survived, by being ready to repel force with force—"

"But not against these odds," John said.

"Yesterday we had four of us against fourteen and we won, so it is possible to win against superior numbers." Jason studied the group. Ray Turner just scowled at him and the others. He was amazed that Tom succeeded in getting him to come. *He probably just wants to find out about the shooting and that's all.* Tom seemed to be on board. He understood evil and violence. Andy seemed to be pretty down to earth, if uncommitted. John seemed to be in denial that this idyllic valley would be violated. All of them had adjusted to living off the grid when the power went out. In varying degrees they were making it here in the valley. Would they realize their need to defend it?

The group was silent for some moments then John spoke again, "I have a seven year old daughter. I'd like her to grow up with a father. If we fight these people, even if we win the fight, some of us may be injured or killed. What price do we pay for victory? Are you all ready to be killed? Because that's what could happen if we fight this gang. We need to find another way."

Jason could see Catherine was getting more and more agitated as the conversation progressed. He was about to respond when she spoke up.

"I'm pretty young so maybe I should let you adults speak and decide, but today I killed some adults, so maybe I've earned the right to speak. I didn't want to fight this morning and I don't want to do it again, but I will if that's what it takes to stay alive." All eyes turned to her. With a nervous swallow she continued, "Jason filled me in on who these people are. They raped, killed and ate the remaining people in Clifton Furnace." She stopped to let that sink in. The room was silent. "If they had won today, they would have killed Jason and raped me, my mom and my sister, Sarah. Maybe they would have eaten us as well. They would have gone on up the valley and done the same to all of you." She paused again, turning to John, "Mr. Sands, your little girl. Think about what they would do to her... and your wife." She stared hard at him, not wavering.

John turned away from her.

"John, do you think you can reason with someone who will eat people?" Jason asked.

The room's silence was broken by Ray Turner clearing his throat. "I fight my own battles. I'm not joining your war. They come to my place they won't find me. I'll melt away in the woods. They come into the woods they'll find me all right. I'll put a bullet in their head before they know I'm there. These city slickers ain't any good in the woods. I'll pick 'em off like crows on a wire."

"We could all go up into the woods and wait for them to leave," John offered. "That might be safer then fighting them."

"What will you come back to?" Tom asked. "You need shelter and food to make it through the winter. They'll take your resources and maybe burn your house down as well."

"Why would they do that?" John asked.

"Are you willing to bet your house they wouldn't? From what Jason has said, that's how they operate. They take what they want—pretty much everything, kill anyone in their way and they don't seem to care about leaving things unharmed. They're vandals as well as thieves. " Tom replied.

"Andy, what do you think?" Jason was taking a chance but he needed another man on his side.

Andy sat silence for some time. "Not sure what I think. This is hard to digest. The gang may or may not come back. If we prepare and they do, we'll have a horrendous fight on our hands...and maybe lose. Even if we win some of us may be killed or wounded. But if we don't prepare and they come back, our only option is to flee into the woods and maybe lose everything." He paused for a moment. "I don't know about the rest of you, but I'm not so quick on my feet when it comes to fleeing. And Claire even less so." He squeezed her hand as he spoke.

"I agree with Andy. I don't want to leave what we've gathered and worked to build since the power went out. I don't think I could survive in the forest without shelter," Claire said.

"So where do you stand?" Tom asked.

"I guess I want to defend the valley. I'd rather trust in myself and the rest of you," he looked around the room, "than trust in what this gang might or might not do."

Ray jumped up. "You all are a bunch of fools. You gonna make this guy your general? Gonna march off and kill this gang? Gonna get yourselves killed is what you'll do."

"Billy, how do you feel about this?" Jason asked.

"Billy thinks the same as me." Ray shouted back at him. "You come into this valley. You think you're some kind of hero? Killing all the game in the hills, taking all our food. Don't think I'm gonna to listen to you. What the hell do you know? For all I know this trouble followed you. Maybe you're the reason this gang is here."

Billy looked like he was going to answer but didn't when his dad's tirade continued.

Jason looked straight back at Ray. "We didn't get off to a good start and I'm sorry about that. I didn't bring them here, but I've run into the likes of them outside this valley. If you want to see what happens when they attack, come down and look at our farm. And if you want to see what we can do together, come down and look at our farm."

Catherine stood up, her fists clenched at her side, her dark eyes now blazed in anger. "Mr. Turner, we just had to fight for our lives today. Without Jason, my mother, my sister and I would be raped, enslaved or dead right now. So, don't you talk to him like that. You have no right. He hasn't done you any harm and he saved our family." Tears began to well up in her eyes. She fought them back and stared directly at the old man, her body shaking with emotion.

Jason stood up and put his arm around Catherine. "She's right." He turned to John Sands, "John, help us. Together we can save ourselves—this valley. We need your help."

"All right, I'll help. But it scares me. I don't know much about guns and shooting, but I can try." John responded.

"I'm in," Andy said. "I don't move so well but I know how to shoot."

"Both Betty and me are in, aren't we?" Tom looked to his wife who nodded.

"I've hunted for years," Betty said.

"She's a good shot too," Tom added.

"This will be like hunting, only it's more dangerous game," Betty said. "I don't want to give scum like that a chance to do us harm. I had friends in Clifton Furnace...we all did."

"I can run that M60. Is there any ammunition for it?" Tom asked. Jason nodded. "Okay, where do we fight them?" he continued.

"The best place to set up an ambush is at the bridge. It's single lane and the road is hemmed in by the cliffs cut into the ridge. We set up on the high ground, we stop the vehicles on the bridge and the gorge on the valley side becomes a killing zone."

"So what's next?" John asked.

"Catherine and I will take you and Andy and Claire back to your farms. Gather some food and water and meet at our farm. Do you have a way to get there? We need to head back after we drop you off to collect weapons and ammunition."

"I've got a pickup that runs, still have some gas left," Andy said. "I'll collect everyone and bring them down."

Ray stood and motioned for Billy to follow him. Billy looked at Catherine, his eyes wide. He had been staring at her ever since she spoke.

"Ray, are you going to join us?" Jason asked as he shuffled past. Ray just glared back at him and left without a word.

"Ignore him," Tom said.

"We'll go over weapons when you get to the farm. I suggest you all stay there tonight. We can head for the bridge first thing in the morning to set up our ambush," Jason said.

"John, why don't you have Natalie and Lisa come to our house. They can stay with me while you're gone," Claire said. "They'll be as safe as they can be at our place."

John nodded and the meeting broke up. Jason and Catherine dropped John, Andy and Claire off and set out for home. It was mid-afternoon. Exhaustion from the battle and the stress of negotiating with the others finally caught up with them. He could see Catherine's head nodding as fatigue overwhelmed her. She finally slouched over on the bench seat, laying her head on Jason's leg, and fell fast asleep. Jason hung his head out of the window, trying to stay awake.

When they reached the farm Catherine was still asleep. Jason left her in the cab and went in to Anne and Sarah. Anne had moved Sarah to the couch, away from the mess left in the kitchen from the battle. Sarah was half reclining. Her forehead was tightly wrapped and she held bandages on the side of her head over the deep cut.

"How did it go? Are the others going to help?" Anne asked as he entered the room.

"Everyone is going to help except for the Turners."

Looking past Jason, Anne asked, "Where's Catherine?"

"She's asleep in the pickup. The stress of the battle and talking with everyone was too much for her."

"That doesn't surprise me."

"The others are coming here later today. We're going to plan our defense and set up tomorrow."

Anne looked around in distress, "The house is so torn apart. There's no time to clean it."

Jason took her in his arms and hugged her, "My sweetheart, earlier the warrior and now the hostess. Don't fret. We'll have all the time we need to clean and repair things, but not now."

"Will we? Tell me truly. I need the truth about what is going to happen. You must be honest with me...about our chances," Anne said.

"It will be hard. We'll defend ourselves at the bridge— ambush the gang there. It's our best chance to defeat them. Afterwards we will have time to clean. How can I think otherwise?" His stomach tightened as he made the promise. How would this all turn out? Would this small group of defenders, mostly novices, be able to stand against hardened outlaws? Besides himself, they had only one combat veteran. Even with their advantageous position, he wasn't sure this was not a suicide mission; one he was sending Catherine on as well as the rest. Doubt began to creep into his thoughts; he forced it down. Now was the time for hardness, not doubt. He had set the group on this path and it would need hard men and women to make it successful.

He turned to Sarah, "How are you doing my warrior princess?"

"I'm impersonating the mummy," she said and tried to smile.

"You look beautiful to me," Jason said.

"No I don't. I'm going to have big scars all over my face." Tears began to well up in her eyes.

"No. There may be two small scars but they won't overcome your beauty. Your beauty is too great. They will only add intrigue."

Sarah tried to smile.

"I think we are all feeling overwhelmed," Anne said.

"Let's get some food together. Then maybe we should get Sarah to bed."

"I don't want to move. I don't want to be alone," Sarah said.

"If you want to stay downstairs when everyone comes, you can," Anne replied.

"We need to eat something now," Jason said as he led Anne into the kitchen.

Quietly he said to her, "As I told you before, suturing Sarah's wounds will have to wait. I have to get everything together—the guns and ammo—and plan our defense. Early tomorrow morning we'll go down to the bridge. If they're coming, it could well be tomorrow."

"So you are sure they'll be back?"

"Whether or not I'm sure, we have to be ready. It's foolishness not to be."

"I understand, but do you think they actually will come back?" she pressed him.

Jason paused and looked at Anne, "Yes, I think they will return." Anne saw his face begin to change, his eyes becoming dark. She shuddered as she looked at the man she loved.

"There will be more killing, a lot of it..." Her voice trailed off.

Jason just looked at her. His face was now hard with a cold intent growing inside. There was no tenderness now. Something dark was there, something to do with killing. No matter what the rest could do, he had to be a lethal force. "There will be killing, but I am the one who will be doing it."

Anne shuddered again both at his countenance and his words.

Chapter 8

It was late in the day when the survivors of the attack, in their shot-up pickup truck, arrived back in Clifton Furnace. One of Big Jacks' captains saw them pull up. He could see the destroyed windshield and bullet holes in the truck's bodywork. He turned and ran to get Big Jacks. The men were not able to melt away before he came out of the house. He took one look at the truck and strode over to it with a dangerous expression on his face.

"What happened? Where's the other truck? Where's the rest of the men?" No one answered. Big Jacks grabbed the closest guy by the neck and yanked him off his feet.

"Answer me, maggot, or I'll ring your neck."

The hapless outlaw, now dangling from Big Jacks' grip, could only croak, suspended in the air, his eyes bulging in fear and pain. Big Jacks put him down but kept his hands on him.

The man said in a weak, terrified voice, "We were ambushed. They had sharpshooters pinning us down. They almost killed us all. We tried to rush the house, but they took out too many of us. We barely got away."

Big Jacks lowered his voice, now more menacing than ever, "What happened to the M60?"

"The driver got shot right away. The rest bailed for cover and the truck turned over. We never got it into the action."

"You idiots." He shouted, smashing his huge fist into the man's head and snapping his neck. Everyone backed away a few steps. This was not the time to catch Big Jacks' eye. He looked around, his face contorted in anger, "We're going back there and we're going to take this group out, burn their house down, kill them and eat them. I'm going to cut out the heart of their leader." Looking at the other men who had returned, he declared, "You're going to lead the charge...I'm putting you at the front when we go after them." Turning back to the house, he yelled, "Get everyone ready." People began to scurry away in different directions.

As they walked back to the house, one of his captains suggested, "We probably need to keep some men back to guard our gear."

Big Jacks glared at him. "I want forty men, get four trucks ready."

"That will leave enough to guard things here in town," the man said. He planned to be among those he was organizing to stay in town.

"Get busy," Big Jacks growled continuing on to the house. "We're bringing the M2. Make sure Mo's on it. I'll rip that house apart with it."

The M2 weighed one hundred and twenty-five pounds, with its center mount tripod. The weapon fired a powerful .50 caliber round from a belt feed. The rounds could penetrate an engine block. Mo was a big man; larger than anyone except Big Jacks. He could handle the large gun. If necessary he could fire it from his arms. The gun would explode concrete block and could tear down the walls of the farmhouse, shredding them and exposing anyone inside. Big Jacks was not going to allow any further defeat, so he would use the gun even if ammunition was scarce.

As they entered their house, his captain asked, "Do you think this is a vigilante group? The last thing we need is to run into a group like that."

Big Jacks gave him a hard look. The man cowered. "You think we can't handle some vigilantes? That what you think?" Now frightened, the man shook his head. "We're the strongest gang around." Big Jacks continued, "We ain't run from anyone since we left Charlotte. Soon we'll have a big town to control, one with lots of resources. You better not be talking like that in front of the others."

Again the man just shook his head, too afraid to speak.

"Anyway they wouldn't be holed up in a farmhouse if they was vigilantes. I figure they must have something really valuable to protect."

"That's what I was thinking. There's some good loot for us," the man agreed eagerly.

"This valley must have a lot of resources. Maybe this farm is the main defense for the whole valley. We take it out and we have the rest, ripe for the pickin'."

The captain licked his lips in anticipation and nodded in assent.

"Pass the word around as you get the men together. I'm betting there's food, fuel, ammunition and weapons for us tomorrow. And probably some women on top of that. You tell 'em. I want them fired up and ready to kill."

Big Jacks' challenge was that the larger and more lethal his gang grew, the more resources it consumed. He was in a race to grow large enough to take over a good sized town that could support him before he ran out of resources in the countryside. Loyalty was built on the shaky principle of being able to continually provide booty; food, fuel, women. He looked forward to the next day's fight. It would bring both revenge and riches.

Jason set about collecting the weapons and ammunition from the men in the yard. He laid them out on the dining room table and piled the boxes of ammunition on the floor nearby. It was nearing dusk when the others arrived. They stood for some time surveying the battle scene. There were bodies lying in the yard, the house had all of its windows that faced the yard shot out and the walls were splintered with bullet holes.

The group picked their way through the carnage and entered the house quietly, not knowing what to say to Anne after seeing first-hand the evidence of that day's violence. Anne had swept up much of the broken glass from the first floor, but everyone could still see the enormous damage the house had suffered. It brought home the intensity of the battle the family had experienced. The group greeted her shyly. It seemed wrong to act normal—as if nothing happened—but no one wanted to acknowledge the enormity of what had taken place.

Betty immediately went to Anne and gave her a big hug. "Oh my dear, how are you?"

"I'm as good as can be expected," Anne replied.

Turning to Sarah, Betty asked, "Sarah, how are you doing?" Sarah still had a bandage wrapped around her forehead. On the side of her face Anne had put a compress bandage and tape.

"I guess I'm okay. Jason says I won't have bad scars, but I think he's just being nice."

"We all heard about your battle. It's amazing you're all alive. I think you are all heroes for what you did. Now we're going to make sure those thugs never come back."

Sarah shuddered. "I hope I never see something like that again in my life."

Betty patted her shoulder, "We'll make that happen, don't you worry."

Everyone assembled in the living room. "You've got quite an arsenal here," Tom marveled.

"From this battle and some prior run-ins with gangs. I collected the weapons and ammo. It all seemed too valuable to leave."

"You got that right," Tom replied. He stepped over to the weapons, "May I take one of the rifles? I'll need something other than just the M60, in case that jams."

"Absolutely. Take one of the carbines that fire the .223 round. I have more of that ammunition than anything else."

John Sands just stood there looking perplexed at the weapons and piles of ammunition. "Jason, I don't know where to begin. These guns look so complicated."

Tom stepped forward to examine the guns laid on the table. "You should take this lever action 30-30. It's simple to load and use." He looked at Jason.

"That belonged to a friend of mine. He would be proud to have someone using his rifle in this battle," Jason replied. Then he went over his plan for setting up the ambush.

The ridge enclosing the valley to the south was lower than the others. The stream that drained the valley had cut a gap in the ridge to join a river flowing to the east. The narrow gorge created by the stream had been widened to accommodate the road which exited the valley over a narrow truss bridge. The bridge connected to a larger county road that ran along side of the river leading to Clifton Furnace about ten miles east of the bridge.

Jason explained his battle plan. "They'll come in pickup trucks. The bridge is one lane, so if we stop the lead truck, it will block the others. We'll position ourselves on the ridges on each side of the road. We will have the high ground and can fire away at them as they're stacked up at the bridge. If they charge over the bridge, we just have to keep up a strong rate of fire and take them out. There's no place to hide. The road in the gorge will be the kill zone. They'll be hemmed in, and if we keep them from getting past the tight part of the gorge, they can't get out."

"How do we stop the lead truck? We don't have any heavy weapons," Andy asked.

"We shoot the driver. I've done it before. When it's time to open fire, everyone should send their initial rounds at the lead truck. No one in the cab should remain alive."

The group discussed the details as the evening closed in. Mattresses and blankets were brought down to the living room and everyone bedded down for what sleep they could get. For most, it was a fitful night of tossing and turning.

Jason and Anne awoke early, before dawn. Anne set out to fry up some meat for everyone while Jason went through the ammunition and weapons one more time.

Tom joined him. "I want to go over the M60 as soon as it's light. We have to remove it from the cab of the truck. I won't last a minute firing from such an exposed position."

"We also can't have the trucks around. They'll know there's an ambush if they see them," Jason replied.

"Yeah. I think we haul everyone down to the gorge and then move the trucks back around the bend so they can't be seen." They went out to the yard and began to unbolt the machine gun.

The others soon arose and as the sun came up everyone was eating or assembling their personal gear. As the group busied themselves in the living room, Ray and Billy arrived at the front door. Anne let them in. They quietly sidled into the living room. Everyone stopped to stare.

Finally Jason broke the silence, "Thank you for joining us."

Ray looked at him, "Turners have lived in this valley for generations. I'm not going to let this gang just come in here to take over. We've had enough strangers in this valley."

Jason ignored the barb. "Do you want any of the weapons I've collected?"

"We use our own. We know how they shoot. We may not shoot as fast, but our shots will all count." They were both carrying bolt action, 30-06 caliber rifles with five shot magazines.

"Well, help yourself to more ammunition," he pointed to some boxes at the side of the pile.

Ray went over and started looking through the boxes. Billy stood at the edge of the room, staring at Sarah sitting on the couch. Finally Sarah noticed him.

"What are you looking at?" she demanded.

Billy kept looking at her with an amazed expression on his face. "You're hurt." It was all he could say.

"I guess I am. Do I look ugly to you?" she said challenging him.

Billy shook his head. "You...you're all growed up," he blurted out. "I mean...you look good, not ugly." His face was now turning red.

Catherine noticed the interchange and stepped in front of Sarah. "Billy, get some ammunition and leave Sarah alone. We've got to get going soon."

Billy turned away, still looking embarrassed. Jason reviewed the battle plan with Ray and his son. Then the group headed outside. Jason had the M110 sniper rifle firing a 7.62 round along with his Ruger .223. Catherine had her .223 carbine. Both of them carried 9mm pistols on their belts. Tom Walsh took charge of the M60, and a .223 carbine. Betty Walsh had her 30-06 semi automatic rifle, the same caliber as Ray and Billy carried. Andy Nolan chose one of the .223 carbines after some instruction from Tom. John Sands carried Sam's rifle that Tom had suggested. Everyone's pockets were stuffed with ammunition.

Anne and Sarah came out on the porch. Anne had her Bible in her hand. The others in the yard turned to her and she spoke. "I grew up going to church every Sunday as did most of you. Maybe we haven't been so good about attending over the years, I know I haven't. And maybe some of us wonder where God is in these troubling times, I know I do. But I still want to offer a blessing on this day." She opened her Bible and read from the Psalms.

> *I have pursued mine enemies and overtaken them:*

Neither did I turn away again till they were consumed.
I have wounded them,
That they were not able to rise:
They are fallen under my feet.
For Thou hast girded me with strength unto the battle;
Thou hast subdued under me those who rose up against me.
Thou hast also given me the necks of mine enemies,
That I might destroy them that hate me.
They cried out, but there was none to save them,
Even unto the Lord, but He answered them not.
Then I did beat them as small as the dust before the wind;
I did cast them out as the dirt in the streets.

And further;

I will lift up mine eyes unto the hills—
From whence cometh my help?
My help cometh from the Lord,
Who made Heaven and Earth.
He will not suffer thy foot to be moved;
He that keepeth thee will not slumber.
The Lord is thy protector.

Everyone stood quietly as the ancient words, three thousand years old, rolled over them. These were not only words of faith, but words of battle, calling for destruction of the enemy. There was no equivocating in what they meant; the enemy needed to be destroyed and the psalms called for God's help and protection in accomplishing that destruction. The words recalled a time of violence and death as well as faith. Would today be such a time?

"May God protect and keep you all safe and give you victory over the evil that assaults us," Anne said in closing.

As Jason turned to go, Anne grabbed him and hugged him fiercely, trying to wrap some of her strength around him.

"You be safe. You come back to us," she whispered. There was a harsh, fierce tone in her voice.

"I hope they don't come. I hope you all just wait for nothing," Sarah joined in.

Jason hugged Anne, "I'll come back, don't you fear. This threat ends today." His face remained dark and his voice was distant, as if he was already gone.

"I love you, remember that," Anne said.

Jason nodded.

"We need you," Sarah added.

He nodded to her and then walked to the pickup. Catherine gave her mom and Sarah hugs and also headed to the truck. Anne and Sarah waved as the group of men and women drove off. They looked like such a small force against a large gang of outlaws and killers. Anne put her arms around Sarah as they watched the trucks roll down the hill.

Chapter 9

B ig Jacks stormed around the camp trying to get everyone organized and ready to depart. Some men still had to be chosen and assembled—that task hadn't been finished last night. Fuel and ammunition were still being collected and loaded. It would be hours before they would be ready to go. Big Jacks was fuming. He was in a hurry to go on this killing spree.

It was still early when the defenders arrived at the gorge. Jason directed Andy, Ray, Billy and John to the ridge on the west side of the road and he, Catherine, Tom and Betty took the ridge to the east of the road. Andy volunteered to take the position closest to the bridge. He could shoot and having been instructed on the semi-automatic .223 carbine, he felt he could fire more rapidly than Ray or Billy with their bolt action rifles. Ray and Billy spaced themselves behind Andy, with John last in the line.

On the east side, Tom suggested he be first in line, but Jason wouldn't allow it. "The M60 has the range, and you will be less likely to be pinned down and hit if you're further back. We'll need that gun in action all the time," he said.

Jason placed himself first. Catherine insisted on being next behind him, which put Tom in the third position. Betty stationed herself behind Tom. On each ridge everyone was spaced about fifty yards apart.

Jason brought a couple of shovels and extra burlap cloth along. "Use the shovel to pile up some dirt to make a rest for your rifles. And cover the dirt with the cloth. It'll keep down any dust from the shots. The dust gives away your position. And remember, if your position gets too hot don't stick your head up. Just crawl back from the cliff edge and move to a new location. Then you can return fire." There was no dissenting opinion from anyone. The group was solemn as they split up and staked out their positions for the ambush. Soon this little gorge was going to be filled with shooting and killing.

With everyone in position, there was nothing to do but wait. The sun rose higher, the sky was clear; the hum of the cicadas grew louder. There was little breeze. It was going to be a hot day.

It will be hot in more ways than one. Jason lay on the ridge with his rifle ready. His stomach churned as the doubts began to rise up again. He forced them down. This wasn't the time for doubt. That time was past. Now was the time to fight—to fight for their lives.

An hour passed. Jason remained patient and still. He was used to waiting. On the other side of the ridge, John squirmed where he lay in the leaf mold, peeking out from under a bush. Sweat ran down his face. Every minute he waited he imagined greater and greater scenes of carnage. His breathing became ragged and a panic rose inside. His body began to itch in odd places. He thought ants were crawling under his clothing. Andy, like the others, remained tense. He wouldn't allow himself to imagine what was to come and kept telling himself over and over to relax.

Finally John yelled out across the ravine, "Are they coming? How long should we wait?"

His answer came quickly from Jason, "Quiet!"

John squirmed and tried to control his growing panic.

Catherine lay in the brush at the edge of the cliff. She kept repeating, "Just hit a target and move on. They don't know we're here. We'll catch them off guard." Any words to hold back her own terror.

Finally they heard the faint sounds of the convoy of trucks. Everyone knew what that meant. The gang was coming; the battle was soon to begin.

The trucks arrived at the intersection. Everyone waited. Tom pulled back the charging lever on the M60. Andy crossed himself. Betty tried to not hyperventilate. Catherine slowed her breathing down as she had been taught; now focusing on the fight to begin. Everyone looked down their barrels, through their sweat, sighting the lead truck.

The first truck turned onto the bridge. Jason let it get half way across; then he opened fire. A barrage of shots erupted from both ridges, all aimed at the windshield of the lead truck. Immediately the windshield was obliterated and the occupants of the cab slumped over. The truck lurched to a stop against the side of the bridge. The men in the back jumped out as the rest of the trucks stopped. The gang emptied from the other pickups and began firing indiscriminately at the ridges. The shooting from the ridges swept over the whole convoy. The noise from dozens of weapons firing was deafening. From the ridge there was the steady popping of rifle fire and the louder rapid staccato of the M60. The gang returned fire, but without being able to see their targets through the cover on the ridge, their shots were ineffective. They were pinned down at the bridge.

If we can keep this up, they'll never get across. We can keep picking them off from the ridge. Jason could not stifle a surge of hope.

Big Jacks shouted to Mo to grab the M2 and set it up on the bridge. "Get the big gun up front. Knock out that machine gunner!"

Mo grabbed another gang member to help feed the belt and ran forward to the front corner of the lead truck.

"It's on the ridge to the right," Big Jacks shouted, pointing out the direction.

Mo opened up with the M2. Its rate of fire was slightly slower than the M60 but with a deep, booming ominous sound. The ridge exploded as the M2 rounds shattered the bank and tore through the trees. Tom quickly backed up, pulling the M60 with him and pressed himself into the ground when the big gun opened up.

With the M60 silenced for the moment, Jacks ordered the lead truck to be started and put in gear. Without getting into the shot out cab, one of the gang reached through the open driver's door and slowly guided the truck to roll forward. The pickup sheltered him and others as they slowly moved off the bridge. Once free of the narrow bridge, he turned the truck sideways giving the attackers a position of cover beyond the bridge.

The M2 immediately changed the balance of the fight. Jason could tell it had shut Tom down, at least for the moment. *We can't let them spread out on this side. If they get to the woods, we lose.*

Even though the M60 was not firing, the rest of the defenders were doing their best to hold back the gang's advance. Anyone who moved from the cover of the pickup did not get far before one of the shooters from the ridge hit him.

The M2 stopped firing. Tom cautiously lifted his head from the dirt and leaves of the brush. Being on the receiving end of such a weapon terrified him. He could see how it had shredded up the bank of the ridge and torn out much of the cover. But Tom's military training kicked in. He realized his group needed the M60's firepower more than ever. He shifted his location, dragging the machine gun and the ammo belts to get into another firing position. He turned his attention on the last pickup in the convoy and disabled it with an intense burst of fire. Then he backed away as the M2 raked the ridge. Again, the big gun tore up the ground and vegetation, exposing Tom's location. He began crawling to a new position.

Jason realized that Tom had cut off the gang's exit. If they could retreat, they could re-group and invade and attack the valley from another direction.

Big Jacks saw that his men could not advance beyond the cover of the truck. Even with the M2 shutting down the machine gun, the other shooters were dispersed enough on both ridges that his men were lethally exposed. There was no cover beyond the pickup.

He shouted to one of his captains, "Get some guys down in the river on both sides of the bridge. I want 'em to climb the ridges in the tree cover. The road's too exposed." The man looked at him but didn't move. "Do it now!" he shouted, pointing his rifle at the man who quickly ran back to the fighters jammed up behind one of the trucks. Shortly two groups descended the banks and into the river.

Jason saw six men dropping down into the river on the west side of the bridge. From his position on the eastern ridge, he couldn't see what was happening on the east side and could only guess that Jacks' men were going to cross there as well. He hoped his shooters on the west side would notice the attackers going into the river east of the bridge and direct their fire at them. Wiping sweat from his face, he began firing at the men crossing in the water but they were shielded by the bridge. He was able to hit only one of them, who dropped into the current and was swept away.

Catherine also saw the men going into the river and started firing at them. Between the two of them, they hit two more as they came out of the water, before reaching the cover of the trees on the steep slope. Climbing the slope would lead the gang to the ridge and from there they could attack the defenders from the rear.

Did Andy and the others know the enemy was coming up to attack from behind? Jason's frustration nearly overwhelmed him. He had no way of letting the shooters on the west ridge know the danger they faced. He could only hope that if they could see what was happening on his side of the bridge they would guess it was also happening on their side.

During this time Tom moved to a new point with the M60. Meanwhile Betty was steadily focused on the men who had made it beyond the bridge. She was farthest away, but her 30-06 with its scope was a fine weapon for the hunt she was on. She was methodical and made each shot count. Anyone exposing themselves quickly drew a shot or two from her, either hitting them or coming close enough to pin them behind the truck. They risked their lives to peek over the pickup and try to fire with any accuracy at the ridge.

Andy, Ray and Billy saw the men dropping into the river on the east side. They knew what they needed to do. Two of the attackers did not make it out of the river, which left three who reached the cover of the woods on the slope leading up to the ridge. The men didn't immediately realize that the same attack was taking place on their side of the gorge. They continued to pour shots at the remaining men jammed up at the bridge.

Tom set up a new position. He could catch glimpses of the large man directing the attackers. Figuring this to be Big Jacks, he kept his weapon aimed in his direction. When Big Jacks moved along the line of trucks, Tom opened fire and sprayed the gap as he moved through it. He hit Jacks in the leg dropping him to the ground behind one of the pickups. The M2 again opened up. This time Mo spotted Tom's position. Instead of ducking, Tom swung the M60 hoping to take Mo out. Before he could fire, the M2 raked his position with a long burst, hitting the M60. The gun was flung from Tom's grasp. A spray of shrapnel tore open his left shoulder. He rolled back away from the ridge. The bipod was shot out; the damaged pieces just missed taking off Tom's hand.

At the same time, Jason got Mo in his sights and fired five shots in quick succession. Two rounds hit Mo in his arm and chest. He fell back from the M2, knocking it on his side. As he tried to crawl back, Jason shot him two more times, one of the rounds splitting open his head.

Jason now dropped the M110 and took up his .223 carbine and headed back along the ridge to where Catherine was located.

"Some attackers may be coming up from the river, through the woods. We have to catch them while they're together," he shouted over the din of the shooting.

Catherine nodded. Together they moved away from the edge of the ridge and headed towards the river. When they got close to the edge of the steep slope, they separated and took up separate positions behind trees. They could hear the shooting, slower now, going on along the gorge. They waited in silence ignoring the rest of the battle. The attackers would be most vulnerable when they got to the top of the slope. They had to hit them there before they could separate.

Tom cut open his shirt and tied it around his upper arm and shoulder to stem the flow of blood. The M60 looked too damaged to shoot. Slowly he made his way back towards Betty. He could hear her steady shots still coming. He could not hear Jason or Catherine. The shooting from his side of the ridge seemed to be only coming from Betty.

On the west ridge, Ray moved back to Billy. "They's some coming up from the river...through the woods. I'm goin' after them," he said.

"You think they're on this side too?" Billy asked.

Ray nodded to his son. "You comin'?"

"Yeah," Billy said getting up.

"Be like hunting deer," the old man said as they quietly made their way through the woods towards the river.

Big Jacks leg was bleeding badly. Two of the M60 rounds had smashed through his left leg, one tearing apart his knee and the other ripping through his thigh. He needed to stop the bleeding. Yelling at his men, he got one to crawl over to him. He tore a shirt and tied it tightly around the knee area to keep the leg intact. He then tied another shirt around Big Jacks' upper thigh to stem the flow of blood.

At this point there were twelve men left with Big Jacks behind the pickups, four men still alive on the valley side of the bridge and three each climbing to the ridges on either side of the road. He noticed the diminished fire coming from the ridges. On the west, only Andy and John were shooting; on the east, only Betty.

"We've taken their shooters out. Get half the men across the bridge and charge up the road. The rest will cover you. You get past the gorge, then you can circle back up the ridge and finish them off." Jacks yelled at the man who bandaged him.

The man looked at him with panic in his eyes. "They won't listen to me," he said fearfully.

Big Jacks gave him a hard look, snorted his disgust and yelled to the rest of the men, "I want six of you across that bridge now." He pointed to two men, "You two and the four up front, run like hell up the road. We'll cover you."

No one moved. Big Jacks pointed his .45 pistol at them and counted off six men in succession. "Now go, or I'll shoot you right here," he shouted. Slowly the two men crept over the bridge, joining the four at the front behind the lead truck. They stopped at its edge, afraid to step beyond its protection. Jacks yelled at them again, "Go maggots, or I'll shoot you now." And he began to fire over their heads. Figuring Big Jacks, being closer, could kill them more easily; the six decided to take their chances in the gorge and bolted up the road. Those on the bridge opened fire to try to pin down the ridge shooters. Andy dropped one of them right away, Betty hit another but he didn't fall. John's shots, unfortunately, missed. Andy's gun went silent and Betty just missed another as the men ran erratically forward.

The remaining five men sensed safety along the east side of the gorge. They splashed through the valley creek and hugged up against the cliff. There they were protected from Betty. She could not see them from her position. John had a clear view of them but his shots were off the mark. Still he kept firing and corrected his aim. Finally he dropped one of the men and wounded two others. They lay against the cliff. The remaining two ran until they reached the woods. John stopped firing. He was nearly out of ammunition and didn't know what to shoot at. The wounded men were not moving, so he watched the bridge.

The battle ground went quiet. There were no shots coming from Andy's position. Ray and Billy were stalking the men coming up on the ridge, John was waiting, not sure what to shoot at. Jason and Catherine were waiting in ambush for the other outlaws who were climbing up the east side of the gorge. Tom was working his way back to Betty's position.

Betty held her fire, not having a target and not sure of what was going to happen next. She guessed some men had gotten past her, up against the cliff. They might be coming towards her from behind. She was close to panicking but didn't know what direction to run. She just lay in the brush, not wanting to give away her position. Suddenly she heard movement in the woods, not from the rear, but from Tom's direction. She readied herself, but waited, hoping it would be Tom. Sure enough, he emerged from the brush, bloody and injured, but alive.

She ran to him, "Tom, you're alive! I didn't hear the machine gun and I didn't know what had happened. I just kept shooting, doing my best."

"I'm alive, but the machine gun is out of commission. What's going on? Is it over?"

"I don't know. John was the last one shooting on the other ridge, but he's stopped now. I'm worried some of the gang may have made it past me. They could be coming up through the woods." She pointed behind her.

Tom had a .45 pistol he had pulled from Jason's collection. "I'll watch for them. You watch the bridge with your rifle." They settled down to wait.

When the three men got to the top of the slope on the west side they headed towards the exposed edge of the ridge. Following the sound of Andy's shots, they crept up behind him. Andy heard rustling in the brush and swung around to bring his rifle to bear on the sound. The three men fired as he turned. He was knocked back like being hit by a powerful punch, and found himself looking at the sky instead of the brush where he meant to look and shoot. He wanted to aim his rifle and shoot the ambushers, but his arms wouldn't respond. Staring at the sky; it looked so blue and calm. Why did he notice that? His rifle and the shooting were forgotten. As he stared, blackness began to close in from the edges of his vision and then it all disappeared.

Ray and Billy heard the shots. They knew what had happened. Quietly they moved at an angle that would intersect the shooters coming their way back along the ridge. Hearing the men before they could see them, they crouched down, ready to shoot. First one came into view through the trees, but there was no clear shot. They waited until all three could be seen. Each picked a man.

They fired and two of the three gang members went down. The third man dropped to the ground, out of sight for the moment. Ray and Billy waited, but the man was smart enough to lie still. Ray looked towards where they had shot, trying to see through the brush. He motioned for

Billy to circle to the right while he went left. He wanted to box the third man in and not let him slip away.

Billy quietly crept to his right. Ray started left, but his old body sabotaged him. His knee gave out and with a grunt he stumbled forward. The gang member heard, then saw Ray stumble and shot rapidly at him though the trees. Ray fell. Billy now could see the man and shot him. As Billy was working the bolt on his rifle to chamber another round, the man turned to fire back when Ray fired. Ray's bullet tore into the man's right side, through his lung and into his heart.

The remaining gang members just crouched behind one of the pickups with Big Jacks. "There's no more shooting. Get up the road."

They didn't move. More than half of those who charged lay dead. The odds didn't look good to them.

"Get your asses up the road. We've got the battle won." He shouted again. Still no one moved.

"Why don't we wait here until the guys on the ridge signal it's clear?" one of them offered.

"You chicken shit. Get going," Big Jacks shouted again.

The man shook his head. "I'm not going out there. Most of those guys got shot."

Big Jacks turned his .45 on him. "You go or I'll shoot you down like a dog." His voice was dark and deadly.

There was fear in his face, but still the man shook his head. "It don't make sense. A lot of guys have been killed. Our guys will signal us when they finish them off. We should wait here." He looked at the others for support, but they had separated themselves from him.

"Coward." Big Jacks said and fired. The man fell back with a large hole in his chest and blood spurting out of his back where the bullet exited.

Without a moment's hesitation, the rest of the men dove around the edge of the pickup and ran down the road away from the fight.

"Come back you cowards," shouted Big Jacks. He fired at them but missed. They ran towards Clifton Furnace as fast as they could go.

Jason and Catherine waited silently. They could hear no more shooting from the gorge. Neither knew if that meant victory or defeat. That didn't matter at this point. What mattered was they had to kill the men coming up the slope. They heard their approach well before they could see them.

Suddenly one of the men appeared. As he got to the top, he moved in a crouch going from tree to tree. He was careful. Jason couldn't see the other two. *They've fanned out. Now we're in trouble.*

There was more rustling to his left. Jason motioned for Catherine to cover the first man and he began to move to his left to intersect the second. The first man seemed to be waiting for the others. He crouched behind a large tree. Catherine could tell where he was hiding but could not see him clearly. He would have to move for her to get a shot at him, or she would have to move. She watched Jason quietly disappear, moving away from her through the brush. She was alone now.

Jason hoped Catherine would not panic at this deadly stalking game. She had the advantage. She knew where the enemy was. He didn't know she was near. As careful as the man was being, Jason understood he didn't have any idea that death might be so close to him. *Just be still, be calm.*

There was no plan on who would shoot and when. Catherine decided that when she had a shot, she would take it. She forced down her rising panic. She could now see her enemy, he couldn't see her. She would use that advantage to the end. One shot when it was clear, and he would never know what hit him.

Now unseen by Catherine, Jason moved forward and to the left of her position. He wanted to intercept the other gang member closer to the edge of the slope.

The man Catherine was watching heard his companion moving on his right and started to go forward. Crouching, he stepped out from the tree and slowly began to go forward. Catherine steadied herself and waited for him to clear the brush. Her shot hit him in the side of his head and blew open the right side of his skull, just above his ear. He collapsed like a limp doll, dead before reaching the ground.

The other outlaw stopped, then moved to his left towards the sound of the shot. His path would intersect Jason in twenty yards. Jason saw him coming and fired. The shot hit him on his right side, spinning him to the ground. Jason guessed it was not a kill shot, so he moved forward. He needed to finish this one off so he could concentrate on the third man. As he approached, the wounded man tried to bring his rifle around to fire at Jason. Before he could take aim, Jason shot him in the head.

The third gang member, thinking the shots were from one person, figured the shooter had moved from in front of him to his right, the direction of Jason's last shot. He headed towards the sound. Catherine saw him moving. She had no clear shot, so she set out after him. The man's movement made enough noise that he couldn't hear Catherine heading towards him.

Suddenly the man stopped and crouched down. He saw Jason. Jason moved cautiously, trying to pinpoint him, but this time he didn't know quite where the man was. The outlaw could barely see Jason. He waited to get a clearer shot, sensing that Jason didn't know his position.

Jason waited. Minutes went by. He slowly moved to his left. He was in the cover of bushes and wanted to reach a tree. Catherine saw the man slowly rise to a standing position behind his tree and sight his rifle. She guessed he had Jason in his sights. She rose and aimed at the man.

As she steadied her aim, a twig snapped under her foot. The man turned towards her, trying to bring his rifle around the tree when Catherine fired. The bullet hit him in his chest. His rifle fired in the air as he spun around and fell to the ground, the rifle thrown ten feet away.

"Jason," Catherine called, "it's all clear."

Jason came through the woods to the man. He was almost dead, the bullet having torn through his chest. After disarming him, he ran to Catherine who was standing at the tree.

"You saved my life," he said to her.

She looked at him. She dropped her rifle and he grabbed her in a huge hug. "Is it over? Did we win?" Then she started shaking and crying.

Jason held her tightly. "I think so. It's okay now, no more shooting, no more killing." They kept hugging and both began to sob.

Jason gently stroked her head and patted her back. "It's safe now," he said between sobs. "We did it. We all did it."

"I was so scared, but I kept on shooting. I did what you taught me. And when I couldn't see you...I almost panicked. I was alone...so scared...seeing those men up close. They would have killed me if they had seen me. It was just up to me...I had to shoot them...by myself."

"It's okay. You did it the way I showed you and we won. It's over now."

Catherine looked up at him. "Do you think it's really over? Can we stop fighting?"

Jason smiled at her. He hoped he was right. "Yes, we can stop fighting now. But we have to get back to the others. We still need to be careful until we've secured the battle field." They picked up their rifles and walked hand in hand back towards Betty and Tom.

When they reached them, Betty told them about the men she thought had gotten past her.

"Stay here with Tom," Jason told Betty. "I'll check out the woods down to the road."

"I'll go with you," Catherine said.

"Are you sure?" He asked turning to her.

She took a deep breath and nodded, "I'm all right now. We'll be careful. We find them before they find us and we'll be okay." She said it like a mantra.

They quietly disappeared into the woods. As they neared the road they heard the rustling in front of them. There were two men crouched in cover. They sensed someone approaching and called out, "We surrender! Please don't shoot."

They were huddled together, the fight completely gone out of them. Jason raised his rifle. Catherine put her hand on his arm.

"Don't."

He looked at her.

"They're not fighting."

"They'd kill us if they had a chance."

"But they don't. It doesn't seem right."

Jason lowered his rifle. They approached the two men who drew back in fear. They stared at Catherine.

"She's just a girl," one of them said in wonder.

Without offering an answer, Jason quickly moved to tie the men up with their own belts, making sure they could not get free or move. Just then Billy shouted from across the road. They could barely see him at the wood's edge.

"Pa's shot! He's alive! I need help! Mr. Nolan is dead. They shot him before Pa and I could get there. Help Pa!"

Betty and Tom came down from the ridge. "The rest of the gang ran off. There's no one left at the bridge but the dead and wounded," she reported.

"Did you see a huge man, Big Jacks, leave?" Jason asked.

"No. I think I hit him with the machine gun. He may be among the wounded."

Just then John came down from the west ridge and ran across the road to them.

"It's over, we did it, I can't believe it, I shot so many times, I kept missing, but I kept trying, I'm an architect, so I figured it was all about angles and vectors—this aiming, I kept correcting, adjusting, and then I started hitting targets—people—I started shooting people, I think I killed some people, I know I wounded some, I saw them go down but they moved, they're still alive, what do we do with them—?"

Jason grabbed him by the shoulders, "It's okay, John. You did what you had to do. We all did. You won't have to do it again. You saved your family."

John looked at the rest, as if coming out of a nightmare, and started to sob, great choking sobs. Betty and Catherine both put their arms around him.

"I'm sorry," he finally said. "I didn't mean to break down. I don't know what's come over me."

"It's the shock—the violence," Tom said. "It gets everyone. You were thrown into the deep end without any training. Hell, John, even those with training sometimes can't handle this. We'll all have nightmares for a while."

Jason said, "John, you and Catherine go up on the west ridge and help bring Billy's dad back down. Betty, help Tom to the pickup. All of you wait there for me. I have some things that must be done. I'll join you later."

Catherine asked, "You're not going to kill them are you? The ones we tied up?"

Jason looked at her and paused. Finally he said, "No. I'll figure that out later. But don't be alarmed if you hear gunshots, some of the wounded are still alive and might try to shoot."

"Be careful," Catherine admonished.

There could be no mercy from Jason's point of view. These were not men he could help medically, nor were these men he could trust. This was not about rehabilitation; this was about preservation, for him, his family and the valley. Part of him was repulsed by what he had to do, but he felt trapped, without an alternative. He would just have to deal with the emotional cost later.

I didn't start this fight, but I will finish it...for good.

He hoped Big Jacks was down there somewhere. He wanted to make sure he was dead. Without him the remnant of the gang would likely disperse. He would make Big Jacks and this battle a signal not to enter this valley.

He worked his way towards the bridge, executing the wounded he found. He had an approximate idea of where Big Jacks was, but couldn't be sure. He had to consider the possibility that he could still move, even if injured. He crept down the side of the trucks exposed to the valley, going slowly past the first and the second one. Big Jacks would be on the other side, sheltered from the ridges.

Jason moved slowly and quietly. This was no time to be careless. He kept his breathing calm and quiet as he listened. As he reached the back of the second truck, he stopped. He could hear labored breathing ahead—*Big Jacks?* He waited.

Suddenly a voice shouted out, "Show yourself, you son of a bitch! I know you're there!"

Jason did not reply. He worked his way back to the front of the truck until he could sneak a look around it. There was Big Jacks, lying on the sheltered side of the next pickup, staring at the back of the second one. He had a rifle at ready in one hand, wavering in the direction he was looking. Ever so slowly, not making a sound, Jason got into a prone shooting position. Then he sighted on the rifle and fired. Big Jacks shouted in pain as Jason's shot shattered his arm and sent the rifle flying.

Now, he slowly walked up to the huge man, still an imposing sight, even lying on the ground crippled by his wounds. Big Jacks glared at him, his eyes filled with hate. He had gone from dreams of being bandit chief of a city to lying on the ground, badly wounded, staring at his nemesis.

"Who are you?" he demanded.

"Just me, my family and some neighbors," came the answer.

Big Jacks looked at him in scornful disbelief. "You're a liar."

"No reason to lie. It's all over."

"I don't believe you," Big Jacks said with a sneer.

"It doesn't really matter, now."

"So you gonna shoot me?" he challenged Jason. "The rest of my gang will be back. They'll kill you yet."

"No they won't. They'll disappear. They don't want anything to do with me, or this valley."

Big Jacks unleashed a torrent of swearing at Jason who just stood there looking at him. Lying wounded on the ground, the anger seemed almost sad. The force of terror was gone from the outlaw.

"You can curse 'till you're hoarse; it won't do any good. Your game is over, big man," Jason said. He squatted down on the pavement, just out of Jacks' reach.

Big Jacks glared at Jason, his impotence gnawing away at him. He inched his left hand, still working towards the pistol lying on the pavement.

Jason studied the man. Now that the fight was over, he wondered why Big Jacks would choose such an obviously dead-end course to follow. "Why didn't you just settle down on a farm and raise some food? You had your gang, they took orders from you. You could have set yourself up like a country squire."

"Fuck that farming shit!" Big Jacks cursed. Then he let out another round of cursing as he inched his left hand forward. At the last moment, he reached for the gun and Jason shot him in the hand and then the elbow.

"Can't let you do that," he said without passion. He realized there would be no sensible answer from this man. He lived outside the law and his instincts were to take, not produce. He was a parasite in the end; a dangerous, deadly parasite.

Suddenly Jason got up. "Where you going?" Big Jacks demanded.

Jason just looked at him and began to clear all the weapons out of his reach. "I may be back, or I may let you bleed out here. The animals will come tonight, the dead will draw them. Maybe you can keep them away from you, but they'll want your flesh at some point." Jason then scrounged through one of the trucks and came up with a piece of rope. He tied this around Big Jacks' neck and then to the side of the bridge. Big Jacks could only crawl, if he could even move, towards the side of the bridge. He could not get to any weapons.

"Don't you leave me here," Big Jacks shouted as Jason walked away.

Chapter 10

When Jason returned to the pickup, Ray was lying in the back with the others holding him. Tom was in the cab. Jason jumped into the cab and they drove off. They drove back to Anne and Sarah where they would tend to Ray and Tom before getting everyone back to their farms.

Anne came out to meet them as they drove up. "You are safe. Thank God!" she exclaimed. Then, seeing Tom and Ray, she hurried back into the house to gather what limited bandages she had.

After Jason and the others left that morning, before the shooting began, Anne convinced Sarah to let her suture her deepest cuts. It would be painful but Anne knew that some of the defenders might be wounded when they returned. She and Sarah needed to be ready.

Tom's wounds were cleaned and disinfected with alcohol. Suturing materials were boiled and ready. With Betty's help the largest opening was sewn shut. Then clean bandages were wrapped around his upper arm and shoulder. Ray's wound was more serious. A bullet had gone through his side and exited. They couldn't tell whether or not any organs had been damaged. There didn't seem to be too much internal bleeding, so his entry and exit wounds were cleaned and bandaged. He was in pain and had lost blood, so they put him in a bed to rest and hoped for the best. The women insisted he shouldn't be moved in his weakened state.

When everyone was stabilized, Jason said he was going back out to retrieve Andy's body. Billy asked if Jason wanted him to go, but he told him to stay with his dad.

"I'll go back with you," John said.

"I'll go also," Catherine added.

"You don't have to. John and I can handle it."

"I'll go. If nothing else, I can keep watch in case anyone comes back. Plus we have to deal with the two we left tied up."

The three drove back to the bridge in silence. Catherine shouldered her rifle and kept watch while John and Jason hiked up to the ridge to retrieve Andy's body.

"Okay, what do we do with our two prisoners?" Catherine asked.

"They're our prisoners because you didn't want me to shoot them. What do you suggest?"

"I don't know, but I still don't feel right shooting them."

"I have to agree with Catherine," John said. "I know you finished off the wounded while we were getting Ray. We heard the shots. But now, it would seem more like murder," John continued.

"We could let them go. Some others got away and ran back to Clifton Furnace," Catherine said.

Jason felt trapped by the dilemma presented, but with the rush of the fight past, even he had no more appetite for killing. "I guess we could let them go. The problem is they have a pretty clear idea of how many of us there are. The others who ran off don't know and probably think we're a well organized militia ready at all times to do battle. These guys could encourage the rest of the gang to try us again."

"I think they may be scared enough of us to not want to come back," Catherine responded.

Jason thought for some time. "Okay, I'll let them go, but we do it my way. I want them to think I'm a crazy killer. And should they ever come back, they'll die. Both of you wait in the pickup. I promise I won't shoot them but before

I let them go, they're going to think I'm a homicidal maniac."

He went over to the men with a rope. He yanked them to their feet, tied the rope around their necks and walked them to the bridge. They stared at all the dead bodies as they passed them. When they got to Big Jacks he had them sit on the pavement. Big Jacks was still conscious, glaring at him, hating him for destroying his plans.

"Here's the deal," Jason said as he squatted down again in front of Big Jacks. "I am the head of this citizen's militia group that defeated you today. There is no other authority in this area, so I am your judge and jury."

"You got no authority over me," Big Jacks snarled.

"I do. I'm the victor so I'm in authority and it is up to me to try you." Standing, Jason continued, "Big Jacks, you are charged with murder, murder of civilians in Clifton Furnace, murder of a member of my defense group and attempted murder of my family and all the families in this valley. How do you plead?"

Big Jacks let out a string of curses.

"Do you have anything to say in your defense?" Jason asked.

"Go to hell, you're just a vigilante, no better than me."

Jason waited until Big Jacks had finished another round of cursing. His cursing was repetitive, unimaginative and now quite futile. There was no art or nimbleness of expression from him. Lying there on the pavement, he was just noisy and profane.

"If you have nothing to say on your behalf, I'll pronounce sentence," Jason intoned.

"Go fuck yourself," was the reply. The two captured men watched in fear, sitting very still. They both wondered if they were to be next.

"On behalf of the people of this valley, who you assaulted when you could have left them alone, on behalf of the people left in Clifton Furnace who you could have spared, on behalf of all the other people who you and your gang killed, I sentence you to death." Jason turned to the two captives, "You two get up and come here." He untied their hands but left the rope around their necks in place. "Grab him and pull him over to the side of the bridge."

The men grabbed their leader and dragged him across the pavement.

"You gonna to hang me?" Big Jacks asked with some fear slipping into his voice.

"I might just stretch that knot around your neck to a part of the bridge and let you choke to death, I might just tie you to the bridge and let the animals eat you, or I might shoot you."

"You can't leave me here for the animals," Big Jacks voice now betrayed his fear. "Don't you leave me to be eaten!" He was now shouting, clearly in fear of some animals chewing on his body while he was alive.

"I can. I'm your judge and executioner." Jason threw the rope tied around Big Jacks' neck to a cross beam of the bridge and pulled him up tight. Strangling sounds came from his mouth as he twisted his neck to keep breathing.

"No, don't," he croaked, hardly able to speak.

Jason stood in front of him and looked at him. He didn't deserve mercy, but Jason had no desire to torture him, to drop to his level. He was now like a terrified animal, responding in wordless fear. Jason had touched a nerve and brought fear to the man who had brought destruction to so many. *Time to end it.* He pulled out his 9mm and shot Big Jacks though the forehead, once, and twice through the heart.

Then he turned to his captives, awaiting their fate, "You two are rapists and cannibals." He had them sit down again and tied their hands and feet. "You deserve to be castrated or executed...or both."

"No, we didn't eat anyone. The others did, but not us," one said.

"How long have you been in the gang?"

"We just joined," the man said.

"If you lie to me, I'll kneecap you right here and now and leave you for the animals. I killed the last person who joined your gang—the sniper. I'll ask again, how long have you been members?"

The other man spoke up, "I've been in for about six months and he was here when I joined."

Jason thought about that. These men could have been part of the gang that killed Sam and raped Judy. His anger began to rise.

"You both deserve to die. But I'm going to set you free, not because I'm merciful, but because you're going to deliver a message for me. What happens to you is what will happen to anyone who comes back here. You are to get out of Clifton Furnace. I'll be coming to kill the rest of you very soon if you're not gone. But first you've got to pay for your crimes."

With that, Jason grabbed the first man, pinned him down on his back, grabbed his hair and began to carve the word 'RAPIST' on his forehead with his hunting knife. The man screamed and squirmed.

"If you make this harder, I'll just cut you more."

When he finished he grabbed the second man, who was desperately trying to squirm away, and did the same to him. Then he untied them and gave them some scraps of cloth.

"Tie these around your foreheads to soak up the blood. I'll give you one minute to get down the road and around the bend before I start shooting to kill." The men took off running as fast as they could go.

The first men to return had already told lurid tales of the ferocity of the firefight and the accuracy of the shooters on the ridge. The last two men dragged themselves into the town two hours later their faces were covered with blood. They could hardly speak. One of the gang reached out to remove the bandage. The man tried to stop him, but was too weak. They all stared at the wound. They could make out the bloody cuts shaping the word 'RAPIST'. The two men reported the execution of Big Jacks by a crazy man, the one who had cut them. When they said that he was coming to Clifton Furnace, the gang immediately began to gather their gear and load themselves into the remaining pickup trucks. Before nightfall, they were headed south, out of Clifton Furnace, to an uncertain fate.

Jason returned to the pickup and they drove back in silence. He was drained, emotionally and physically. No one spoke. John rode in back with Andy's body. Catherine kept staring at Jason. She had heard the screams of the men. Still she was reluctant to ask the question, to question this man who was instrumental in saving her life. He had given his word. When he finally looked over at her, he just shook his head and mouthed the word "no".

Book IV: The Army
Chapter 1

E veryone slept at Anne and Jason's house the night after the battle. The next day they drove Andy's body back to his farm. Anne stayed back with Sarah and Billy to take care of Ray. Claire, Andy's wife, was devastated by his death. They buried Andy on the hill behind their house. Everyone pledged their help to Claire. Andy, like the others, played a key part in the valley being victorious in the battle. Betty stayed with Claire when the others departed. After a few days, Claire decided that she would move into the Turner's place to help Billy take care of his dad; being helpful felt better than sitting and grieving.

After getting Stan Turner back home, Jason took Anne aside. "We have to get rid of the bodies, now before they get worse."

"I know. But I don't want the girls involved. They're too traumatized already. You and I will do it."

"This is awkward to say, but we need to strip the bodies of useful things, boots, belts and some of the clothing. More than just the weapons."

Anne thought for a moment. "That sounds so medieval, so primitive and unpleasant...but it is practical. All the more reason to not have the girls involved. We'll collect everything and share it with the others in the valley." Jason nodded in assent.

They completed the grisly task of removing the bodies from the yard and transporting them to the bridge. Anne was stunned when she saw the battle site.

"My God," she exclaimed, "so many bodies. It's a miracle that you weren't all killed. And the smell..." she covered her face with a rag.

They unloaded the bodies on the bridge, collected the firearms, ammunition and additional useful clothing. Jason scavenged all the useable gear from the pickups but left everything else in place—the bodies strewn on the road and bridge. "I want to leave it as it is—a warning to anyone else trying to invade our valley. If we need to get out later, I can move the trucks."

Anne nodded. She had no more words for the grisly scene.

In the weeks following the battle everyone in the family seemed to want to be close to one another—to be in touch, physically. The girls would snuggle up to Jason or their mother at any chance, especially at night when they would sit in the living room. Jason took out some books and they spent time huddled together on the couch with him reading to the family, like, he imagined, a parent would to young children. The physical closeness seemed to be an antidote to the killing that had engulfed them. Touching, being close seemed to have a healing power.

Still there were periods of depression that came upon each of them, when they would sit despondently, not being able to respond to any encouragement or cajoling from the others. And then there were the nightmares; reliving the traumatic scenes from the battle, enhanced by the subconscious to terrifying proportions. The only remedy seemed to be routine and being close to one another. Jason and Anne found additional respite in making love every time they could steal some privacy, which wasn't often with the girls needing and wanting so much attention.

A week after the battle, Jason announced that he wanted to go to Clifton Furnace. He wanted to see what the gang had done and if there was anything left of value.

"You can't go alone," Anne declared.

The girls agreed. It was decided that Catherine should go while Anne stayed back with Sarah, whose wounds were still healing. Catherine was adamant that they should not go by road as that involved going through the battle field and over the bridge. Jason agreed. Neither of them had any stomach for revisiting that scene. They hiked south along the upper fields to cross over the curve of the mountain ridge that formed the southern end of the valley. It was slower going but they felt better using that route.

After a long day of hiking, they reached the river and, while still under the cover of the woods, Jason carefully examined the town with his binoculars. It was still. Nothing moved but a stray piece of paper blowing along the main street. Doors hung open. The place had the look of a ruin, a civilization lost. They descended the ridge, waded across the river and started through the deserted town. The silence was oppressive—no sound of people or commerce, no birds calling. They came upon the remains of a large fire. Scattered around it were human bones. Catherine shivered visibly and turned away. She kept close to Jason's side, even though they were both armed. Nothing disturbed the silence except the wind preceding the rain which came that evening along with haunting images of the horrors that had taken place there.

There was very little to salvage: some overlooked tools from the hardware shop and a package of sanitary napkins in the back corner of the general store, which Catherine secreted into her backpack. In a shed behind the store Jason discovered two partially filled bags of seed—corn and wheat. Beyond those few items, there were only the structures themselves.

They spent an uneasy night in the shed behind the store, being awakened by the passing rain, the sounds of prowling animals, the creaking of the shed or a door banging as a stray breeze went past. At the first graying of the eastern sky, the two of them quickly shouldered their packs and departed. With a sense of relief they waded across the river and climbed the ridge. Soon they were hiking the fields of the valley on their way back home, putting the desolation of Clifton Furnace behind them.

Later in the day, as they walked along Catherine began talking, "We've come so close to death. Three times now."

"Yes, and the last two times you played a big part in helping to protect us."

"There's been so much killing. I feel I've changed."

Jason looked at her, "I think you have. You've matured. You're more sure of yourself."

"Well, I've been doing a lot of thinking. I want to get all this killing behind me, out of my system."

"We all need to put it behind us. It was necessary, but it's not healthy to dwell on it. You're right, we need to move on, but I'm not exactly sure of how we do that."

"Just carrying on our routines may not be enough."

Jason turned to Catherine, "I don't know what else we can do."

After a pause, she said, "Well, I do. I want to have a baby."

"What?" He blurted out.

"You heard me."

"But that would be too dangerous."

"No it won't."

"There's no medical support for giving birth anywhere."

"It doesn't matter."

"What about a hospital?"

"Women have had babies forever without hospitals or nurses. It's a natural thing to do."

"But you're too young. And where will you find a young man? There's no one around."

"I'm not too young. I'm nearly 18 and I've killed people and almost been killed. You yourself just said I'm more mature than others my age."

They walked in silence. She was right, he thought. Even before the fighting experiences, Catherine had been a mature teenager. These battles had developed her even more into a no-nonsense, self-confident woman.

"Yes, you've grown up a lot since I've known you, but there's no one around," Jason said. "We can't go to Hillsboro or another big city, who knows what's going on there, and besides, it would take too long to get there."

Catherine met his eyes, "I want to have a baby with you."

Jason stopped and stared at her dumfounded. He had not seen this coming. Yes, they had developed a deep relationship. They had saved each other lives. Catherine had killed for him, showing great courage. They shared something special, beyond what he shared with Anne, and certainly beyond the flirtatious relationship Sarah kept up with him. But Jason had not expected this.

"I don't want to just survive," Catherine continued, "I want a future. I want to know there *is* a future. Babies *are* the future. We've survived so much, but it is just surviving. I want to build a future, Jason. Who knows what is happening out there? Who knows if things will ever return to normal? I don't want to just hang on, waiting for things to get better. I'm not sure I believe we'll ever be the same as we were. Maybe this is all we have, but it's enough." She held him with her gaze, speaking with all the force and energy she could muster.

"And it's not like you don't find me attractive. I've noticed you checking me out." Jason started to protest, but she reached up and touched his lips and shushed him, "I know you would never go after me. I figured that out before I allowed myself to warm up to you. But I know we can make this work, and I can think of no finer father for my baby." Catherine looked straight at him.

"Catherine, the desire for new life is normal. Maybe it's a reaction to all the killing—an affirmation of life after so much death. But what you're asking will tear us apart. We've all bonded as a family...but this?" He paused. "Have you talked to Anne about this?" He was buying time while his brain was still reeling from her announcement.

"No, I haven't. I needed to talk to you first. And I think you should be the one to talk to her." It was not lost on Catherine that Jason used Anne's name, not her title, Mom. "I know our relationships will change, but we'll survive it." She pressed on, "Life has changed, and we're surviving it. And besides, we're not related." They stood still while she held him in her steady gaze, "I realized that new life is what I could have inside of me. I can bring new life to our family and move us forward. Sarah's too young and Mom is too old. Jason, I know this is the right thing to do. Please say you will talk with Mom."

Her chin began to quiver. Jason saw she was expending every ounce of her considerable courage to broach this subject. He shook his head in wonder and doubt, but he realized how carefully he needed to treat her at this moment. She was thoughtful, like her mother, but when she had made a decision, she was firm in it. Now she was laying herself open to him. He had to be careful not to crush her.

"Yes, Catherine, I will talk to Anne about this."

She reached up and quickly kissed him on the cheek. Relief spread across her face. They turned back to their hike and Catherine slipped her hand into Jason's. They walked hand in hand, silently. He looked over the field towards the setting sun in the southwest. The late afternoon haze filtered the light and gave a soft yellow glow to the valley and hills. A mist was starting to rise from the creek to join the haze. High on the ridges the scarlets and yellows were just beginning to emerge, while the lower slopes were still clad in their greenery.

Such a beautiful place, no wonder Anne didn't want to leave.

He felt at home in a way he had never felt before. He breathed deeply, there was a musky scent in the air—the smell of coming fall. Every season had its signature smell, but spring and fall were the most pungent. By summer the heat had burned off the freshness of spring, and in the winter the cold and snow locked up all the smells. He belonged here, to this time and place. They walked on in silence. Jason sifted Catherine's proposal over and over in his head with mounting concern. Catherine had raised an issue that could tear apart all that had been achieved. This was uncertain ground, a far different challenge from any he had faced before.

Chapter 2

L ife continued. The family fell back into their routine of hunting, gathering food, doing repairs, collecting firewood and sharing moments of discovery. The family activities seemed to return to normal except that Catherine would occasionally exchange a significant look with Jason. A week after Jason and Catherine had returned from Clifton Furnace, Jason asked Anne to go on a picnic with him. They packed some dried meat, apples and water and headed up the ridge to an outcropping that offered a grand view of the valley. The spot was bathed in warm sunshine on the early fall day. They spread a blanket out.

"This valley is so beautiful. I understand why you and your husband chose to live here."

"Yes, and now I get to live here with you. You are my husband," Anne replied. "If you hadn't come along, we wouldn't have made it. You literally saved our lives."

"We saved each other. I never expected to have such a rich life after the disaster. I couldn't see beyond survival. Finding you and the girls fulfilled me in a way I never expected. I'm happier now than I was before the EMP attack." He paused in reflection, "Sometimes I feel guilty about that. I often wonder how I gathered such a blessing out of all of this...so many people's lives were destroyed, my wife, people I knew in Hillsboro, people in this valley, Sam and Judy...and yet, here I am with you and the girls having found so much joy together..." his voice trailed off.

"Something is on your mind," Anne said. "You've been a bit different since you returned from Clifton Furnace, and now...this picnic. Is there something you want to tell me?"

Jason swallowed hard, then said, "Catherine wants to have a baby."

Anne looked at him for a moment, "Well she has grown up a lot—"

"She wants to have a baby with me." Now it was out. He went on to relate the conversation he had with Catherine as they hiked back from the town.

Anne's face grew stern as she stared at Jason, searching him, trying to read his mind, "Did you encourage her in this?"

"No."

"Are you sure? I've seen how you look at the girls sometimes." There was a hint of accusation in her voice.

"I check everyone out, it's my nature, you know that," Jason said in protest. "I study the clues the woods gives me, I study people as well. You can learn a lot by watching them closely. If that is what you mean by 'looking at them', then, yes, I'm guilty. I study you as well. I've been no saint. You know that, but I have always acted with good intent. My interactions with the girls have always been honorable. When I joined the family, I put the girls out of bounds, and that is a boundary I won't cross."

After a long silence, Anne responded, "I believe you. You do treat them well, which is one of the things I love about you."

"Anne, I would love to have a child with you. Maybe that would give Catherine what she is seeking."

"I don't know. This new world with no medicine or hospitals...why do you think I keep you away from me sometimes? I'm concerned about getting pregnant. There isn't the support for child birth that there was just two years ago. And it has been over thirteen years since I had Sarah." She let the implications sink in. "Sometimes I am on fire for you so much but I force myself to wait until I think it is safe. So far it's been working. I understand Catherine's desire. New life is an antidote to all the killing we've experienced. I also know you and Catherine have a special dimension to your relationship. I can see where this comes from."

"Is there anyone you know that might change Catherine's focus away from me?"

Anne gave him a sharp look. "The only person around Catherine's age is Billy. I wouldn't consider him a good candidate. No, there's no one left in the area. Catherine had some friends in the village, but they all left or..."

They were lucky to have survived. She and the girls were lucky to have been found by Jason. She noticed that she rarely thought about herself and the girls as separate from him anymore.

Anne lapsed into silence. Things were getting complicated. Her 'normal' was eroding away as she pondered this new revelation about her eldest daughter. Her emotions surged in conflicting directions. Could she take Jason away? Would she?

Finally Anne said, "I need time to digest this. I'll talk with Catherine later."

Then she reached out for Jason and they embraced. They hugged and their bodies surged with excitement. There was a fresh urgency to their arousal. Their limbs entwined with each other, trying to join as one in their passion. Afterward, they lay spent in each other's arms, oblivious to any distractions.

Anne whispered, "You are my man. I belong to you and you belong to me." There was finality to her statement.

"Let me talk with Catherine," Jason offered, "she approached me and I should close off this path. If there's any disruption in relationships let it be with me, not you. There are too many potential mine fields in the conversation between the two of you."

"I'm not willing to share you, certainly not with my eldest daughter."

It was evening when they returned. Jason realized that though they hadn't achieved an Eden, they had achieved a wonderful existence amid the chaos of the past year. However, he realized that the girls needed a wider world than the farm or the valley. He and Anne would need to find an outside world for them. Someday they would even need to find others to start building their own lives and families; Catherine sooner it seemed. That reality struck Jason like a slap in the face. What would contact with the outside world be like? What had happened in Hillsboro since he left? He didn't imagine things had improved. This was going to be hard.

Chapter 3

Catherine grew impatient and finally caught Jason alone in the workshop.

"Did you talk with Mom?" she asked while he worked on some storm shutters. "I know you two went off together on that picnic last week. Did you talk with her?"

"Yes we talked about it. It's an awkward thing, you have to understand. It's very conflicting for both your mother and me," Jason replied.

Catherine came up close to Jason as he was speaking. She was wearing a tight tee shirt which she filled out. She pulled Jason close to her in a hug. It was more friendly than affectionate, but as she drew him close, she began to get aroused. Her breathing became labored. She could feel Jason harden against her. She instinctively responded with her body, pressing her pelvis and breasts against him, her arms circling him tightly. Both of them were breathing harder now. She tilted her head up and kissed him fully on the mouth. Without thinking, Jason responded with a deep kiss.

Suddenly, he pulled back, not letting go of Catherine, but separating their bodies, "We can't do this."

"Yes we can," she murmured, trying to close their embrace again.

"No, we can't. This will break the relationship between you and your mother. It will break my relationship with her as well."

"But you want me. Don't deny it. I can feel your body."
Catherine's voice was full of sexual energy.

"But—"

"No buts, I want this, you want this and it's time."

"Part of me may want this," Jason said. This was not
going well. Part of him wanted to take her right there on
the floor. Her arousal stimulated his body in a way he
hadn't expected. He wanted to ignore, not dwell on the
consequences and just take her and satisfy both of their
desires. "I can't. I can't do this. I made a commitment to
Anne."

"But things are different. You said it. Things may never
get back to what they were."

"Things may not get back to what they were, but I made
that commitment to your mother. That commitment is for
now, not for before."

"But Jason, I feel so right about this and...I want you so
much. Can't you feel that?"

"I do, and part of me wants you. Maybe it's because of
what we shared."

"Then why shouldn't we do this? It's part of our special
relationship."

"Because of my commitment to your mom. In our eyes
we are married."

While they were talking, Catherine slipped her arms
under Jason' shirt, arousing both of them. Her body
demanded a response, demanded satisfaction. This time
Jason abruptly broke the embrace. His eyes flashed.
Catherine saw the anger in his face.

"Stop it! It's not just about sex. Do you think that I
would ignore my relationship with Anne, with you and
Sarah, to gratify my desire for you?" Then more gently, as
Catherine looked at him in shock, "Look," he said, "I have
to come to terms with the fact that I'm sexually attracted
to you. This happens to people, even after they've made
commitments. And it doesn't take the extraordinary
experiences that we've had. But that doesn't mean they

have to act on those desires. It's the commitments they make to one another that keep them from following those attractions."

He headed for the door. "Think about this," he said. He needed to escape from Catherine's temptations. "Do you want a relationship with someone who's so unreliable that they would cheat on their wife? Don't answer now and don't think this would not be cheating on Anne—your mother." He turned and left the shed.

Catherine stood in the shop alone. Her face reflected a swirl of emotions: rejection, anger, frustration. She began to cry bitterly.

Anne saw Jason emerge from the shop with an angry look on his face. "Catherine?" she asked. He pointed to the shop and Anne headed there. Inside she found Catherine crying bitterly. Without a word, she went to her daughter and wrapped her in her arms. Catherine initially was stiff and resistant, but Anne would not let her go. Finally Catherine relaxed and began sobbing in her mom's tight embrace. She disintegrated into a little girl as Anne comforted her.

"He's so mean!" Catherine cried out. "He just rejected me. I'm so embarrassed. He doesn't want me!"

After some time, Anne said, "Jason loves you, but he wants to be your father, your friend, not your lover. He made *that* commitment to me." She continued after Catherine calmed down, "I understand that you and Jason have a special bond. I know you went through a lot together. That's unique and precious and should never be diminished. And your desire for a baby is a good one, a healthy one, but it must wait for the right man. Jason is not the right man for you. I am not sorry for that, Catherine. I understand your need, but you have time, time to grow, to heal, to find someone more your age to share life with. It's not just about having a baby, it's about making a life together with someone else. You will find that someone else."

"But there's no one around!" Catherine turned away from her mother. "And Jason is the one I want. He's the only one I would want to have a baby with."

"Catherine, I think Jason is the best man we could have in our family. The finest man I could have. But we are a couple now."

"That's what he said."

"It's one of the reasons I fell in love with him. He's a man of character," Anne responded. "Please believe me, you will find someone and I am sure that person better be special, or they will have a hard time with Jason. He loves you so much, only the best man will do."

Catherine didn't answer. Her pain remained.

When Anne returned to the house, leaving Catherine in the workshop to gather herself, Jason was packing his gear.

"Where are you going?" she asked.

"Hunting."

"Running away?"

"No. I just think I should be absent for a while, seems like I've made a mess of things," he responded.

"Well, she got the message and the issue is now settled. Catherine has to come to grips with it. I helped her understand that what she is looking for was out of bounds. It's not going to happen."

"I should have let you do it from the start," Jason responded. "I didn't expect such an encounter."

"Well, it was going to be a big disappointment for her no matter who handled it—she'll get over it."

"I wonder how long that will take?" he said as Sarah came downstairs.

"Where are you going?" she asked.

"Hunting. We need meat and I need to be in the woods."

"I'll go with you," Sarah offered. "It could be fun and I'd like to get away."

Anne looked at Jason. "No," Jason replied, "I need to spend a little time alone."

"You're no fun. I'd really like to go with you." Jason caught something in Sarah's tone. She was thinking about more than just a hunting outing.

"Well, sometimes I am just 'no fun', like you say. But I need to go alone. Don't worry, I'll be back soon, hopefully with some game." Turning to Anne, "Keep watch and keep your side arms on you at all times. You know the drill. Things seem to be fine, but we should always be cautious."

"When can we expect you back?" Anne asked.

"I'll be out two nights. I'm going to go over the ridge to the lake and try for some ducks or geese. I'm taking the 12 gauge."

"You're sure you don't want some company? I can help with the hunting," Sarah asked plaintively.

"Sarah, if I wanted a hunting partner I would be happy to take you along, but not this time," Jason responded, forcing a smile.

He turned to Anne and kissed her quickly, "I should head out now. See you day after tomorrow. Take care of the girls."

Chapter 4

As Jason made his way through the orchard and into the deeper woods, heading towards the ridge, another pair of eyes besides Anne's watched him depart. Billy had been sneaking over to the Whitman's house ever since the battle at the bridge. Seeing Sarah grown up, her body filled out, now more woman than girl, had inflamed his desires. The cuts to her face had only increased his interest, stimulating a mixture of physical desire and protective urge. His mind was assaulted by these two attractions, one sexual, the other caring until he couldn't distinguish between them. The result was a newly aroused passion that carried an overlay of legitimacy in Billy's mind. As if he was justified in his lust by his desire to protect. He began to slip away from tending to his dad every chance he got to hike through the fields and spy on the farmhouse, hoping to see Sarah.

Billy was at ease in the woods. The forest was like his back yard. The valley was a very private place to live and he was familiar with it and the surrounding ridges. He knew how to be quiet and to move though the woods without being seen or heard, a skill he developed while working with his pa, tending the still in the woods. Billy was not much of a success in school before the power went out. He didn't excel at sports and he was shy with the girls. Even out here in the country he stood out as being more redneck than the others, more of a hillbilly, a name he often heard spoken behind his back. But in the woods he felt at home. There he had a sense of mastery over his environment. Old man Turner had been a moonshiner all his life, just like his father and now, it seemed, Billy would be also.

He could see that Jason was woods smart and able move as quietly as he could. He also saw how deadly Jason was, and that scared him. It scared him because Billy's fantasies about Sarah could incite Jason to attack him.

Sometimes he was watching when the girls came out to bathe in the tub. Thinking they were alone, they would undress in the yard before washing. Billy could then catch glimpses of them naked from afar. Seeing them, especially Sarah, even from a distance aroused him. Now Jason was gone and no one knew Billy was watching. It gave him a feeling of power to spy on the family—they didn't know he could see them and watch everything they did. And with Jason gone, he could now get closer.

Later Catherine came up to the house. Her face was flushed from crying. They all had a quiet meal and then went upstairs for the night. Sarah, however, remained downstairs, on the couch, with a lamp lit. She relaxed and began to think about going hunting with Jason. It wasn't the hunting that held her interest, it was the camping. She had fantasized before about him. He was the central male figure in her life...and was not her father. She was attracted to his strong presence. He was forbidden, unknown territory.

She slipped into her fantasy, and began rubbing herself. As her arousal grew, she closed her eyes and slid further down on the couch. Rolling her head to the side her eyes opened...and she screamed loudly.

There was a face in the window leering at her. The mouth hung open; the eyes were aflame with lust. Hands were pressed to the window, framing the terrible visage. Her scream was loud and full of terror. Anne and

Catherine came bounding down the stairs. Catherine had her pistol out and ready.

"What's going on?" Catherine shouted to Sarah, who was sitting bolt upright on the couch. She pointed to the window.

"Someone was looking in the window—a horrible face!" she exclaimed.

Catherine immediately snuffed out the lamp and Anne ran back upstairs to get her 9mm. Catherine cautiously went to the window and looked out; she could see no one.

"Do you know who it was?"

"No...no, wait...it might have been Billy Turner. It scared me so, I can't be sure."

"What a creep," Catherine said in disgust. "Sarah, get your pistol and we'll go around the house. I want to make sure the doors and windows are locked tight."

"You're not going outside, are you?" Sarah asked.

"No, I want to make sure we're secure from the inside."

They went through the house and only after satisfying themselves that the main floor was secure, headed back upstairs. Catherine made sure the extra weapons were locked away and each of the women took their rifles upstairs with them. Anne added the 20 gauge pump shotgun as well. For a long time Catherine kept watch out of the second floor window. She thought she saw a shadowy figure moving through the orchard, away from the house but she could not be sure. That night the women slept together in Anne and Jason's bedroom. Sarah had a hard time getting to sleep; every time she closed her eyes, the leering face pressed against the window flashed in her mind.

Chapter 5

B illy jumped back at Sarah's scream. He was thoroughly aroused from what he saw but now, in a panic, he scrambled for the cover of the orchard. From there he watched as the dim lamps went out. They would be looking outside for someone now. After calming down, he began to slink away through the dark, back to his own farm. His mind raced with thoughts of Sarah. He had gotten to see her partially naked up close and sexually aroused. She seemed full of sexual desires which he imagined satisfying. His mind churned with fantasies as he made his way back through the dark woods. He was frustrated. If Jason were out of the picture, he would be able to have his way with her. They would all look to him for protection, especially Sarah.

The next day Anne and the girls stayed close to the house. They took turns at the lookout position on the roof, but saw no one. They had pretty much decided that the peeping tom was Billy and, while disdainful of him, they did not dismiss him as an idle threat in this post-EMP era. Catherine was adamant that he could be serious trouble—for them and for Jason. When Jason returned with his ducks the next day, he was set upon by the girls with the story of Billy's spying. Even Catherine seemed to have set aside the issues that drove him from the house in the face of this new threat. Jason proposed going to the Turner farm to talk with the father. Anne was doubtful and Catherine said it wouldn't work.

"You saw how he behaved when we met with everyone—before the battle. He's got a mean streak and doesn't like you," Catherine declared emphatically, "And now that he's injured I'm not sure Billy would listen to him."

Anne agreed with Catherine's assessment. Sarah just wanted something done. She knew that what Billy had seen—more than the others realized—could be harmful to her.

"Someone's got to do something. We can't just wait until he comes back. We didn't know that he was spying on us. How many times has he done this and we didn't know about?" Sarah's question sent a shudder through Anne and Catherine. The idea of Billy hanging around the house was creepy, and now in these lawless times, who knew what could happen?

"Did you notice the way Billy kept looking at Sarah when they came to the house the morning of the battle?" Catherine asked. "He was staring at her—checking her out. Sarah noticed it. I had to interrupt him."

"I guess I was preoccupied with other things. I didn't notice. But what do you want me to do?" Jason asked.

"You should take care of him," Sarah said.

"What does that mean, 'take care of him'?" Jason responded.

"I don't know..."

"Shoot him," Catherine said matter-of-factly.

"I can't just shoot him. You're asking me to kill him." He looked hard at Catherine. She looked straight back at him, not giving an inch.

"Why not?" Sarah said. "You've killed lots of people."

"That's different, and you know it. I was defending us against attackers who wanted to kill us. This kid is a peeping tom, and needs disciplining, not killing. And don't forget, he fought for the valley and his dad almost gave his life in that fight."

"I'll do it then," Catherine said. She had a dangerous look in her eyes. Everyone turned to stare at her. "Just because he took part in the battle doesn't give him the right to spy on us...and it didn't automatically make him a good guy. I'm a good shot, I'll just wait and shoot him when he goes up to his dad's still. I can ambush him there."

"No! I won't let you do it," Jason said with all the finality he could bring to his voice.

"What's the matter? I've killed before."

"But you haven't *murdered*," Jason said.

"I don't want you doing this. It will harm you," Anne said. "We'll find some other way to deal with Billy."

"I don't think you will," Catherine said. Jason wondered if she was taking her hurt out on Billy.

"Look," he said, "You have let me be a father to you. I couldn't demand that acceptance. I had to earn it from you girls." He was looking from Sarah to Catherine; pausing to stare at her to emphasize his point. "But there's another dimension to our relationship. Along with your step father, I am also your commanding officer." The girls now looked at him with some surprise. "Yes, we are a family, but we also are a fighting unit, an army of four, and I am the general of this army. You are bringing up a threat to the family which makes this a military matter." He looked directly at Catherine, "You are under my authority in these matters and I will not allow any insubordination."

She glared back at him. Her fists clenched at her side. She looked as if she was going to argue, but Jason stared back. His face grew hard and cold. She finally turned away. "Nothing else will work," she mumbled almost to herself.

Sarah just stared at Jason. She was caught off guard by the intensity of the exchange. "So what do we do?" she said after some silence.

"I don't know yet. But I want it settled that we don't kill Billy and no one acts without my okay. That's critical. Do I have everyone's agreement on this?" Anne offered her yes, as did Sarah. Catherine glared at him for some time and then just turned away.

After an awkward pause, Anne asked, "What's next?"

"I'd like to catch Billy alone, get the drop on him, disarm him then play it by ear. I'm not sure, but I think he has to have a chance to not be a problem for us. I need to set the boundaries and let him know the deadly consequences of breaking them."

"So you'll kill him *after* you talk to him, because that will be the end result. He'll be back," Catherine said.

"Maybe so," Jason responded tersely.

"The results are the same in the end."

"I'm creating an opportunity for Billy to do the right thing, then it's up to him."

Chapter 6

Early the next morning, well before dawn, Catherine got up, quietly dressed, took her carbine and pistol and stole out of the house. In the dark, tempered only by the slight bluing of the eastern sky, presaging the coming dawn, she made her way into the woods and towards the Turner farm. Once in the forest, she worked her way up onto the ridge. She was headed for the still, hoping she would catch Billy starting to work on a batch of liquor.

Dawn found her comfortably hidden in the brush with a commanding view of the still. She snacked on some venison jerky and water while she waited. Soon after the sun came up, still quite early, Billy came into view carrying a bag of corn. The still was strategically situated in a low hollow near a small spring. He got the fire going, filled the kettle with water from the spring and started cooking the grain. Then he sat down, his back against a log, with his rifle laid aside and began to relax. After pulling his cap down over his eyes he started to nod off.

The birds began their chirping as Billy settled down. Catherine could smell the corn beginning to boil. She slowly stood up and aimed at Billy's rifle. She needed to take his weapon out of action so he wouldn't go for it. She squeezed off a round and the rifle went flying away from Billy. He jumped up with a wild, confused look and started for the rifle. Catherine hit it with another round.

"Stay where you are. Don't move and you won't get hurt!" She shouted, pointing her carbine at him.

"What the fuck? What're you doing?" he asked.

"Sit back down. Now!" Catherine shouted in her most commanding voice.

"What's going on?" Billy asked, but he sat back down on the log. "What're you doing here? You're not supposed to be here."

"I want to talk about what you did at our farm, you spying on us, peeping through the windows."

"Who told you that? I didn't do anything," Billy replied acting offended.

"Don't lie about it. Sarah saw you. And I saw you sneaking away through the orchard."

"You can't prove that," Billy was now defensive. "And you shouldn't be here. You know my pa don't want you here."

"It's proven as far as I'm concerned. Don't keep trying to deny it." Catherine ignored the rest of Billy's comments.

"So what? I ain't saying I did, but what're you gonna do about it, if I did?"

"That's what I'm here to talk to you about. I could just shoot you right now and then Sarah and I don't have to worry about you spying on us—"

"You ain't gonna shoot me."

"Don't bet on it. I killed my share of those guys at the bridge. I don't mind killing you if I think you're a threat to me or my sister."

Billy looked at Catherine. She could see the doubt creep into his expression. He wasn't sure she was bluffing. She kept her rifle trained on him.

"You don't control me. You can't tell me what to do," he finally blurted out.

"I don't. But I can tell you what you can't do when it comes to our farm."

"I ain't talking to you. You can just fuck off."

"Billy. You got one chance to get out of this without getting shot. You better talk to me."

"You think you're so hot? Just because you took part in the battle? Shit, I'll bet you just hid in the woods. Me and Pa, we shot and killed those guys. More than you probably done."

"You're thick in the head." The conversation was not going well. "I figured it would be a waste of time and I was right. There's no sense talking to you." She paused, then said, "Here's the deal. You don't ever come onto the Whitman property...ever. If you do, I'll shoot you on sight."

"You wouldn't."

"I would. I've warned you and from this point on I'll have no problem shooting you."

"You don't scare me," Billy said, but his voice carried some concern. He was not sure just how seriously to take Catherine. She was acting dangerous. "Jason know you're here? Bet he don't want you up here, talking like this."

"Jason doesn't have anything to do with this. It's about me and you. You can't spy on me or my sister any more. You can't come on our property any more. I'm serious."

Catherine began to feel it was all futile. She was struggling to make Billy respect her resolve. Now, talking to Billy made it harder to think so casually about shooting him. The gang members, all strangers, bad men, all clearly attacking the family, bent on hurting and killing, were easier to shoot. It had all been from a distance and with no communication. But here she was, talking to Billy, someone she used to ride with on the bus when the schools were open. She realized her mother may have been right. Billy was a person—a someone. She would have a hard time shooting him. Somehow she had to make him believe that she could shoot him and that he would suffer if he came on the Whitman farm.

When Jason and Anne woke up, they discovered Catherine gone.

"Sarah, do you know where she went," Anne asked her youngest daughter.

"No. She must have left while I was asleep. I never heard her," Sarah replied.

"She took her weapons," Jason said after looking around. "I think she went to ambush Billy."

"Oh my God," exclaimed Anne. "We told her not to do that. We have to stop her."

"I'll go. It'll be faster with me alone. I know about where the still is. Maybe I can get there before anything bad happens."

"Yes. Go right now," Anne said.

He grabbed his rifle and 9mm and headed out of the house on the run. Twenty minutes later, with a rush of relief, he heard the voices as he approached the still. Billy and Catherine were talking.

As Catherine was considering how to make Billy believe she was serious Jason called out.

"Catherine, it's me, Jason. I'm coming in."

Billy looked up, hoping the interruption might be an opportunity. But Catherine, after the briefest glance towards the sound of Jason's voice, focused her attention back to Billy. There was nothing for him to do but sit still.

"Now you're going to get it," he said.

Catherine ignored him. "What are you doing here," she demanded of Jason as he walked into the clearing.

"I could ask you the same thing. Do you remember what we agreed to last night?"

"He's still alive," she responded.

"What's gone on?" Jason asked.

Catherine relayed her conversation with Billy. "It seems as though he's too thick to understand how serious this is...and that I mean business."

"So what do you want to do?" Jason asked.

Catherine thought for a moment, then said, "Watch him." She grabbed a metal cup from the board lying on the ground next to the cooking fire. "Wait here," she called and walked through the trees. About 30 yards into the brush, Catherine hooked the handle of the cup over a branch. From the camp, you could hardly see it. Billy looked from Catherine to Jason, but didn't move. Jason kept his eyes on Billy.

She walked back into the camp, "Now watch, Billy Turner. You see that cup behind me?" she asked.

Not waiting for an answer, she turned and quickly brought her rifle up to her shoulder, sighting for only a brief second, and fired two quick rounds. The cup went flying; no one could tell if it was the first or second shot that hit it.

"Shit," Billy muttered.

"Billy," Catherine fixed him with her hard gaze. "You didn't get to see me in the battle, but I killed my share of those bad guys you saw dead—at the farm and at the bridge—and I *will* also shoot you on sight if I see you on our farm. Now that you're warned, anyone on the farm will shoot you if you come on the property. That's the deal. And don't think if you see Jason go off into the woods that we're easy targets for whatever you're thinking. I'll kill you just as quickly as Jason will."

Turning to Jason she said, "I've done my talking. He still may not believe me. Maybe you can talk some sense into him, so I don't have to shoot him."

Jason turned to Billy, "You get the picture? You don't come on the property unless invited. It's shoot on sight, for you."

"I wasn't doin' nothin'," Billy responded with a sullen look on his face. "And you don't control me."

"The girls identified you," Jason replied. "That part's settled. And it's not a matter of controlling you, it's a matter of you doing what you're told," Jason said.

"Do you know what she was doing that night? She was acting like a dog in heat."

"Billy, you're treading on thin ice," Jason's voice turned cold and hard. Billy shut up. "You better believe Catherine. She means what she says and I'd hate to see you get killed."

Billy looked from Jason to Catherine. He was stunned by her shooting skills and now less sure that she was bluffing. He never expected this girl, who he had gone to school with, would turn out to be so dangerous. He shuffled his feet in the dirt and leaves but didn't say anything.

Jason paused, then continued, "You've got some good skills. You're very good in the woods and you've proven yourself to be a brave fighter."

Billy looked up at him with a puzzled expression. He didn't get many compliments.

"I would hate to lose those skills. They're useful. The valley needs them. In the future, we'll all need to work together for everyone's benefit. There are probably still bad guys out there—"

"Like the ones we killed?"

"Yeah, like the guys we all killed. You know how bad they are...and how dangerous. The valley has to work together to make sure we're ready if that ever happens again. But right now, you have to agree to what Catherine said. You cannot come onto the Whitman farm...ever. You've been there once, maybe more, but no more. That is what you have to agree to."

"What if I do?"

Catherine now spoke up, "One of us will kill you on sight."

"What if I shoot you first?"

"Listen carefully to me," Jason said. "I've killed over 20 men, I'm a better shot than you are and I can move through woods as well or better than you. And Catherine is just as good as me. She saved my life in the last battle. Here's the important thing: I don't bluff and neither does

Catherine. She means what she says...and so do I. I promise you, you will not win that battle."

Billy took off on a different tack, "What do you mean about us working together?" he finally asked. "Can't do that if I can't come on the farm."

"We'll talk about that later," Jason replied. "When you've shown you're ready, I'll call on you. Now, you agree? The Whitman farm and the Whitman girls are off limits."

Billy sat quiet for a moment, trying to maintain some control over the decision forced upon him. "I guess so...don't have much of a choice, do I?"

"Not now, but every time you think about it, you'll have a choice. I hope you're smart enough to realize it's a life or death choice you'll be making."

Jason started to go, then paused and turned back to Billy, "Remember, everyone's a good shot on the Whitman farm. You're outgunned. It's better to be an ally than an enemy. Just keep to the agreement and we'll all be fine. If you need to contact me, leave a note in the mail box at the road."

"Well, don't you come onto our property, including this still," Billy retorted.

"Fair enough. If any of us need to contact you, we'll leave a message in your mailbox. We won't come on your property."

"What about my gun? She broke it. I need something to hunt with."

Jason thought for a moment, "I'll get a replacement from the house, drop it by your mailbox tomorrow."

"How 'bout one of them semi-autos?" Billy figured he'd lobby for an upgrade.

"I'll get you something that will work."

"You ain't very generous."

"Maybe not, but you're lucky to be alive, considering how mad Catherine was yesterday. Now you should go and then we'll leave."

"I got to cook the mash."

"You can come back to finish later. We'll watch you leave and then we'll go.

"Don't forget what we said...and what you saw here," Catherine added.

Billy got up. There was no more to say. He headed back down towards his farmhouse. Catherine and Jason watched him. Then Jason grabbed Billy's old rifle and they headed back home.

When they got home, they were greeted by Anne and Sarah who were relieved to find no one had been shot. Catherine related what she had done and what she had told Billy. Jason added that it was the right solution and then told them about Catherine's performance. It was a good opportunity to build her up. She allowed a pleased look to cross her face at the dramatic way Jason told the story. Where there had been a solid wall between them since his rejection of her there now seemed to be a fence. Catherine still maintained a line of separation but he sensed they might now be able to communicate across that line.

There was a 30-06 among the weapons they had collected after the battle at the house. It was a semi-automatic with a five shot magazine, higher quality from what Billy had been using. Jason took it up to the Turner mailbox and left it there with what ammunition he could find. The family kept a regular lookout, but didn't see any more signs of Billy.

Chapter 7

As they prepared for the coming winter, Jason and Anne looked for opportunities to spend time alone together. He wondered about Anne's more frequent allowances of their intimacy, but, not wanting to mess up a good thing, kept quiet.

After making love one day, he asked, "You've been less reserved this past month. Aren't you worried about getting pregnant?"

Anne lay on the bed looking at him with a loving smile, full and satisfied and unapologetic, "I'm not worried about getting pregnant...you see, I am pregnant." She was beaming as she said it. "After the battle my desire to be close to you was so strong. I wasn't paying attention to my schedule and I let it slip. Now I find out that I'm still quite fertile. New life is on its way and we are creating it," she beamed.

Jason's mouth dropped open. He didn't know what to say. *A child of our own!*

"Why didn't you tell me?"

"I wanted to be sure...and I didn't want to worry you."

"Aren't you worried? I thought this was dangerous for you."

She pulled his face close to hers. "I am a little. But it will be all right. I'm experienced, and my girls came easy enough. Now that it's happened, I feel I am ready for this. You'll be a father in the spring." There was a joyful gleam in her eyes.

"Have you told the girls?"

"Not yet. I'll know when the time is right, but it's not now. We can just enjoy the fact that we don't have to worry about me getting pregnant." Her eyes were alight with excitement as she spoke.

The fall rains came. The torrents lashed at the windows and searched out every crack in the house. With the rain, the weather grew colder. There were no more signs of any gangs. Their hidden valley seemed to have returned to its former state as a forgotten place off the beaten path.

One cold, rainy morning Anne sat the girls down in the kitchen. "You remember when I told you that Jason and I were going to live as a couple? That we considered ourselves married?"

The girls nodded.

"Well, I have some good news to announce. I'm pregnant. We're going to have a baby next spring."

The girls looked at their mother in shock. "You can't be," Catherine exclaimed.

"Well, I can, and I am."

"But there's no hospital around. How will you have a baby with no doctors or a hospital?" Sarah asked.

"Women have had babies without hospitals for thousands of years. It is a very natural thing to do," Anne replied.

"Aren't you too old? And isn't it too dangerous?" Catherine asked.

"Apparently I'm not too old, or it wouldn't have happened. Since I have had you two already, my body is better prepared than if this were a first pregnancy at my age."

"But it's more dangerous now...I mean without doctors or medicines," Catherine continued.

"Yes it's more dangerous, but not impossibly so. I had the two of you in a hospital, but I did it naturally. It wasn't the easiest thing I have done, but neither of you were hard births."

"Still, you're putting yourself in danger," Catherine said.

"A first birth is the most dangerous and generally sets the tone for the others," Anne replied. "And I have Jason and both of you to help."

"Not me," Sarah responded.

"Well, I won't force you," Anne said with a knowing smile. "Catherine, can I count on you to help?"

"Of course," she replied. "I don't think Jason will be much help in this area. Do you have any books I can read to get ready?"

"Thank you, Catherine," Anne replied. "Yes, there are some books still around from my pregnancies. I think they're in a box in the spare bedroom closet. They should help. And don't count Jason out. He may surprise us all."

Anne's face beamed in joy. Catherine smiled back at her mother. The baby was already having a healing effect, and it had just begun to grow.

Chapter 8

L
ate in February, the family woke up to a cow bell ringing down at the road. Jason hurriedly got dressed, grabbed his rifle and pistol and went down to see what was going on. Catherine followed him. At the end of the driveway, they found Billy looking frantic. He was obviously distressed but feared to come onto the property.

"Can you come and help?" he asked in a desperate voice. "It's Pa. He's in a bad way. He's really sick."

"What's wrong with him?" Jason asked.

"He's peein' blood and hasn't eaten for days. He's getting weaker. I don't know what to do," Billy said.

Claire, who had moved in to help Billy after her husband had been killed, had returned to her house months ago when Ray's wound stabilized. He had progressed to moving around the house and Billy had taken over caring for his dad. Catherine was shocked not realizing Billy could show such emotion.

"Come up to the house. I'll get some things and we'll go back together." Jason said.

They rushed back up the hill to the house. Anne and Sarah were at the door. When Sarah saw Billy coming, she disappeared inside. Jason told Anne what was happening and she went to gather the few medical supplies they had. After a pause to think about it, sympathy opened her heart and she took the precious bottle of pain pills that she kept stashed away. Catherine offered to go with Jason, but

Anne insisted that she be the one. She was more experienced at nursing the sick and injured, and she guessed Ray's problems were from his injuries, not from any sickness. They drove off in the pickup with Billy between them.

Billy's dad was in a bad way. His wound had re-opened. Jason suspected internal bleeding as well. Ray also seemed to be suffering from malnutrition and probably too much alcohol. He was emaciated and not fully cognitive. There didn't seem to be much they could do. Anne tried to get some fluids into the old man with only a little success. He was in a great deal of pain and cried out when they tried to prop him up. He kept fading in and out of lucidity. When he focused on Anne, he asked her how her husband was doing and mentioned the girls as if they were still little. Anne got two pain pills into him with a little water. In a few minutes he relaxed and went to sleep. Then the three of them went downstairs to the kitchen.

The house was a mess. Most of the rooms were closed off; Anne didn't even want to see what shape they might be in. The kitchen, pantry and hallways were filthy.

"Thanks for giving Pa something to let him sleep. He's been cryin' out. It hurts I can't help him." Billy's concern showed a side of him that neither Anne nor Jason had ever noticed.

"Do you have any food in the house?" Anne asked.

"A little, most things have run out," he replied.

"Is the well still working?" Jason asked.

"Yeah. It froze up in the last cold spell and now it don't pump so good, but I get water out of it. I can always go down to the creek."

"You know what foods to forage for in the woods, don't you?"

"Some...berries and things," Billy replied, "but there ain't much this time of year."

Then Jason asked Billy about his weapons for hunting.

"I run out of shotgun shells. Makes it harder. The 30-06 you gave me is a whole lot better than my old one. I got a deer with it a month ago. Been eating off that, but I can't get Pa to eat."

Anne took out some food she had brought along and they ate in silence. "You know Billy we cannot fix your father. He needs a hospital and real doctors. Even then he might not make it. We can only make him comfortable." She put her hand over his, "You know he's dying."

Billy stared hard at her. "Yeah, I guess I know it," he said. "Don't know what I'll do if he's gone. Don't know how I'll get along."

"You'll do all right. You've managed pretty well without much help so far," Anne said in a motherly tone.

"I'll be all alone..." Billy's voice trailed off.

Jason felt a sudden surge of pity for Billy; Billy the peeping tom, the hillbilly redneck that he threatened to shoot on sight five months ago. Anne's face showed she felt the same.

She cleaned and dressed Ray's wound and gave Billy two more pain tablets. "Use them only for the worst of the pain. It's all I can spare. Try to keep him hydrated—keep getting him to drink some water. We'll be back in two days to check on him."

"Thanks," Billy said with sincerity. It was not a word he was familiar with. It was rarely used around his house and never with outsiders.

Two days later, as promised, Anne and Jason were back. Billy seemed surprised to see them. He didn't expect people to keep their promises. Anne immediately went to Billy's dad. He was running a fever and his breathing was rapid and shallow. His heart beat was irregular and faint. She didn't think he had much time left. She set about washing him and cooling him down with wet towels. It had a soothing effect on the old man. Now they could only wait. Both Jason and Anne felt that death would not be long in coming and, if possible, they wanted to be there with Billy when it came.

Billy sat without moving. The scowl that was beginning to be etched on his face was now gone, replaced by a sad expression. His whole body mirrored his face. The angry attitude had disappeared with this crisis of losing his last family member. He now needed people in a way he had never felt before and here were people he had mistreated, helping him without reservation. His life was shifting under him like the ground in an earthquake.

Chapter 9

Billy and his old man had just continued their mountain ways after the EMP attack without thinking much about the future. From what anyone could tell, Billy had no ambitions. Ray hadn't made any plans as supplies ran down. They lived a lifestyle close enough to a subsistence level that they didn't experience the shocking disruptions felt by urban people. The biggest change for them was the loss of moonshine customers and the money they brought in. That money went to buy food and the seed they used to grow the corn for the mash. They kept at the business, or to be precise, Billy kept at the still, as his dad began to drink what they couldn't sell. Food dwindled but there was enough with the hunting and trapping that they survived. Now Billy was facing the end of that long, gradual decline. The anger he carried for so long, the chip on his shoulder, fell away as he faced his need for others.

They kept watch through the night and into the next afternoon. Near dusk, the old man woke up and looked around the room. "Becka, that you?" he rasped, mistaking Anne for his long dead wife, Rebecca.

Anne gently replied, "Yes, it is me."

"I'm glad you're here. I miss you. I drink too much when you're gone," he said with a weak voice. He looked around, then called out, "Billy, come here."

"I'm here, Pa," Billy replied, moving closer to his dad so he could see him.

The old man focused on him and said in a surprisingly clear voice, "You're a good boy. You done good by me. Your ma loves you...and I love you." He sank back in the bed.

Tears welled up in Billy's eyes. Anne's eyes grew moist. They sat in silence for some time. Ray just laid there, his breathing raspy and irregular. What was there to say? There was no fixing of things. They were there to keep the dying company.

Ray lay still for hours, semi-conscious. Anne began to speak softly to him about how much he and his wife had helped her. She encouraged Billy to talk to his dad; to tell him the good stories, reminding him about their better times, mostly when Becka, Ray's wife, was alive. They got a quiet conversation going, gently flowing over the old man. At times Anne sang parts of remembered hymns, old country ones. She sang softly with a clear alto voice about meeting the Savior in the 'middle of the air'. No one could tell if he heard them, but sometimes Ray's eyelids would flutter or the hint of a smile would trace across his face.

Near dawn the old man stirred, "Becka, Becka," his voice barely audible. "Wait for me, I'm comin'." His body stiffened, then slowly relaxed. His breath wheezed out like a balloon gently deflating, then he was silent. Everyone leaned forward. Billy looked at Jason and then Anne. Anne put her ear over his chest to listen for a heartbeat. She slowly shook her head. There was no heartbeat and no breathing. Harsh, convulsive sobs came from Billy as he fled the room. Jason wiped the old man's face and closed his eyes.

Death was never pleasant, even when it involved the enemy. Here, death visited not an enemy, but an ally. Death is a part of life, but people in the modern era had developed the ability to insulate themselves from it. Since society had collapsed, death had become personal again. A hundred years ago people saw death up close. Now, they were seeing it up close again. It should not be shocking, thought Jason. This was more the way humans had experienced death for millennia.

Maybe this is more 'normal' than what we've left behind.

Later, when Billy had collected himself, he and Jason went to dig a grave while Anne wrapped the body in a sheet. There was a burial plot out behind the house. It looked like several generations were buried there. Jason saw the head marker for Rebecca, the old man's wife. Billy said they should place his pa next to her. With pickax and shovel they started. The ground had begun to thaw, but it got harder going as they dug down. After some hours they had a four foot hole dug. Billy allowed as that was sufficient and they went back into the house.

Jason carried the body out to the grave and gently laid it in the ground. Billy kneeled down and placed his dad's hunting knife under his crossed hands. He stood up and stared down at his pa lying there.

"Mrs. Whitman," he asked, "would you say something? I don't know what words to use."

Anne opened the family Bible she found in the bedroom. This was the second time in a year she had opened one. Now her hands went of their own accord to the passages. She began in Genesis, Chapter 3, starting with verse 19:

> *By the sweat of thy face*
> *Shalt thou eat bread,*
> *Till thou return unto the ground,*
> *For out of it thou wast taken;*
> *For thou art dust,*
> *And unto dust thou shalt return.*

Then she turned to the Psalms and read Psalm 23:

> *The Lord is my shepherd,*

I shall not want.
He maketh me to lie down in green pastures;
He leadeth me beside still waters.
He restoreth my soul;
He leadeth me in the paths of righteousness
For His name's sake.
Yea though I walk through the valley of the shadow of death,
I fear no evil; for Thou art with me;
Thy rod and Thy staff, they comfort me.
Thou preparest a table before me in the presence of mine enemies;
Thou hast anointest my head with oil;
My cup runneth over.
Surely goodness and mercy shall follow me all the days of my life,
And I will dwell in the house of the Lord forever.

She finished with the Gospel of John, Chapter 14, verses 1 through 4:

Let not your heart be troubled; ye believe in God, believe also in Me. In my Father's house are many mansions; if it were not so, I would have told you; for I go to prepare a place for you. And if I go and prepare a place for you, I will come again and receive you unto Myself; that where I am, there ye may be also. And whither I go ye know, and the way ye know.

Anne closed the bible, then continued, "I remember Ray, your father, as a solitary man. He was a man of the woods, a man of this valley. And when we moved here twelve years ago, he helped us adjust to life in the mountains. His mountain wisdom proved valuable over the years. It helped us to get along. I remember he did not want to be bothered, but if we had any serious trouble he would always help."

Billy stared at her as she spoke of her memories from years ago. "I didn't know Pa done that for you," he said with wonder.

"Of course not," Anne replied, "you were too young. I also met your mother. She was very nice and helpful, especially with canning and putting up food."

Billy turned back to the grave, "Bye, Pa. Thank you for saying what you did…at the end." Again tears began to well up, and he stopped talking.

Jason waited for a nod to begin filling in the grave. Anne suggested that Billy walk back with her and let Jason finish the work, but Billy insisted on helping. "Pa says we Turners take care of our own. I need to do this."

Later, Jason and Anne prepared to leave. "Are you going to be all right?" Anne asked.

"I guess," he paused, "I'm all alone now. Don't know how that will go. I was always pretty much alone, but it's different now…"

"Your dad was always there, even if in the background," Anne said.

"Yeah, I guess that's it," he appeared dazed.

"We'll stop by in a few days, if that's okay with you," Jason said.

"Yeah, that's okay. I'm not gonna shoot you or anything like that," Billy said. Then a bright look came into his eyes. He jumped up, went to the cupboard, and brought back a gallon jug almost full of clear liquid. "Here. It's the last batch I made. I won't be making any more. I don't like it. Pa drank it and it made him either mean or sad. You take it with you. Throw it out if you want. I don't want it."

Anne and Jason graciously accepted the jug as a gift and left for home.

Chapter 10

The air remained brisk over the next weeks, even though the sun was regaining its strength. Crocuses, the early harbingers of spring, shot up on the south facing slopes, greedily drinking in the sun's rays. Jason found himself starting to look for the leaf buds on the trees; they would be coming soon. One afternoon, sitting around the kitchen table, the family was interrupted by the sound of engines. These were not gas engines. The sound had the deeper thumping of diesel motors. Jason grabbed his binoculars and ran up to the lookout on the roof. Catherine followed close behind. He looked down the valley for some time. The sound came and went with the wind. It was still far off.

"What do you see?" Catherine asked after a few moments.

"I can't tell for sure. It looks like two military vehicles," he said with surprise.

"Military?" Catherine was also surprised. "What would they be doing way out here?"

"I'm pretty sure they're military. I just can't tell who's in them. And there's a machine gun on one."

"We better get ready," Catherine said, and both turned to go down the ladder.

Anne and Sarah met them on the second floor.

"Could it really be the Army?" Anne asked.

"Maybe, but we can't be sure," Jason replied.

"We're saved!" Sarah blurted out. Everyone turned to look at her. "Well, if it's the army, then things are back to normal, and we can go to school, and we don't have to fight gangs, and things will be...normal again," Sarah's voice rose with her enthusiasm as her imagination surged ahead.

"Still, we better assume the worst and hope for the best," Jason said soberly. Catherine had the look of a person used to battle and prepared for another. Sarah looked hopeful; Anne looked concerned.

"Anne," Jason turned to her, "Are you going to be all right if there is a fight? You could wait in the cellar."

"No," she replied, "I'll help. The gunfire will disturb the baby, but I'll be more disturbed hearing it from the cellar and not knowing what's going on. We face this together...as a family." She was firm, and the girls nodded in agreement. Even Sarah, after her burst of enthusiasm, seemed resolved to do her part.

"Okay. Let's sit down and figure out how we deal with this," Jason said.

Second Lieutenant Kevin Cameron and Sergeant Rodney Gibbs led six other men, riding in two Humvees. Lieutenant Cameron was enthusiastic. He enjoyed the structure and routine of the army along with its mission and sense of purpose. While he had yet to see combat, he felt prepared and determined to be a good leader of his men. He could be called a 'strac trooper', one who followed the regulations, proudly. And one who worked hard to support his men. For that reason, his men accepted him, even though he was un-tested by war.

Lieutenant Cameron's best asset was his sergeant, Rodney Gibbs. Sergeant Gibbs was a veteran of Afghanistan and Iraq. He was a black man, older than Cameron but tough and battle hardened. He was no one's fool, having endured discrimination and hostility growing up and then in the army. In his combat tours, he had found himself to be a source of curiosity in his contacts with Afghani's and Iraqi's, sometimes hostile, sometimes not. It all served to give Gibbs a pragmatic, cynical view of life. He didn't expect favors or help from others. He expected to have to succeed on his own, knowing much of the system was not organized in his favor.

Still, Gibbs liked the lieutenant. The younger man respected his experience and was not so taken with his rank as to ignore Gibbs' wisdom, garnered from much hard experience. They made a good pair with much trust between them.

On this patrol through the countryside, they had stopped in Clifton Furnace. The town was empty but still showed the evidence of the violence it had suffered. The soldiers' banter was dampened by the signs of cannibalization they discovered. The evidence gave silent testimony to the horror that had occurred there. In a somber mood they drove up the river road until they came to the iron truss bridge.

The bridge was blocked. Two pickups riddled with bullet holes were still in the roadway. The remains of the fallen, mostly skeletons now with only a few rags of clothing left on them, were scattered around the bridge and the road leading into the valley. Parts of Big Jacks' remains were still tied up against the bridge.

"This must have been quite a battle," remarked Gibbs.

"A lot of bodies left to rot and be eaten," Cameron said.

"They stripped everything of value though. No weapons, gear...and clothing missing."

"I wonder how many dead there are. It looks like it must have been a pretty large group. What do you think?"

Gibbs was silent, studying the layout of the remains, trying to reconstruct the scene, "I'm guessing this was an ambush. They were caught as they crossed the bridge. It's a natural place for an ambush—the one lane bridge, a narrow gorge with cliffs on either side. From the cliffs the shooters could pin down a force of superior numbers. Still, they had to be pretty good."

"And these guys lost."

"Yeah. If they had won, they would have salvaged their vehicles and cleared the bridge."

"So the bridge was left closed by the victors...to keep others out of the valley," Cameron concluded.

"That's what I'm thinking."

"Think these guys were gang members?"

"Yeah."

"Then...up the road, in that valley, are some farmers, people who know how to fight and protect themselves," Cameron concluded.

"And they're well armed. Shall we investigate?" Gibbs looked over at Cameron.

"Carefully," he replied.

Gibbs directed the patrol to clear the bridge. The men worked somberly at their grizzly task.

The family sat down and Jason quickly went over their options.

"We only have a short time to prepare. There's no time to round up the rest of the valley. If it's a gang, we'll have to defend ourselves like we did before. The others, at least Tom, will come quickly when they hear the gunfire, so help will arrive if we can hold out for a little while."

"You said this was the military. Why will there be any shooting?" Sarah asked.

"The vehicles could be stolen."

Sarah swallowed hard. The prospect of another firefight at the farm was unnerving to everyone.

"If it really is the army, then we have to be prepared to greet them, properly but carefully," Jason continued.

"How do we do that?" Catherine asked.

"We really don't know what they want. But they're not on a sightseeing trip. They must have a purpose. Since we don't know what that is, we have to be cautious."

"Then we do not run out to them with open arms." Anne concluded.

"Right. We don't know how things have changed since the EMP attack. This could be a very different army from what we remember."

"So what do we do?" Sarah asked, "If it's the army that should be a good thing."

Jason frowned, not having a ready answer.

"We show them hospitality," said Anne. "We'll set up a table out in the front yard,"

"That's it," Jason said. "Anne, you and I will stand behind it, like welcoming hosts." He gathered momentum as the plan unfolded in his mind. "We'll be armed, but not holding our weapons at ready. I want them to get the message that we are capable of taking care of ourselves, but we are not threatening them."

"How about we put on good clothes? If we're welcoming guests, we should be well dressed," Catherine offered. "We'll get more respect that way."

Jason nodded with enthusiasm. "But I want you girls to stay behind, in the house. Keep your weapons at ready. I don't know how the army might react to two beautiful teenagers. I'll call you out when I am confident it's okay. When you come out, have your rifles slung over your shoulders, not ready to fire."

The patrol stopped briefly at the first two farms. They were long abandoned and of no interest. They had seen many just like them on their trip. As they came closer, Jason confirmed they were all in uniform.

He ran down to the main floor. "It's the army," he shouted. Everyone began to move.

"Now let's quickly set out some food." Anne had put together a platter of dried venison, ham and bread. "Sarah, get some glasses of water. That will complete the table. This should have a pacifying effect," she said.

The table was set. Everyone was wearing their best clothes as if they were greeting important visitors. Anne stood with Jason behind the table. She was obviously pregnant and obviously armed. Jason had his rifle shouldered and his 9mm strapped to his waist. Inside, the girls took up position on the second floor with their rifles and handguns. They were to watch carefully from the house in case anything went wrong. If shooting broke out, Jason had instructed Catherine to shoot at the senior officer and Sarah to fire at the machine gunner. He had no hope of winning a battle, but he would try to give his family the best chance he could.

Chapter 11

Everyone took their positions as the convoy turned onto the drive. The two vehicles wound up the hill and stopped at the front yard. Jason and Anne stood quietly behind the table covered with a white cloth and with the food spread out.

The first vehicle had a machine gun mounted with the barrel pointed forward and up. A young man lounged at the gun, not at the ready position. Finally two men got out of the second Humvee. Jason waved at them and shouted a hello.

Lieutenant Cameron waved back. They studied one another.

"The house is set up for defense. Check out the second floor—the screening," Sergeant Gibbs remarked.

"And the fence," Cameron replied, "looks like they've seen some action here. And this", he continued, referring to the table and food, "looks staged".

"Thinking the same thing," Gibbs responded.

"You're from the Army?" Jason shouted out. "We've been alone for two years. We never thought we'd see the likes of you."

"I'm Lieutenant Cameron and this is Sergeant Gibbs. We're from the Second Brigade Combat Team out of Fort Bragg. We've come from Hillsboro."

"We're very glad to meet you, Lieutenant Cameron and Sergeant Gibbs," Jason watched and evaluated the men as he spoke. The lieutenant was young, probably not very experienced. The sergeant seemed a more serious man, older and stockier than the Lieutenant. He had a more hardened look about him.

Probably seen action. Now helping his Lieutenant learn what he needs to know about field work.

"I'm Jason and this is my wife, Anne. We are pleased to meet you. Come, sit with us. We have lots of questions. We have no idea what's going on outside of our valley. You're like someone out of a dream. We had begun to think there was no society left and now you show up." Jason gestured for them to join him and Anne at the table.

The men walked forward. The girls kept watch unobserved from the house. After shaking hands, the four sat down. Anne offered them some of the food they had laid out on the table.

"No thank you," Cameron said. "We shouldn't be eating your food,"

"Nonsense," Anne replied, "You've been on the road and probably eating just your rations. This is fresh food and we have enough. Besides, you're the first guests we've had since the power went out."

"So, please tell us what's happening in the outside world. Has the power come back? Jason asked.

"Not yet," Cameron responded.

"Do you have any idea of when it will return?"

"No," he said.

"I assume that most vehicles still don't work," Jason continued.

"I'm not sure the newer ones will ever work again," Cameron responded.

"So, no power, no transportation...that means there must still be shortages of food and fuel?"

"Yes. Those are still in short supply," Cameron said. Everyone was silent.

"What do you think of our venison and ham?" Anne asked.

The two men took their first bites. "It's very tasty, ma'am," Cameron replied. Sergeant Gibbs nodded in agreement. There was an awkward pause in the conversation. Jason worried about why they were here.

To break the silence, Gibbs stood up, "Excuse me for a moment, I want to have the men stand down and eat something." He walked back to the Humvees.

Jason watched the men as they got out of the vehicles. They were all properly dressed and looked like regular troops, not some rogue group. The sight encouraged him.

When Gibbs came back and sat down, Cameron asked, "So how are you doing? Do you have enough food?"

"We're doing well," Jason responded. "Life is more like it probably was in colonial days, but we can get enough to eat."

Then Jason turned to wave at the house. "Let me introduce you to the rest of our family," he said. The girls came out of the house, dressed in their best skirts and blouses, their rifles slung over their shoulders and their pistols strapped to their waists.

"Lieutenant Cameron, Sergeant Gibbs, this is Catherine and Sarah," Jason said proudly.

Cameron looked stunned. He had been around women in the army, but the sudden appearance of these attractive teenage girls, all dressed up, looking very feminine and carrying serious weapons caught him off guard. Gibbs smiled at the sight. Catherine and Sarah shook hands with the officers and sat down, casually slinging their rifles over the backs of their chairs.

Catherine stared at Cameron, studying him, while Sarah's gaze flickered around to all the young men back at the Humvees who had turned their attention to the table when the girls emerged from the house. Catherine's focus remained on Cameron and the conversation.

"You have two beautiful daughters," Cameron said to Anne.

"Thank you," Anne replied. "With Jason's help they have become quite self-sufficient."

"Are they proficient with those weapons?" Cameron asked.

"Very," replied Jason. "We all help with hunting and defense."

Cameron looked again at Catherine to find her still gazing at him with a solemn expression on her face. He turned to Jason, "How many other farms are there in this valley?"

"There are four more that are inhabited."

"Are they getting along as well as you?" Cameron asked.

"Yes."

"Was that your work? Down at the bridge?" Gibbs asked.

Jason looked at Gibbs, sizing him up. Finally he answered, "Yes. All of us took part in defending the valley. My whole family included."

"That looks like it was quite a battle," Gibbs said.

"We lost two men but we destroyed the gang that attacked us. It was led by a man called Big Jacks."

"Was that his remains we saw tied to the bridge?" Gibbs asked.

"Yes. I left it there as a warning to others to stay out of the valley. We killed over thirty of the gang and the rest dispersed. I have no idea what became of them."

"We heard of this Big Jacks," Cameron said. He turned to Catherine, "Did you take part in the battle?"

"We both did," Catherine replied, staring straight back at him. Her gaze never strayed far from him. It was neither cold nor friendly, but serious—measuring.

"It looks like you've been attacked here...at your farm as well," Gibbs went on.

"That's right. I guess you noticed some of the bullet holes," Jason said.

"And the fence," Gibbs replied.

"We've been attacked twice here at the farm and once at the bridge. Here at the farm we were completely on our own," Jason said.

"That's very impressive," Cameron said.

"We have adjusted. We have learned to protect ourselves and are getting along pretty well. Everyone in the valley is," Jason paused. Then he continued, "But why are you here, Lieutenant?"

"Well, we're doing an inventory of the countryside. Our Captain wants to know who's out here, how many people and their condition. It's in preparation to move everyone closer to Hillsboro so we can provide better support."

"Well, you can report that we're doing fine. There's no sickness or injuries amongst us and we are feeding ourselves adequately."

"I'm glad to hear that, but I still have to make out my report. And there is the issue of preparation for relocating," Cameron said.

Silence. Then Jason asked, "Wouldn't that be counterproductive? Seeing as we are already self-sufficient?"

"Well, the city can provide better medical care and protection from gangs." He turned to Anne, "it looks as if you are pregnant. Being closer to Hillsboro would be a benefit when it comes time to have a baby."

"Women have had babies for thousands of years without hospitals," Anne replied. "Yes there is more danger, but it's a natural activity, however difficult. I appreciate your concern, but I'll be fine," Anne smiled at Cameron as she reached out to touch Catherine.

Catherine continued to fix her gaze on Cameron, occasionally shifting to Gibbs. Jason noticed her focus and sensed she was carefully evaluating these two men, trying to figure out if they posed a threat. So far, the conversation had gone well, but the plan to get people to relocate closer to Hillsboro disturbed him.

Sarah grew bored with the conversation and got up to fill the water pitcher from the pump in the front yard. Facing the young men at the Humvees, she bent over the handle allowing a calculated amount of cleavage show. When she finished, she looked at the men, smiled, and strolled back to the table. Catherine watched with an expression of disdainful amusement.

"You see, Lieutenant, my wife agrees with me. We feel we are fine on our own."

"Still, those are my orders," Cameron responded.

"So you would have all the families leave this valley?" Catherine asked.

"It looks like some have already left of their own accord."

"And no one knows if that was good for them or not. What we have here now is good for us," Catherine responded.

Jason spoke up, "Just so we can understand, would you explain this relocation process? I want to make sure I understand all its ramifications."

"We'll survey everyone we locate, like you and the rest in this valley, and note any injuries or other needs. We can address some urgent situations with supplies we're carrying," Cameron said. "We have some forms to fill out and later, we'll return to transport everyone back to the Hillsboro area. The plan is not fully developed at this point. When it is ready for implementation we will schedule transportation by sectors. You will get a date so you can prepare."

"How will that work? Will we transport all our belongings—all our household items?" Jason asked.

"That wouldn't be practical. We'll leave you a list. We're going to get vacant houses back at Hillsboro ready for everyone coming in from the countryside."

"You mean houses of those who died in town?" Cameron was silent. Jason went on, "In general, what can we bring with us?"

"Really, just your personal items—clothes and personal effects, mementos and such." Cameron's enthusiasm grew, "There is no need for furniture, bedding, or cooking utensils. The houses will have everything you need in them."

"What about tools, or knives, or guns?" Jason asked.

"No," Cameron replied, "weapons will not be allowed."

Jason paused, thinking for a moment. "Lieutenant, I'm glad to see you...I think we all are. Your presence suggests that things are improving, but I'm not convinced that we would want to move back to Hillsboro. I left Hillsboro almost two years ago because of growing corruption. I'm concerned about taking my family back there. After all, we've survived pretty well on our own. Let's assume for the moment, we decide not to move back. How does that work for you or your commander?"

Cameron pondered his question, "I think that you could choose to stay here."

"And we keep our weapons?"

"I'm not sure about that part. Smooth bore guns and maybe a hunting rifle would be allowed. I'd have to confirm that, of course, but not military grade weapons. We have to demilitarize the countryside. We can't have everyone armed and shooting each other. You've experienced the problems with gangs and guns so you know what I'm talking about."

"Yes, and it was only because we had weapons that we are still alive—all of us in this valley. We had to fend for ourselves. There was no police or military to turn to."

"First of all, the solution to that is to relocate to Hillsboro, like that plan calls for," Cameron responded. "But if you don't want to do that, we will protect you. We have to stop the gangs as well as the vigilante groups; it's the only way to bring order back to the area. Frankly, I don't understand why you would not take us up on our offer, considering your wife's condition."

"My wife is fine, as she said. But even with your best efforts, you could not come around here more than a few times a year. In between we'd have to fend for ourselves. We can do that, but we will need our weapons—both for hunting and for defense. I'm not sure you will eradicate all the gangs, and if we're defenseless even one or two outlaws would be disastrous. They won't be disarmed. Besides, what problem or threat could we pose this far out in the country?"

"I hear you. But it still sounds like you should relocate." Cameron ignored Jason's last question.

"Lieutenant," Jason was trying to be as persuasive as possible, "you give us a choice that is no choice. You say relocate, or disarm and stay here, which would be almost suicidal. You're giving us an option we don't want and an option that we can't survive. That's not a choice."

"I'm sorry. My orders are my orders. I can't offer you anything else." The lieutenant looked as if he were about to get up.

"Lieutenant, have you ever killed someone?" Catherine asked.

Cameron stopped and turned to her. Her steady gaze bore into him. "I'm not sure that is relevant to our conversation," he replied.

"It is relevant," Catherine responded, "These are different times. My question is relevant for the way of life we have now. Have you ever killed someone?"

Cameron hesitated, "I have been trained to kill. It's what the military does."

"I assume from your answer that you haven't actually killed anyone. I can tell that Sergeant Gibbs may have. He has that look." She went on, "I'm asking because if you haven't faced certain death, like we have, you cannot appreciate the importance of being able to defend yourself. I mean personally defend yourself. Not rely on the police or military. You should understand our need to protect ourselves. And you should recognize your limited ability to do so."

Cameron's face grew red and his eyes narrowed. He shrugged and looked away for a moment as he struggled for a response, "Young lady, I appreciate your point of view, but I have my orders. We can't have anarchy, everyone running around the countryside, armed and dangerous."

"Lieutenant Cameron, you can call me by my name, Catherine, since we have been properly introduced. I may look young, but killing people who want to rape, kill and possible eat you has a way of maturing you, so I'm not much of a young lady anymore."

Jason watched the exchange with admiration. He could tell Cameron did not know how to deal with this beautiful young woman who boldly challenged him. Glancing at Gibbs, he noticed a hint of amusement playing out in his expression; he seemed to be enjoying the exchange.

"I hope you are not blindly bound to your *orders* to the point that you cannot see the reality facing you here," Catherine continued.

Cameron turned to her with a serious expression on his face. "I am sorry if I offended you. I didn't mean to dismiss you or the points you make." He paused for a moment, "Maybe I don't fully understand what you have been through."

Suddenly Gibbs changed the subject, "Your daughters came out after we sat down. I noticed you signaled them. They must have been watching. Why did you keep them back? Was it because you didn't trust us?"

"You're partly correct. We're alive because we haven't taken anything for granted. You could be regular army or you could have been a rogue group, split off from the army, maybe no different from the gangs."

"If we had been a rogue gang, would keeping them hidden have helped in the end?"

Jason wondered where Gibbs was headed with these questions, but before he could respond, Catherine jumped in.

"Sergeant, if you had been an outlaw group and the situation had turned violent, I would have shot both of you starting with Lieutenant Cameron," she said, turning to him.

"You were prepared to shoot us?" Cameron now asked.

"I had you in my sights. Sergeant Gibbs would have been next, hopefully before he had a chance to react. And Sarah would have taken out the machine gunner." She paused to let that sink in, "I'm not sure that would have saved us but it would have given us a fighting chance."

Cameron stared at Catherine, this teenager whose looks belied a deadly ability.

The table was silent. The conversation had now turned more dangerous. A mixture of pride and concern crept into Anne's face. Sarah looked at her sister, her face showing some shock at her words. Cameron shifted in his chair. He looked towards Jason and then back at Catherine. Gibbs sat there, now watching Jason, wondering where this would wind up.

Then Catherine continued, "Of course it would have been a shame for that to happen. I could tell, having you in my sights that you were a good-looking guy, and we don't get too many good-looking guys here in the valley. It would have been a shame to shoot you. I'm glad I didn't have to," then she smiled at him for the first time.

Cameron suddenly began to blush. Gibbs laughed out loud as the tension melted away. "Lieutenant, I think this lady just got you," which only increased Cameron's discomfort.

"Well..." he began to mumble about command decisions and taking all situations seriously, but Gibbs just kept chuckling. "I didn't expect to get blindsided by someone so young. Didn't see that coming." He paused,

"With apologies to you, young in age, not in maturity," Cameron said.

"Apology accepted," Catherine replied and graced the lieutenant again with another smile melting away the dark, dangerous look in her eyes.

"Now we can all be friends," Sarah announced as everyone chuckled at Cameron's expense.

"As Sarah said, now that we are friends, can we resolve this issue between us?" Jason asked.

Turning serious again, Cameron said, "I don't know if there is anything else I can offer at the moment. I can check back with the Captain, but if he says everyone has to come in, they have to come in."

Anne then spoke up, "Lieutenant, how will you feed everyone? We can feed ourselves now. If we go to Hillsboro, we'll be another four mouths to feed. I don't see how that helps anyone. Is control so important as to increase food shortages? Is disarming law abiding citizens more important than letting us get on with our lives?"

Cameron shrugged. He didn't have an answer to Anne's practical questions.

Then Gibbs said, "Let me talk with the Lieutenant privately for a moment." He stood up and the two walked out to the well.

"You know this woman is right. Moving everyone back to Hillsboro has never made a lot of sense to me. It's more mouths to feed."

"I agree...with the extra mouths. But you know what Captain Roper instructed. And he's getting his orders from Colonel Stillman."

"Who's not around anymore," Gibbs replied. "Taking an inventory of the countryside is useful. The rest I'm not sure about.

"But we have our orders. And if everyone stays out here, they create targets for the gangs."

"I think the gangs might not want to mess with this family or this valley."

"You think this all wasn't a bluff? I know they did some fighting, but that girl and all that talk about being ready to shoot us...I don't know. It sounds like theater to me."

"I don't think so. Jason certainly isn't bluffing. I can see it in him. He's faced death and killed before."

"And the girl?"

"She has the same look. My guess is she isn't bluffing. I think she's killed her share of the bad guys and is confident she could do it again. Did you see how the mother looked at her when she spoke up? She was proud of her, not shocked. Here she is, very pregnant and sitting out here with her husband, not hiding in a cellar..."

"And armed...I get it. This is some family."

"Did you notice the scars on the younger girl's face? She looks like she was injured in one of their battles. It looks like a home suturing job. These are tough people."

"So what do you suggest?"

"Let's see if they can give us some justification for leaving them here, with their weapons. Something we can take back to Roper to convince him."

Cameron thought for a moment. "Okay, I'll give it a shot," he said.

They walked back and sat down. "So what do you want?" Cameron began.

Jason thought for a moment. "We want to be allowed to stay here, with our weapons. We're self-sufficient and not a burden to anyone."

"What can you offer me to take back to my captain? I'll need something to convince him to alter his plans," Cameron said.

Jason looked hard at the lieutenant, "You said food is still a problem, right?"

Cameron nodded.

Jason went on, "The challenge for everyone is how to restart food production. It probably won't be through industrial farming as before, but small farms growing more than they consume. But your problem is more difficult than you might guess. Did you know that commercial seeds are hybrids? They don't reproduce a second season. The crop reverts to an unproductive form. That means seed from the harvest can't be set aside to plant for the next year. So the seed companies get to sell their products each year. That worked before but it won't now."

"I appreciate the information, but what is your point?" Cameron asked.

"My point is that we have some fertile, non-hybrid seed to start from in this valley. Leave us alone, with our weapons, and you get the whole valley producing again. We will be able to begin supplying the town with food. With each harvest we'll have more fertile seed to use to expand our planting and increase our yields. We can also defend ourselves as you've seen. You don't have to protect us, and we can produce food, something Hillsboro needs. Lieutenant, we're more useful to Hillsboro left alone out here, than being relocated to town."

Cameron and Gibbs again stood up and walked off together. "He makes a good point," Cameron said. "We haven't found farms intact with the resources to restart production." He paused to think. "I don't know if he's making it up about the seeds, but if he's right, the whole valley could be producing food—more than they consume."

"And the town would have less to feed. It sounds like a win-win to me."

"I wonder if that's enough to have Roper go for this."

"It may not be easy, but it's worth a try, isn't it?"

Cameron finally nodded, "Okay, let's settle with this guy and then check out the rest of the valley. But I don't know about the Captain."

"We can deal with the Captain later. I'm sure you're up to the task of convincing him."

Cameron sighed, "I doubt Roper appreciates my eloquence, or my point of view, but I'll give it a try."

Chapter 12

They returned to the table. Cameron said to Jason, "I'll give your idea a try. I have to convince Captain Roper, but you make some good points."

"Thank you Lieutenant. I think you may have just saved all our lives," Jason said.

Anne grabbed Sarah, "Come with me, we will have some tea and preserves to celebrate." They went back into the house.

Sergeant Gibbs motioned to Jason to come with him, "Tell me more about your battles with the gangs. I'd like to know how you handled them." They walked off talking guns and fighting strategy.

Cameron was left with Catherine at the table. He didn't quite know what to say to her. Finally he asked, "How did you learn to shoot?"

"My real dad—Jason is my step-dad—taught Sarah and me a little about shooting before he left. When Jason came he'd already had run-ins with gangs, so he was very serious about teaching us how to defend ourselves. The first time we were attacked it was four men. Jason had to fight them all by himself. That's when we realized we all needed to learn how to defend ourselves."

"But how did you train for that? It's very hard to simulate actual battle conditions."

"Jason used moving targets and created lots of different, loud diversions to distract us. He kept saying the noise could be paralyzing if we weren't used to it. He was right."

"So you got used to it?"

Catherine thought for a moment, "I don't know if I got used to it, but I was able to keep functioning. We got good at target acquisition which is what Jason calls it. I'm also a very good shot." She paused then added with a smile, "I'll bet I'm a better shot than you are."

"That's a lot to claim. Remember, I've had years of training."

Catherine leaned forward, her smile broadening, "I've been studying you. I'm up for the challenge."

"I noticed you staring at me. What were you thinking?" he asked.

Catherine paused and looked away, gathering her thoughts, then continued, "Lieutenant, like I said before, you're pretty good-looking and we don't see many guys here in the valley. Now I find you're an upright person. I like that. I was figuring all that out." She paused again, before plunging ahead, "Then I was wondering if you had a girlfriend."

Cameron almost choked and began to blush again.

"You seem to blush a lot. I like that. It means you don't hide your feelings too deeply."

"Well, Miss Catherine, if you must know, I do not have a girl friend. But why would that matter to you?"

Catherine just smiled, "I just assumed that all the girls in Hillsboro would be chasing you, you being an officer and handsome as well."

"I suppose I've been too busy. And I really don't think it is a good idea to get involved with the local citizens in a town we're supposed to be policing."

"Well I hope you don't feel the same about us here in the valley." Catherine now had quite a different look on her face. One he couldn't fathom.

"I may have to make an exception in this case. It seems like I'm doing that a lot today."

"Adjusting to new realities is a good thing." Catherine replied with a satisfied smile.

Jason and Sergeant Gibbs returned. Anne and Sarah brought out the tea and jam. They all sat down again.

"Tell us more about what is going on outside our valley," Jason said.

"Well, things are not all that well yet. Until we can get power and transportation going everyone is going to struggle. You know what happened?"

"An EMP burst."

"Best we can figure is that there were multiple ones over the U.S., so the whole country was affected. I don't know what's happened abroad, but I don't think other countries experienced an attack," Cameron said.

"Do we have a government?" Jason asked.

"Depends on what you mean," Cameron said. "We have a local government in Hillsboro. There's essentially no state government...probably anywhere. Nationally we have some government. The President and much of his cabinet are still in D.C., but the city is in shambles and under tight military control. Of course, I get my instructions from the Army which still has some command and control function, although it's spotty."

"Well," Jason said at length, "I wonder if other countries can help, if they haven't already."

"From what we hear the world financial systems have collapsed, the mid-east is blown up and no oil is flowing. The rest of the world didn't get an EMP attack, but they got the after effects. When the U.S. sneezes, the world catches a cold. We hear stories and it doesn't sound good anywhere," Cameron replied.

"What about food? You said it was still tight. When I left Hillsboro over a year ago food was already scarce. Do you have a good supply?"

"It's tight. I won't lie to you."

"What about seeds? Other farm areas could begin to help provide if they had seeds," Jason said.

"The stocks on hand seem to have been taken and eaten rather than planted. The supply is minimal."

"Seed and some starter livestock—chickens, pigs, cows, if there are any left uneaten. That's what the farms need to feed the cities," Anne said.

Jason thought about Sam and Judy; they kept their livestock as best they could and were just fine, until the gang came and destroyed not only their lives, but their ability to feed others. He knew Anne was right. If they could prime the pump the farms could start producing food again. He felt more convinced the idea of concentrating people back in the city was foolish at best, dangerous and suspicious at worst. Everyone would be better off dispersed, but then they couldn't be controlled. He kept those thoughts to himself.

Jason stood up, "I think it's time for a drink." He went into the house and returned with the Turner moonshine. He had mixed it with some crushed berries to create a primitive version of schnapps. He poured three glasses and toasted Lieutenant Cameron and Sergeant Gibbs. "Here's to both of you. Your showing flexibility allows me and my family to remain in place. We're grateful and we'll do our part to make you look good for this decision."

The men took swigs and all coughed and choked a bit. Anne and the girls laughed. "It's not the smoothest drink. Very little aging goes into moonshine, I'm told," Catherine offered.

Getting his breath back, Cameron asked, "Where did your dad get this? He didn't have time to moonshine as well as construct this fortress?"

Catherine responded, "No, a neighbor up the valley has a still in the hills. He died recently and his son hates the stuff, so he gave it to Dad." That was the first time Jason and Anne had heard Catherine use the word 'Dad' for Jason.

"I can see why he didn't like it much," replied Cameron. "No offense, but this is rough around the edges."

"It's the only game in town...or to be more accurate, the valley," Jason responded. "Sergeant, how do you like it?"

Gibbs put his partially drained glass down, "I haven't had a drink for months so I would rate this as excellent."

"Well said," Jason agreed. "Lieutenant, I'd like to ask a favor of you," he continued. "The young man who gave us this moonshine is now all alone. I can't bring him into our family with my two daughters but he needs some help. I was thinking that he might be a useful addition to your outfit—sort of like a scout for the cavalry in the old west. The boy knows the mountains and is a good woodsman, born and bred to it. His dad died from wounds defending the valley, so I feel a responsibility to him. He's adrift now and needs to attach himself to a group. Would you consider it?"

"I don't know; that's highly unusual..."

"But not without precedent, if you go back in history. It could be another field improvisation. These *are* unique times."

"I'll give it some thought," Cameron finally said. "You've already got me doing a lot of improvising."

They continued talking until late in the afternoon. The rest of the squad was introduced to the family. Sarah spent time flirting with them while Anne watched from a distance. She could tell the interaction was good for Sarah who still worried about her scars. The attention seemed to boost her self-confidence. One young man in particular, the machine gunner, Tommy Wilkes, seemed smitten with her. His fascination only increased when she told him how he would have been her first target if things had gone badly.

Cameron said they were going to talk to the rest of the people in the valley and would come back in two or three weeks with a firm answer regarding the arrangements.

"Since you are coming back, would it possible to bring some birthing supplies with you when you return? We're prepared to do without, but it would be helpful if you could bring some anti-bacterial soap, and any cloth diapers and baby garments the hospital might have," Anne asked.

"I'll do what I can."

"Thank you, Lieutenant. If supplies are short, don't worry, we can get by."

In the morning the family said goodbye to Cameron and Gibbs.

"We'll look forward to seeing you again," Catherine said to Cameron with a smile.

Jason thanked them again and Sarah waved to everyone in the Humvees. Her eye caught sight of Tommy Wilkes who blew her a kiss and was rewarded with a bright smile.

"That was quite an experience," Gibbs remarked as the patrol later headed back to Hillsboro. "Way out here in the country we find a family of fighters: a pregnant mother, a dad and two teenage daughters. I never saw anything like that before in my life."

"They're quite a family," Cameron replied with a smile. "I hope we can sell this to Roper."

"We can. I'll help you." Looking at Cameron, he continued, "You're smiling. Thinking about that girl? I noticed you couldn't take your eyes off her."

"She is something, don't you think?"

"If you mean she's young and good looking, yes."

"I think she's more than just that. She's got a head on her shoulders."

"Lieutenant, with all due respect, I don't think you were attracted to her brain. Aren't you a bit too old for her?"

"She seemed pretty mature to me. She was mature enough to tell me directly she was ready to shoot me."

"Not sure I'd want to pursue a female that would be willing to shoot me. It sounds dangerous. I didn't know you liked dangerous women."

Cameron smiled and shook his head and changed the subject. "So the rest of the valley seems happy to stay. They actually like Jason's idea."

Gibbs' face grew serious, "Jason and his wife made a good point about food. If we relocate them, this valley goes from being a possible source of food to a food drain. The more I think about this relocation plan, the less I like it. Certainly in the short term it just increases Hillsboro's problems."

"Yeah, I agree. I can understand inventorying, but not relocating. I don't know why Roper wants to pursue this."

"He's got pressure from the Colonel."

"Yeah, we've seen some dumb things proposed since the EMP attack."

"Now Lieutenant, don't go criticizing the brass, you're going to be one someday."

"I didn't know you were such a diplomat."

"I'm not, but you are and you should remember that. You the diplomat, me the hard ass."

"Quite a team," said Cameron with a smile.

Chapter 13

Back in Hillsboro, Lieutenant Cameron gave his report to Captain Roper. He made sure to not dwell on the battles and weapons that valley had amassed. After some time, he was able to convince Roper that working with the valley could be a good way to increase the food supply. Roper actually seemed enthused with Cameron's idea and suggested he spend his time developing it. He encouraged Cameron to visit the valley as often as necessary and gave him full responsibility to work on the project.

After informing Gibbs their plan was approved, he went to the hospital and collected what supplies he could. Three weeks later, Cameron was back on his way to see Jason.

His machine gunner from the previous trip, Tommy Wilkes, had secured his place and convinced Cameron that he didn't need to take anyone else. He didn't want any competition. He was determined to get back to the girl that smiled at him. He didn't even know her name, but vowed to correct that situation. Cameron grabbed Gibbs and the three of them set out early one morning.

When they arrived they found Anne quite close to giving birth. Lieutenant Cameron presented her with the supplies he received from the hospital.

"Thank you very much Lieutenant," Anne said, "These will be a great help. This baby is going to be coming very soon."

"Are you sure you don't want to come back to Hillsboro with us to have the baby in the hospital?" Cameron asked.

"Yes, I'm sure," Anne replied calmly. "I have my daughters and my husband and I do have some experience in these matters."

"I can arrange to come back after the birth and maybe bring a doctor or nurse to check up on you...if that would be all right?"

"Yes, that would be fine. I would appreciate that. But can you get away so often?" she asked.

"I'll find a way," he said.

Sarah spoke up, "Will you be able to bring everyone along with you, when you return? I mean, it would not be wise to travel alone and Sergeant Gibbs and Tommy know about us, so you wouldn't want to bring new people along, would you?" She smiled at Tommy after speaking.

"No, you're right, of course. I guess we will be the travel group between here and Hillsboro. In any case, my Captain likes sending me out on various patrol missions. Many seem pointless, but that's the way it is in the military sometimes."

"I hope *you* don't think your mission to our farm was pointless. Catherine and I think your visit was quite enlightening," Sarah replied with a smile.

"You could say it opened up our horizons," Catherine chimed in. "We are just simple country girls, so your visits are very helpful to enlarge our understanding of the outside world," she smiled at Cameron.

While the bantering was going on, Jason, Cameron and Gibbs went outside.

"Lieutenant, what did your Captain say about my proposal?" Jason asked.

"Please call me Kevin. I think we're on a first name basis now. He gave me the green light, so we can go ahead. You can let the rest of the valley know. He actually sounded enthused about the project. He wants me to try to expand it. That's where I'll need your help."

"I'll let everyone know. That's great news." Jason paused, then added, "It won't be anything fancy, but the town can start to get local produce from the surrounding farms."

"I can imagine a farmer's market coming to town," Rodney said.

"Yeah, something like that, just like the old days. But people will have to relearn how to preserve food so they can eat in the winter when the farms can't produce."

"I guess we're going back to the nineteenth century," Kevin said.

"Better than the twelfth century, which is what it was like fighting the gangs...a twelfth century fight for your life with modern weapons," Jason said, reflecting on the ferocity of his battles. "I can help make this one valley start producing more than subsistence levels of crops. Even if I didn't grow up on a farm, I have Anne to help...and the others in the valley. There's a wealth of knowledge here and I can put it in action."

Jason continued, "Are things really getting any better in Hillsboro? With this farming plan we'll be doing business with them in the near future. I need to know how things are there."

The officers were silent for a moment. Then Rodney said, "I don't know. We come in to a community, we set up our marshal law and everything is supposed to get better. Only it really doesn't. We don't have any new resources to solve the town's problems—food, fuel, medicine. Hunger is still a big issue. It drives how the city functions. Everyone's getting fed but everyone feels some level of hunger. The local authorities have things tied up pretty tight...did so even before we got there."

"I left because of the corruption I saw starting to take place," Jason said.

"It didn't go away, I won't kid you," Rodney replied.

"Yeah; and there's still a criminal element in the town. They've got some resources and are using them to control the locals," Kevin said.

"I figured some of the police and town leaders might start their own power play with the scarce resources."

"It's happened," Gibbs responded.

"Who's involved?" Jason asked.

"The town's mayor and now chairman of the Safety Committee, the Chief of Police."

"And probably some local gangsters," Gibbs interrupted.

"Yeah, some of them as well."

"That could affect us," Jason said. "I'm not sure I would want to trust them."

"You don't," Rodney said.

"Don't be too cynical, Rodney. You don't want to paint too bad a picture," Kevin said.

"Maybe more the realist than cynic." Rodney went on to describe how other towns had been raided and some transports of supplies had been hijacked. "It takes some inside information, information the Safety Committee has, to pull off those raids. Yet no one seems to be able to find out who the culprits are."

"Something's up, I don't deny it," Kevin agreed. "But at least the town is peaceful...no riots or anarchy."

"But at what price?" Jason asked. "From what I'm hearing, I'm glad I left. I don't think I'd like to return anytime soon. What's your command structure?"

"Our colonel's gone, Kevin replied. "He took the main body and continued his loop through the countryside. We have a Captain Roper in charge."

"Well I hope he's clean. If he's compromised, you could be in for real trouble," Jason declared.

Kevin looked down at the ground as if he didn't want to go to where the conversation had just turned.

"I'm guessing you have some doubts about Captain Roper?" Jason asked.

Kevin remained quiet. Rodney finally spoke. "He seems to be willfully blind to what's going on. I'm not sure how to read that."

"Well, I'm worried about how we do business with them. And with just a small squad left, you really don't have much power to counter the militia, do you?" Jason continued.

Kevin looked around, as if hunting for an answer.

"The short answer is no," said Rodney.

"So what's to keep them from coming into the valley and just stealing our crops? You've just told me they've raided other towns." Jason said.

"We don't know who raided those towns, we just have our suspicions. And I want you to know that you are my project and I will defend this valley. I expect Captain Roper will as well. Yeah, we don't have full control over everything going on in the town, but no one has tried to hijack or attack any of our work directly. As of now, you come under that umbrella." Cameron said.

"I appreciate that statement of support, but I'll keep a wary eye out anyway. It's how we've survived so far. I hope you will as well." Jason responded.

Anne and the girls came out on the porch with Tommy close behind. "I'm going to go lie down now," Anne said. "The baby is tiring me out. We've reached that point where it will be more comfortable for both of us with the baby outside of me rather than inside of me." She smiled at the men and went back inside.

"We better get going," Rodney said. "We don't want to be on the road too late at night."

"You will return soon?" Catherine asked Kevin.

"How soon do you think I should?" Kevin replied.

"Mom said she thought the baby would come within a week, so any time after that should be good."

"I'll try to make that happen."

"We'll eagerly await your return, Lieutenant," Catherine said with a smile.

"Be sure to bring Tommy along to help drive," Sarah added.

Chapter 14

A week later Anne began experiencing contractions which went on for two days. Starting with one every two to three hours, they progressed to every hour. She tried to keep mobile, walking around the house in order to help the birth. This became more difficult as the contractions came more frequently. One bright spring morning around ten, Anne's water broke. She cried out and everyone rushed into the kitchen to see the fluid all over the floor.

"My water has broken," she declared.

The girls looked stunned, as did Jason. "Remember the steps I outlined for you, this is natural and it means the baby will be coming soon," Anne said.

"Do you have to go to bed now?" Sarah asked.

Anne smiled, "Maybe, but not before I change my clothes."

"Of course," she responded. The two girls helped their mom up to the bedroom.

Anne changed into a nightgown. She lay down in the bed and asked Catherine to start timing the contractions so they could keep track of her progress. She had Jason rub her lower back.

Thankfully, Anne had strong, wide hips. Her two girls had been born with reasonably short periods of labor. This baby, she hoped, would be the same.

Jason arranged strips from a sheet, carefully cut for cleaning Anne and the baby after the birth.

"Babies are moist," Anne said.

"I hope it's not too yucky," Sarah declared.

"Be brave," Catherine admonished in a joking manner. "Remember, you're the princess warrior."

"No, the mid-wife," Sarah retorted. "And I'm too young for either title."

"You'll do fine. I'm going to do all the work, you just have to help," Anne said.

The girls washed their mother with the soap brought from the hospital. Everyone focused on the final steps for the birth. They kept track of Anne's dilation through the frequency and intensity of her contractions. They were stunned at the effort, but did not shirk from helping her in whatever way they could: counting, cheerleading, pressing hard on her back and reminding her when to breathe and when to push. After six hours of increasingly intense effort, Jason cradled a baby boy who came squeezing out from Anne into the world. Catherine tied off the cord and, at Anne's prodding, Jason cut it.

The girls wiped off the new baby. He started to breathe and began to cry as the air hit his lungs. They laid him on Anne so she and the new baby could get acquainted with each other and the baby could begin to nurse. Everyone felt exhausted even though Anne did all the work. They watched the new baby start to nurse from the sidelines until Anne suggested they set about cleaning things up and changing the bedding so she could lie in a dry bed. Jason could see the girls were awed by what their mother had done. Participating in the birth seemed to give them a new insight into what being a woman was all about. Jason also found the moment inspirational, seeing his wife absorbing so much in order to bring new life into the world.

No wonder we never stop honoring our mothers.

Two days later, Kevin, Rodney and Tommy returned as promised, bringing a nurse from the hospital. After examining both the baby and Anne she declared them fine and fit. Everyone was elated at the successful birth.

Jason, the girls and Anne beamed. The others all expressed their admiration for the baby.

Kevin indicated he wanted to talk with Jason alone, so they went outside. "With authorization to help you restart farming in the valley, we'll be working more closely with each other."

"I know. I'm looking forward to it."

"There's another reason I'm excited about this project," Kevin continued.

"And what is that?"

"First, I need to ask something personal of you. It may sound a bit old fashioned, but these are different times, and maybe they call for an old fashioned approach."

"What are you driving at?" Jason inquired.

"I would like permission to visit you in the future."

"We're going to be working together. I assumed you would be visiting as part of that effort," Jason responded.

"Yes, we'll be working together, but this is different. I would like permission to court Catherine." It sounded odd for Kevin to say, odd for Jason to hear, but somehow appropriate.

"Ah," Jason said with a sigh, "an ulterior motive."

He had suspected this might be coming. He was not unaware of the glances between Kevin and Catherine. Little did Kevin know how opportune his arrival this spring had been, filling an emotional hole in Catherine when Jason rejected her plea last fall. But Kevin was unaware of how volatile Catherine's emotions might be as a romantic relationship developed. Jason's protective instincts kicked in.

"You know she is quite young."

"Yes, even though I don't know exactly how old Catherine is. However, she's obviously very mature."

"With all the trials we've been through since last year and earlier, she is more vulnerable than she might seem. I don't want her hurt. Remember, Catherine has lost her biological father, accepted a new step father, learned to be a warrior and killed—up close and ugly. That is a lot to absorb for a teenager. This family has felt the trauma of violence and its terrible aftermath—the bodies dead and dying, stripping them of valuables, getting rid of them, the smell—she's experienced it all, more than you."

"I understand what you're saying which is why I wanted to talk to you in this manner. My feelings are strong for your daughter. She's all I've thought about since we returned to Hillsboro. I couldn't wait to get back here to see her. Maybe we're all too emotionally vulnerable in these times, but I can think of no one other than her to be with in this new world.

"You see," Kevin continued, "like you, I'm not sure, in spite of what the official word is from my command structure, that our society has not fundamentally changed, and that we will have to make our way in this new reality using different methods. Success may be measured far differently going forward than it has been in the past. I'm ready to embrace the future, but I realize I want to embrace it with Catherine. Whether or not she will want the same, I don't know. But I'm ready to try to win her heart and ready to accept my failure if I can't."

"That's a nice speech," Jason responded. "You've come a long way from the officer who sat in my yard a month ago."

"Yes. It's ironic that the young woman who was ready to shoot me is the one whose heart I want to win."

"If you break her heart, I'll do what she didn't." Jason paused, "I guess that is another way of saying you have my blessing, but don't misuse it."

"Thank you. I won't. On another note, I'd like to recommend Tommy Wilkes to you. I know he's going to try to come around as often as he can cajole me into doing so. He wants to be a part of what I'm doing here."

"Sarah's much too young if that is what you mean," Jason responded.

"I agree wholeheartedly. I just wanted to let you know he'll be finding reasons to come around as long as you allow it."

"Just let him know if he hurts Sarah, or he gets her pregnant, he'll have me to deal with."

"I understand. He'll be respectful. He seems very serious in his intentions. He has not allowed anyone back at camp to say a bad word about her."

They walked back into the house to find Rodney holding the new baby. He looked up at Jason, beaming.

"You look like you've held a baby before," Jason chided.

"It's been a long while, but you don't forget." His hard, warrior's exterior was softened by his moist eyes.

"I think our new baby has some built-in godparents," Anne said. "Thank you for all your help and for listening to my husband a month ago. Look at how it has blessed us all."

Everyone agreed. As the team assembled to leave, Jason turned to Tommy, "You can come back here as often as your officers allow. I'll be putting you to work and I expect you to work hard. You're welcome as long as you treat my daughters respectfully."

"Thank you, sir!" Tommy replied with enthusiasm. Sarah beamed and Anne and Catherine smiled.

"And is Kevin allowed back?" Catherine asked.

"Well, he had a hard time to convince me, but I finally told him if he was brave enough to want to spend time with the young lady who almost shot him, then I would not stand in his way."

"He doesn't stand a chance," Rodney said.

The team climbed into their Humvee and slowly drove down the drive to the road, everyone waving goodbye.

"Well?" Kevin looked at Rodney, "What do you think about this project? I think there's a lot of good we can do."

Rodney Gibbs was quiet as his thoughts turned to his lost family back in the Midwest. He didn't know if he would ever see them again. And the army hadn't accomplished much since the EMP attack, but here was promise. Here was something positive he could get a hold of. Helping here seemed like the right thing to do. It might even lead him back to his own family someday.

"Yeah, we can do some good." He smiled.

Jason held his son in one arm with the other around Anne. As the Humvee drove down the hill, the girls moved close to Anne, him and their new baby brother. He watched the Humvee go out of sight. His thoughts drifted to Hillsboro. He had put the town in his past and now it loomed in his future, a dark cloud that could be signaling an impending storm.

Then he looked out over the beautiful valley glowing in the afternoon sun of late spring, dappled with long shadows cast from the budding trees. *Such a beautiful place. Such a beautiful family.*

He had not expected happiness to come out of such disaster and misery. He had been smart enough to recognize where his future belonged, and had fought hard to protect that future. He thought for a moment of Maggie, and Sam and Judy. Their memories now held no pain; they were remembered shadows from a lost past.

He turned to the present, drinking in all the details of the valley, its peace and beauty. His senses felt amplified. He breathed the fresh spring air. *This is how to live going forward, in the moment: savoring every blessing and never ceasing to enjoy them.*

As the family quietly held each other, looking out over the valley, Jason sensed what everyone felt. They were in the right place, and ready for this new world. Whatever it would bring, they would face its challenges.

Afterword

You can follow Jason's further adventures in my sequel, *Uprising*. In this story of Jason and his family come into conflict with the town and its corrupt leaders. It's a big story, rich in characters and plots, encompassing events in Hillsboro. Below is a sample from the first chapter. Get more information on my website, www.davidnees.com.

As always, if you liked my story, I hope you will leave a review on Amazon, you can find the section at the beginning of the reviews on the book page. Reviews are a form of "social proof" of a book's worthiness. Readers unfamiliar with an author rely on reviews to help them decided whether or not to invest their time.

You can follow the progress on my website at
davidnees.com or on my facebook page;
facebook.com/neesauthor.

Thank you for reading my book.

Uprising
Book 2 in the After the Fall series
Chapter 1

The man made his way hurriedly through the shadowy streets. There were no lights to relieve the darkness; the soft glow of oil lamps illuminated only a few windows. The crescent moon and stars gave little light. Even so, he worked to keep to the shadows as he hurried along. The town was quiet, as it was most nights. He could hear an occasional pedestrian hurrying along somewhere in the dark.

The man moved close to the buildings seeking more darkness when he heard footsteps. He didn't want to be seen; no one did. It was after curfew and, if caught out, he would be arrested, with an uncertain fate in store for him. Others had been so detained and had reported aggressive interrogation, often accompanied by beatings with fists and clubs.

The questions were always the same: "What are you doing out? Where are you coming from? Who did you meet with?" The authorities had suspicions that there was a subversive element in Hillsboro. A group of people who, although law-abiding, did not approve of the dictatorial power of those in charge, who objected to the restrictive rules and were getting themselves organized.

The man sensed he was being followed. He quickened his pace. He was taking a circuitous route to his assigned apartment. If he was not certain that he was alone, he would not return home but would instead keep moving on the streets, even if he had to walk all night, in order to protect his family. He was endangering them, but he rationalized his nocturnal outings by telling himself that he was working to create a better social order for his family. If someone were caught and was thought to be doing anything subversive, not only did they disappear, but their family might vanish as well. The disappearances did not have to be publicized. Everyone who interacted with a targeted family would know its fate. The word always got out. Don't stand out; don't oppose the existing rules and authorities.

A sense of panic began to grow, creating a tight knot in his stomach. His body tingled with fear, the hair on his neck bristled. He began to run. When he had gone a half block, he stopped abruptly. Did he hear footsteps suddenly stopping? Or was his mind playing tricks on him? Summoning his courage, he spun around. There were only shadows behind him. Nothing moved. He turned back, taking a deep breath and started walking again. He decided the clandestine meetings were beginning to unnerve him.

After turning a corner three blocks from his home, he thought he saw two shadowy shapes ahead in a doorway. He turned around to go back and found two large men standing at the corner. With a shock, he realized his instincts were correct. He had been followed. His knees began to buckle. He turned again and saw the shadows disengage from the doorway and start in his direction. He lurched across the street in a desperate attempt to flee. It was futile. The men moved quickly and surrounded him and he sank to the ground under their blows. Not a word was spoken. They dragged him, weakly struggling, to a waiting van. They threw him in the back and drove off down the dark streets.

Hillsboro, like the rest of the country, was still suffering from the after-effects of the electromagnetic pulse attack. Now, two years later, stability had still not been restored, and Hillsboro had not returned to normal.

The town was not completely under control. In spite of the best efforts of the civil authorities and their militia to impose martial law, there were still small numbers of outlaws operating within the city. They snuck in from outside or were residents who did not want to conform to the strict martial law imposed.

The EMP attack had destroyed electrical power, communications, and transportation throughout the U.S., leaving the country in a state of anarchy. The possibility of any rapid restoration was near zero. Many people had died that first year, mostly the old and sick. More waves of deaths had followed as antibiotics had run out in communities and sickness had spread from lack of clean water and proper sanitation.

There had been a massive exodus from the large cities as disease and starvation reigned. Many smaller towns, like Hillsboro, had tried to resist the influx of refugees.

Those that couldn't had soon been overwhelmed, and the anarchy that engulfed the big cities erupted, making life nearly intolerable. Towns that had been fortunate enough to be able to build barriers and resist the flow of people looking for any help they could find had avoided such a fate.

There were tense and often ugly standoffs between those lucky to be inside of a defended town and those outside. The refugees were all desperate. Some were heartbreaking: families with starving children, struggling to find scraps to eat and shelter from the weather. Some had become outlaws, desperados embracing violence or driven to it in order to gather the resources needed to survive.

No relief agencies were coming to the rescue. FEMA was not functioning. There was no group that would arrive to bring some level of order and distribute food and shelter. People were on their own. They would get no help from the federal government. And, having grown up in modern society, they were not prepared to survive without its structures of support.

Hillsboro had walled itself in. During the first year, the city's government had directed citizens to work on dismantling houses and buildings in a perimeter around the central core of the city. Kids had been put to work extracting and saving the nails, scavenging the wiring from the buildings, and collecting anything that could be useful. The main rubble had then been used to construct a wall of sorts. It rose in a jagged fashion, six to ten feet high. It was primitive, ugly and porous, reminiscent of the barricades of the French Revolution. A cleared space grew outside of the walls, marked with concrete slabs that had been foundations and open basements now flooded with stagnant water.

Other novels published by David Nees:

Uprising, book two in *After the Fall* series
(replaces *Catherine's Tale Parts 1 & 2*)
Rescue; book three in the *After the Fall* series

Payback, book one in the Dan Stone assassin series
The Shaman, book two in the Dan Stone assassin series
The Captive Girl, book three in the Dan Stone Assassin series

For information about upcoming novels, please visit my website at https://www.davidnees.com or go to my Facebook page; fb.me/neesauthor.

You can also sign up for my reader list to get new information. No spam; I never sell my list and you can opt out at any time. Scroll down from the landing page on my website to find the sign-up form.

Thank you for reading my book. If you enjoyed the story, please consider writing a review on Amazon. Your reading pleasure is why I write. Until next time...be well.

CPSIA information can be obtained
at www.ICGtesting.com
Printed in the USA
BVHW040119030320
573844BV00014B/327

9 781530 563203